The Shongorin ros

"Honorable Doctor Salasara, Oikisha has asked me to learn when you wish to copulate. What may I tell her?"

Salazar's jaw sagged. "God in Heaven!" he exclaimed before changing to Shongo. "What makes her think that I want any such thing?"

"Oh, sir, it is a rigid custom among the Choshas. It is part of the mutual obligations between an onnifa and her liege lord; they copulate as often as desired whenever the liege lord is without his lawful mate. Oikisha asked me if you had a lawful mate. I told her that I understood you did not; so Oikisha stands ready to perform her duty."

"I evidently did not know native customs so well as I thought," said Salazar. "But Sensao, such copulation is impossible, because of the physical differences between our species. If I tried to meet Oikisha's expectations, the result would be no pleasure for her and severe pains to me."

"I am sorry, honorable sir," said Sensao. "If you cannot meet your part of this obligation, she will consider her oath to you cancelled and resume her allegiance to Prophet Kampai. Since you are Kampai's foe, she must slay you. If she succeeds, she must then return to her tribe, although she knows that they will kill her forthwith."

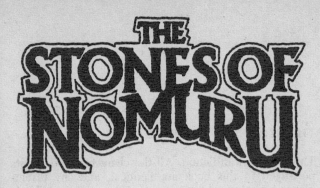

THE STONES OF NOMURU

L. Sprague de Camp
Catherine Crook de Camp

BAEN
FANTASY

THE STONES OF NOMURU

This is a work of fiction. All the characters and events portrayed in this book are fictional, and any resemblance to real people or incidents is purely coincidental.

A Baen Book

Baen Publishing Enterprises
P.O. Box 1403
Riverdale, N.Y. 10471

ISBN: 0-671-72053-8

Cover art by Tom Kidd

First Baen printing, May 1991

Distributed by
SIMON & SCHUSTER
1230 Avenue of the Americas
New York, N.Y. 10020

Printed in the United States of America

To Wendy Bacon, Marshall Becker,
and Susan Johnson, the supervisors
on the Printzhof dig at Essington, Pennsylvania,
in the summer of 1985,
where we learned our field archaeology.

CONTENTS

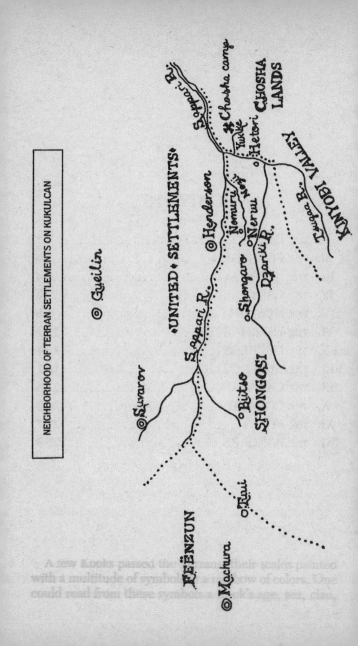

NEIGHBORHOOD OF TERRAN SETTLEMENTS ON KUKULCAN

Gueilin

•UNITED•SETTLEMENTS•

Suvarov

Sappari R.

Sappari R.

Henderson

Nomuru

Neruu

Shongaro

Dzariki R.

Bitto

SHONGOSI

Tippu

FEËNZUN

Machura

Chosha camp

Tuike

Hetori

CHOSHA LANDS

Tsuopaa R.

KINZOBI VALLEY

A few Kooks passed the terrans, their scales painted with a multitude of symbols in a rainbow of colors. One could read from these symbols a Kook's age, sex, clan,

THE
DIG

"Get those goddam animals out of my way!" yelled the huge, black-browed man who stood at the end of the rickety footbridge across the Sappari.

Keith Adams Salazar, in dirty khakis and a tropical sun helmet, looked up from his task of calming the terrified kudzai, while his three native helpers unloaded supplies intended for his camp. He studied the burly man and the group of Terrans and Kukulcanians that thronged the trail behind him, then said mildly:

"I'm getting out as fast as I can. But we shall have to pull my animal's foot out of this rotten planking before we can move."

Crimsoning, the black-browed man waved a large, hairy fist. "Goddamn it, why don't you just pull? You must be as stupid as that creature!" Topping two meters, he towered over Salazar.

The latter's lips set in a thin, acerbic line, but he

answered reasonably: "Because if we don't unload it first, the animal will buck itself into the river."

"I don't give a damn what happens to the fucking beast!" screamed the big man. "Goddamn it, you're holding me up on purpose!"

Salazar ignored the choleric stranger and, with the help of his Kooks, at last released the kudzai's imprisoned hoof and calmed the squealing, tapirlike beast. As they reloaded the scaly pack animal, the turtle-beaked faces of Salazar's helpers showed no emotion. Still, a Terran skilled in the ways of the folk of the planet Kukulcan could have interpreted their anger from the rippling patterns of the bristles on their necks.

The Kooks—natives of Kukulcan, so called by human settlers on that planet—were taller than most human beings but more slender. Although built on the general lines of a bipedal Terran primate, they did not much resemble any Earthly being. If anything, their aspect was reptilian. They had four-digit, clawed hands and feet; skins covered with iridescent scales and further decorated with painted symbols in a kaleidoscope of colors; no visible organs of sex; and a fishy smell. Muskets of peculiar shape were slung across their backs, while leather cases and pouches dangled from various straps, like the equipment of Terran tourists on a wildlife-watching expedition.

Finally Salazar's party got under way. The bridge shuddered beneath the weight of the Terran, his three Kooks, and the three kudzais. As he neared the far end of the structure, Salazar glanced back to see the other party already starting across instead of waiting for the bridge to clear. Fearing that the combined weight of the parties would overload the rope cables that supported the structure, he picked

up his pace. Reaching solid ground again, Salazar
pulled off to one side, saying amicably:

"Since you're in such a tearing hurry, perhaps
you—"

"I ought to slap the shit out of you!" roared the
burly man.

"Have you had your blood pressure checked lately?"
asked Salazar. "Such an unruly temper implies a
medical problem."

For an instant it looked as if the black-browed man
would hurl himself at Salazar. Then the latter's three
Kooks, with pink, forked tongues flicking out, unslung and leveled their muskets. The burly man
paused with a hand on his holster.

Two other Terrans elbowed their way forward.
One was tall, young, and fair-haired; the other, dark
and obese. The heavy one spoke with an accent as
thick as borsch. "Come on! If you two kill each
other, is no fun for us." Laughing equably, he put a
convivial arm around the burly man. "Come on,
Conrad, before you turn to stone like *bogatíri*."

The speaker and the blond man led their grumbling companion away. Another Terran, stocky, tea-
colored, and flat-faced, stepped up and nodded
politely. "I am sorry, sir," he said. "Mr. Bergen's
temper is—well, he has problems. Permit me; my
name is Chung."

"Glad to know you, Mr. Chung," said Salazar. He
waved a hand at the rest of the group, now filing
down the trail ahead. "And who are those people?"

"It is a hunting party from Suvarov, which Mr.
Bergen has organized. And you, if I may ask?"

"I'm Keith Salazar, from the university."

"The archaeologist?"

"Yep."

"Digging up Nomuru?"

Salazar nodded. "Don't advertise it, please. I don't want spectators. Where are you people headed?"

"Kinyobi Valley. Mr. Bergen wants to shoot a tseturen and take its head back."

"He'd better have a big room to mount it in," observed Salazar. "How'll he get it back? It'll weigh a ton."

"He plans to build a sled and hire Kooks to haul it. Do you know the trail to Kinyobi?"

"Yep."

"Do you know how many days' hike it is from here?"

"Yep."

Chung paused, then smiled. "A precise man, I see, Professor Salazar. How many days' hike is it?"

" 'Bout two and a half, on foot. I think one could make it in a day and a half on juten back, but I've never ridden a juten."

"Neither have Mr. Travers and Mr. Pokrovskii; that is why they are walking the distance. Thank you; it is my pleasure to meet you." Chung ducked a bow and trotted off after the hunting party.

Salazar waited as the fat hunter's booming laughter wafted back along the trail, fainter and fainter. When Salazar could no longer hear it, he resumed his trek.

A crashing in the underbrush revealed the flight of some beast, probably a wild kudzai, whose tusks could be dangerous. Overhead a *hurato*—an arboreal carnivore with long, spidery limbs, blue-and-white spotted scales, and a prehensile tail—swung agilely away through the leafy branches.

Smaller fliers called *zutas* flitted among the lush foliage. When they flew through shafts of sunlight, their batlike wings glowed with patterns of ruby, gold, and sapphire against the backdrop of somber green. One, bearing a striped pattern of emerald and black, flew near the foremost Kook in Salazar's train. With a lightning snatch, the native caught it, stuffed it into his beaked maw, and munched it with a crackle of small bones.

Salazar picked up a dead branch a meter long and, as he walked, slashed at the jungle vegetation, whose new spring growth glowed a pale jade-green. Only then did he give vent to his rage.

"Son of a bitch! Son of a bitch!"

When he had worked off his passion, he relaxed, enjoying some slight satisfaction at having kept his temper under extreme provocation. On Kukulcan, he reflected, loss of self-control could get one a brief mention in the obituary column of the *Henderson Times*.

Moreover, if Salazar had let Bergen goad him into fisticuffs, the hunter would have made a hash of him. Although both were of an age and Salazar was in good trim, Bergen far outweighed him. For the hundredth time, Salazar felt a stab of regret that the splendid Kara, his former wife, was no longer there to support him; and it was all his own stupid fault.

When the big bungalow tent of Salazar's camp hulked up through the trees, he blew a whistle to notify his native camp workers of his approach. Through the scattering of foliage he saw a flicker of motion as two figures emerged from the tent. He called out in Shongo, rendering the sounds of that alien tongue as well as human vocal organs could:

"Kono! Uwangi! It is I, your master. All is well with me. Is all well with you?"

Then he saw another figure issue from the tent. The curtain of twigs and fronds, swaying in the breeze between him and the tent, did not disguise the fact that the newcomer was a female Terran.

"Galina?" he called. When the woman did not at once reply, he added: "Who are you? *Kto v-i? Ni shéi ma?*" Then, as he strode forward with a hand on his pistol holster, he exclaimed: "Good God, it's Kara!"

"Yes," she said, approaching. She was a slim woman of medium height and build, with strong, classical features and gray-green eyes beneath dark curls. A connoisseur would have called her handsome rather than beautiful. "Hello, Keith. Please don't look at me as if I had two heads!"

"I'll try not to goggle. But what—"

"I hope you don't mind my making myself at home. I came in while you were away."

"Of course not! But what's this all about? Have you decided that—that—" Salazar felt himself flushing.

"This is purely a business visit," she said in a voice as crisp as melba toast. "I have an assignment from the *Henderson Times* for a story on your dig. I hope you won't mind putting me up for a few days."

"Not a bit!" said Salazar heartily. "You're looking splendid."

"Covered with dirt and sweat? But thanks; you're looking well, too."

"No amount of dirt could hide your beauty, Kara. Excuse me; I've got to go through the rigmarole." He turned to the native couple and, in rasping Shongo, repeated the elaborate greetings and responses of Kookish etiquette:

"Is your health good?"

"Thanks to my ancestral spirits, my health is good," replied Kono. As the male Kook opened his mouth, a set of shearing and grinding teeth were momentarily visible behind his turtle beak. "Is the honorable master's health likewise good?"

"Thank the Universal Law, it is. Is all well with your clan?"

"Thank the spirits of our ancestors, it is. Is all well with your clan?"

"Indeed it is. Have you led tranquil lives?"

"We have lived tranquil lives. Has the master lived a tranquil life?"

When the ritual dialogue ended, Salazar went through a similar procedure with Uwangi, Kono's mate, and then with the three helpers as he paid off and dismissed them. He turned back.

"After that hike from Henderson, I could do with a drink. You?"

Kara studied her fingers before she spoke. "Sure."

"Then let's go in." Salazar turned to the two remaining Kooks to give orders for stowing the baggage. Inside the tent he said:

"Will you please wait in the study, Kara?"

In the bath compartment, Salazar looked in the mirror. He saw a youthfully mature man, of medium height and slight but wiry build, with dark hair and beard lightly touched with gray. He had not bothered with razor, dye, or a prescription to restore his hair pigmentation. He had never cared much about appearance, and since the woman for whom he had left Kara had in turn deserted him, he had become even more indifferent to the way he looked.

Feeling, however, that with a female guest, and a special one at that, he ought to present a more sightly façade, he washed up and trimmed his hair and beard. When he emerged, he was in clean khakis and in shoes instead of mud-caked boots.

Drinks consisted of the "whiskey" distilled at Henderson from native Kukulcanian plants, with water and cakes of ice from his small ice-making machine.

The fluid had a plausible amber hue, but a Terran connoisseur of Scotch would not have been impressed. When Salazar rejoined his former wife, Kara said:

"You make those Kookish sounds better than I ever could. The words look simple when written, but they don't sound like what you'd expect."

Ill at ease with his unexpected visitor, Salazar unconsciously took on his classroom manner. "Since the Kookish vocal organs differ so from ours, interspecies speech is like trying to converse with intelligent parrots. You used to know a little Shongo."

"I know, but from lack of practice I've forgotten it. I was never much of a linguist anyway."

"You could pick it up again. The grammar's not very complex; the hard parts are the non-human sounds and the inflections for status. Everything is modified according to whether you're speaking to someone of your own social level, or above it, or below it. Kooks display their status by insulting their inferiors and fawning upon their superiors, like that female from the Maravilla Society, who came upon me in my work clothes and called me 'My good man!' "

Kara chuckled. "You, the planet's leading archaeologist! So much for the snobby descendants of the first settlers, as if the *Maravilla* had been brought across interstellar space by angels!"

"Kooks," Salazar continued, "are even more class-conscious. An upper-class Kook would consider it rude to shoot out his tongue at an equal or a superior. Since, like Terran snakes, they use their tongues to smell odors, it's like saying: 'You stink!' By the way, how did you get here?"

"My bicycle. I'd have hired a steam car, but I was told the Sappari bridge wouldn't take the weight.

Kono put the bike in the shed. Why did you walk instead of biking?"

"I've found one must get off and push a bike so often it's hardly worth the trouble. Besides, kudzais can't travel much faster than a walk for long, and I've never learned to ride a juten. Did you come all this way by yourself?"

"Sure." Kara sipped and smiled. "Why the frown?"

"Might be dangerous. Choshas have been seen scouting around. Some are headhunters. You came armed, of course?"

She shrugged. "With everything so peaceful, a gun seemed silly."

"Peaceful now, maybe; but it wasn't always so. There are rifles and ammunition from the old days somewhere in the bowels of the museum. Really, Kara, you should know better. Your head's too pretty to end up in a nomad's private collection."

"I didn't have you to advise me." Kara glanced sidelong at her former husband and then at her ringless left hand. "By the way, your friend Cabot Firestone sends his regards."

"You've seen Cabot?"

"Yes. I interviewed him for a story, and later he took me out to dinner."

"How long will you be here?" Salazar asked.

"Depends. Didn't I see another party, with both Kooks and Terrans, go past on the main trail?"

"Guess you did."

"Do you know who they were?"

"Yep."

"Oh, stop playing the Maine storekeeper! Who were they?"

"A hunting party, headed for Kinyobi Valley."

"Was their leader a huge, heavyset man with bushy black eyebrows?"

Salazar tensed. "Their guide said the man's name was Bergen. Do you know him?"

"That's Conrad Bergen, the developer. He's looking for me—wants to kill me."

"*What?*" cried Salazar.

"I said, he's looking for me to kill me."

"But—why?"

"We were engaged; but when I looked up his previous wife and learned a thing or two, I changed my mind."

"How did you ever get involved with such a character? He obviously needs his screws tightened. He'd look fine in a glass case at the Museum."

Kara shrugged. "It was when he was launching his chicken farm, having somehow gotten around the rule against importing Terran plants and animals. Conrad can put up a good front, as men do when they're courting."

"Putting his best paunch forward, you mean," said Salazar. "I'm surprised at you, Kara."

"I think I missed having a husband—missed being married. I suppose I felt sorry for myself. But when I told him we were through, he had one of his temper tantrums and knocked me down. I left the chicken farm with a fine shiner and Conrad roaring that he'd kill me."

Salazar clenched his fists, then slammed one fist into the other palm. "Oh, God! If I hadn't gone nuts . . ."

"Forget that!" Kara snapped. "What's past is past. Anyway, I moved back to Henderson. I don't suppose he'd actually shoot me on sight, but I'd better not take chances."

Salazar took his larger pistol off the hook and checked the magazine. Kara said: "Nothing rash, please, Keith."

"Don't worry. If his head were mounted over my fireplace, people might think it in poor taste."

She smiled. "Who's Galina, the person you called out to?"

"A graduate student, helping with the dig. My students are running a survey on the site. Do you know the other two in Bergen's hunting party? One's tall and blond, the other short and stout with a Slavic accent."

"They're two of Conrad's cronies; he does have friends in spite of his temper. The blond is Derek Travers, a bureaucrat from the Native Relations Office, who never lets us forget that his grandparents were all English. The other's Oleg Pokrovskii, Conrad's construction supervisor."

"And was Bergen—" He bit back the words "your lover?"

Kara's eyes sparkled wickedly as she viewed Salazar's discomfort. "You mean, was he 'enjoying my favors,' as they used to say long ago? It's none of your business, Keith, any more than your Galina is any of mine."

Miserable, Salazar busied himself with his drink. "Not *my* Galina, please. She's a good kid but doesn't attract me. Anyway, students are off-limits to a professor. What name are you using?"

"After Rodney—uh—died, I went back to Sheffield. I didn't have to change the initials on my baggage."

At the name of their son, Salazar shut his eyes. "Please, Kara!"

"Sorry, Keith; but you asked. What became of Diane—what was her name?—Diane Morrow, who awoke the springtime in you?"

Salazar grunted as if in pain. "We were properly married; but after a few months she flew the coop."

"What didn't she like about you?"

The archaeologist spread his hands. "Said I was a stuffy old pedant who ought to be mounted in the museum with the other specimens, because I was always reading or poking around for potsherds. She wanted to spend all our time at one of Bergen's resorts, the one I took her to for our honeymoon, dancing until midnight and making love all the rest of the night every night. I wasn't up to it; as Lothario I'm a flop."

"I told you what would happen with a girl of her age."

"So you did, but not forcefully enough. Why didn't you put up more of a fight? Maybe you could have brought me to my senses."

Kara shrugged. "I said all I thought I could without making a royal battle of it. Anyway, if a man rejects me, that's the end of it as far as I'm concerned."

"I must have been as crazy as Tom O'Bedlam," muttered Salazar.

She gave him a steely, level stare. "You said it, not I. Did her leaving hurt you badly?"

"Not so much as I must have hurt you. For one thing—well, remember how we always had plenty to talk about? With Diane, I found we had nothing much to say."

"I'm sorry, Keith. How's your social life these days?"

"What social life? Oh, an occasional student makes a pass, but I know better than to respond to her overtures."

"Are you happy nowadays, Keith?"

Salazar shrugged. "About as happy as a man can be without any sort of home life. I'm doing what I most want to do; and I flatter myself that it's important, even though some people may not agree."

"You mean your archaeological work?"

"Yep. To me, the advancement of knowledge is a sight more important than money or power or glory. Years ago, when I was an undergraduate at the University of Maine, I read a book by an early Terran explorer on Kukulcan. Along with a lot of stuff we now know to be nonsense, this writer told of legends of the great, long-vanished Nomoruvian Empire. While nobody knew the exact site of its capital, the explorer was told that the last ruler, King Bembogu, had built a famous library. This library was said to contain more of the history of Kukulcan than all the other native documents then known. So I resolved, as soon as I got my degree, to go to Kukulcan, try to find the buried city and, if it still existed, dig up Bembogu's library."

Kara said: "I know archaeology on Terra doesn't afford much scope nowadays. You once told me that all the sites have been so dug up, measured, photographed, dated, and fixed up as tourist attractions that there's little for an archaeologist to do but rearrange the exhibits in his museum and write learned papers."

"Did I say that?" Salazar chuckled. "Yep, anybody who thinks he can emulate Schliemann or Stevens on Terra is kidding himself. But here we have a virgin planet, archaeologically speaking! Of course, if money or glory came my way, I shouldn't mind; but they're only incidentals. The chance to take a big bite out of mankind's ignorance—that's what I really want out of life."

Salazar paused and studied his work-roughened hands. Then he smiled. "Guess I haven't broken my old habit of telling you everything—whether you want to hear it or not. Now what about you? I see you are not currently attached."

"How did you know?"

Salazar pointed to the bare, sunburned ring finger on Kara's left hand. "When a man meets a woman, that's the third thing he looks at, the first being her face."

"What's the second?"

"Guess!" He grinned as he saw her flush a little, then tore his gaze away. "Tell me about this writing job."

"Just journalism, churning out copy." She shrugged, but a note of pride crept into her low-pitched voice. "I've been with the *News* a year. Now they call me their top feature writer."

"Good for you! But I hope you won't sensationalize the story of my dig. The last thing I want is a horde of sightseers breaking down the walls of the test pits; or treasure hunters stealing artifacts and ruining the stratigraphy. Our backers give me trouble enough."

"Who are they, besides the University?"

"The University put up matching funds with the Maravilla Society, and the dear old ladies come out to make sure I spend their money wisely. But please be careful; I know what journalists can do."

"What can they do?" she asked with a look of innocence.

"Grab anything that makes a heady headline. There once was an archaeologist in my native America, who tried to explain to a journalist relations between Europeans and aborigines in Pennsylvania during the seventeenth century. He said that, to the Amerinds, William Penn and his followers appeared so strange as to seem hardly human. The headline in the newspaper read: PROFESSOR SAYS QUAKERS HARDLY HUMAN."

Kara Sheffield laughed. Salazar smiled wryly, saying: "That wouldn't be funny to the poor guy on the spot." He looked around at the sound of cheerful voices. "Hello there! Kara, these are my assistants: Galina Bartch, Marcel Frappot, and Ito Kurita. Folks, this is Kara Sheffield, come to write a story about the dig. Now get washed up; we have company for dinner."

At the end of a generous meal, Salazar checked the worksheets of the graduate students and sent them off to bed. The red sun sank slowly, to the discordant chirp and buzz and click of the insectlike arthropods and the rustle and squeal of the other animals of the surrounding forest. Kara asked:

"How are the kids working out, Keith?"

"Okay. Galina's the best; she's Suvarov-born, while the other two are immigrants from Terra like me. Ito's a workaholic without redeeming vices, except he's touchy about his dignity. Marcel's a romantic flutterwit and a chatterbox, but he may steady in time. Excuse me a minute."

Salazar went to a drawing table, to which was tacked a complex chart embellished with patterns of wiggly, intersecting lines in red, blue, and green. He picked up a sheet bearing columns of numbers and began adding pencil marks to the chart. Kara asked:

"What are you doing?"

'I'm going to start some test pits tomorrow, using the Kooks that Sambyaku, the Shongaro chief, has promised me, while the kids finish the survey."

"What are all those figures?"

"Random numbers for locating the pits. If we dug them in neat rows, we might miss a linear feature, like a wall."

He made a few more marks on the chart. Kara said: "I think I'll turn in. It's been a strenuous trip."

"So shall I," said Salazar. "Just one more . . . Okay." he escorted Kara to the canvas door of her compartment, cudgeling his brains all the while. How was one supposed to act toward a former spouse, whom one had not seen for nearly two years? He took refuge in one of the jingles for which he had a knack:

> *"I'm walking on air,*
> *For the fairest of fair*
> *Has come to my lair,*
> *My labors to share!"*

Kara gave a little laugh. "Still at it, I see! It's nice to know that somebody likes my looks enough to flatter me, even if I take his words with a whole kilo of salt."

"Merely objective judgment," said Salazar. As she opened the flap to her compartment, he cleared his throat and mumbled: "Kara, would you—ah—like me to drop in later?"

The gray-green eyes uncompromisingly met his. "No, Keith. This is purely a business visit; so wipe that gleam out of your eye!"

In the dim light, she seemed lovelier than he remembered her. His blood pounded. Emboldened, he said: "I've missed you so!"

Her mouth was set in a resolute line. "You should have thought of that a couple of years ago. We can be friends, but that's all. If my being here upsets you, I'll go back to Henderson."

Salazar gave a sigh and found that it was genuine. "Same old Kara, with a whim of iron!"

"Goodnight!" she said, closing the flap.

Salazar slept badly. While tossing on his bunk, he heard voices through the canvas. Marcel Frappot was whispering: "Yes, I thought I recognized the name; they were in the paper two years ago. Their son killed himself after Keith ran off with another woman. I should not have thought our distinguished professor such a Casanova."

"It is normal that a vigorous man like him should like the ladies," said Galina Bartch. "How old was this boy?"

"Seven or eight, I think. Martinov the sociologist said it was cause and effect. Firestone, that professor of psychology, claimed that this was unjust; the boy had troubles before his father fled. The Reverend Ragnarsen—the one who disappeared—pronounced it a divine judgment on our Keith. I wonder if they will take time for a little *poum-poum*. A divorced couple sometimes come together for *une petite amourette*—"

"Oh, Marcel, you gossip more than an old woman!"

"Very well; let us talk of things more agreeable. *Ma petite*, you are so beautiful in that light—"

"No, Marcel! Go back to bed! It is against my religion; and besides, if I got pregnant . . ."

The voices died. From Galina's delicate snore, Salazar inferred that Frappot had departed unsatisfied. *He is not the only one,* thought the archaeologist.

As Kono and Uwangi served breakfast, Salazar observed in himself a disinclination to meet Kara's eye. With wry amusement, he detected a similar coolness between Frappot and Galina. He said:

"Ito, can you finish the five-meter lines today?"

"I am sure of it," said Kurita.

"What's that for?" asked Kara.

"A resistivity survey," said Salazar.

Kara raised a questioning eyebrow, and the archaeologist's voice took on a classroom tone. "We measure the resistance of the ground to current, in ohm-meters. Any variation can show up a buried feature, like a building foundation. Since we can't afford to dig up the whole square kilometer, we learn what we can with instruments. I've already made a magnetometer survey; so between the two we should get a good idea of the underground layout."

"You didn't use all that apparatus at Horenso," said Kara, referring to the dig on which she as a bride had accompanied her bridegroom.

Momentarily, memories checked Salazar's breath; but he spoke with cool professionalism: "I didn't, because that job was all photography, measuring, cleaning up, and consolidating. Those ruins were recent and in plain sight. Here they're buried, with nothing on the surface but fragments."

The site of Nomuru stretched across a broad, shallow vale or depression, sparsely covered with the Kukulcanian analogues of grass and herbs. Along the edges of this flat, buff-and-green expanse lay piles of thorny bushes and stunted trees, which had been uprooted and stacked to leave the ruin free of major vegetation. Beyond the western border, the little Mozii, an affluent of the Sappari, gurgled softly. Salazar told Kara:

"You can bet your brassière old Sambyaku and his friends took a bite out of my appropriation. His excuse was that the tribal elders were outraged by our digging up the graves of their ancestors. Of course, the people who lived here when Nomuru was the capital of the Nomoruvian Empire were quite different from the present locals. But the fact that Neruu, which is in Sambyaku's chieftainship, gets its name from the ancient capital gives him a pretext to shake down the hairy aliens." He glanced at his poignette. "Damn! Those Kooks he promised me should have arrived long since."

Salazar pulled a trowel out of his boot and a file from a small sheath. While watching for the promised workers, he began sharpening the edge of the tool.

"Why sharpen a trowel?" asked Kara.

"We use them to shave down the surface of a test pit."

"May I see what your students are doing with those instruments over there?"

"Sure." Salazar led Kara to the northern end of the site, where the three assistants were finishing their survey.

Galina Bartch, a buxom, blue-eyed blond with a spotty complexion beneath a floppy straw hat, had charge of a black box with four terminals, to which electric cables were attached. These four wires led to four iron pins, like oversized nails, thrust into the ground half a meter apart, along a cord stretched between two posts.

As Kara watched, the slim, elegant Marcel Frappot pulled up the rearmost pin, moved it past the other three, and thrust it into the earth a measured distance from its neighbor. At the same time, Galina deftly unscrewed the cable from its binding post, repositioned it, and shifted the remaining wires.

Ito Kurita bent over the black box, pushed a button, and made a notation on his clipboard. Kara, busily photographing the scene, began: "Keith, now could you—"

Salazar laid a hand on her arm. "Hold everything. Here comes Sambyaku himself."

Five Kooks marched out of the woods in a rigid formation. Two were armed with native muskets, while two others bore spears. An elderly Kook, his body decorated with symbols in blue and yellow, strode amid the four. Salazar muttered: "They don't use spears any more for serious fighting, but you know what sticklers for tradition they are." He raised his voice in the harsh, nonhuman Shongo tongue: "Hail, honorable Chief Sambyaku! All is well with me. Is all well with you?"

After the usual questions and responses, Salazar said: "What brings you hither, Your Honor? I observe that my promised workers have not appeared, nor has the Sappari bridge been repaired."

"I regret to inconvenience my honorable Terran friend," rasped Sambyaku. "Know that it has been decided that Intromission Day shall be observed two days hence. No workers will be available, because all will be practicing rituals and donning their formal paint."

"When will my workers be available?" asked Salazar.

"In ten or eleven days. You will understand that after Intromission Day, our younger persons are less willingly tied down to a plan of work than usual. The bridge shall be repaired when labor is available."

"I understand," said Salazar unctuously. "What cannot be cured must be endured, even if it be a bath in the Sappari. I look forward to the resumption of our work. May I invite the honorable chief to refreshment?"

"I thank the wise Terran, but my duties compel my return to Neruu. Take utmost care of your health!"

"And may Your Honor take utmost care of his health!"

"May your life be tranquil. . . ."

After a long exchange of good wishes, the chief stalked away. Salazar growled: "Always some damned delay!"

"What did he say?" asked Kara.

"They're taking the next sixtnight off for Intromission Day."

"You mean their springtime orgy?"

"Yep. It's their annual mating rite; actually, not an orgy but the equivalent of a mass wedding."

"I want to see that! Are you saying it's the only time of year they—uh—"

"Oh, no; they screw the year round, like Terrans. Don't you as a journalist know about these matters?"

"Only a little. The *Times* has a man for native relations, Phil Reiner. All my work has been with human beings. Hey, Keith, look!"

Salazar turned. A being had appeared on the far side of the field: a Kook mounted on a juten, a creature that resembled something between a small bipedal dinosaur and a featherless ostrich. Its coppery scales reflected the sun; its large head, on a thick neck, ended in a huge hooked beak. The Kook bore a slender lance, while the holster of a bulky pistol hung from his saddle.

Salazar took out his pistol and checked the magazine, muttering: "Damn, I should have kept those three I hired for the Henderson trip! That's a Chosha, a nomad, and we need more fire power. . . ."

As he spoke, the newcomer wheeled his mount and leisurely jounced away to the dusty-green forest. Salazar growled: "I'm stupid. I should have brought my rifle."

"Wouldn't your pistol outrange those flintlock things?"

"Yep; but their big bullets can still kill at a hundred meters."

"If we had a zapper, we could mow them down."

"Sure, but the army won't let ray weapons out of its armories. This may foreshadow something serious; rumors are afloat that the nomads are preparing an attack on the Shongosi Chieftainship, which includes our site."

"What would happen?"

Salazar shrugged. "Couldn't predict. If the Choshas overran Shongosi, they'd be up against the Empire of Feënzun, and I don't think Empress Gariko would tolerate that. So we'd better move along, if we don't want to get caught in a Kookish war." Salazar paused. "Since there's no help for it, we shall have to open the first test pit ourselves. Will you lend a hand?"

"Sure," said Kara. "But why can't Kono and Uwangi man the shovels?"

"They were hired as camp workers, and it would be easier to pick up Mount Nezumi than to get a Kook to do a job he's not contracted for."

"Okay, then; but I want to see this Intromission Day ceremony."

"You won't get an erotic kick out of it, unless you're like a man I knew who got horny from watching an amoeba divide itself under the microscope."

"You're evil-minded, Keith! It's my job as a writer."

"Not evil, but not an amoeba, either. Besides, I've got to make the most of every minute on the dig, before the money runs out or the Choshas invade."

"Now look here, Keith! If I put in two days' work on your dig—you know I'm no weakling—that would make up the time you'd lose by taking one day off. If you won't—well, I'll go alone."

"You can't do that! You don't speak Shongo, and all sorts of things could happen."

Eyes alight with animation, Marcel Frappot spoke up: "Keith, why do you not take her? We will start your test pits and set up the screens. We know how to sort and bag the finds."

"Go ahead!" echoed Galina Bartch.

"I shall keep meticulous records," added Ito Kurita primly.

"If we strike a significant feature," said Frappot, "we shall leave it untouched until you return."

Salazar thought glumly: Macel, the romantic, would like to engineer a reunion. Well, I suppose one day without me won't be fatal to the project.

"Okay," he said at last. "I'll let you kids run the dig, provided you don't go below ten centimeters on any new pits. Kara, please hold the tape. While the young people finish here, I'll mark out a few test pits."

THE
FESTIVAL

Keith Salazar and Kara Sheffield walked back to one of the five-meter squares the assistants had staked out along the side of the site toward the camp. Salazar blew his whistle. Then he laid a compass on the ground and, with Kara's help, marked off a one-by-two-meter rectangle, with its long axis north and south, and demarcated the area by stakes and strings.

By the time they had finished this task, Kono and Uwangi had answered the summons. Kono, his scales alight with a pattern of emerald crosses, shouldered an armload of timbers and a screen of coarse wire netting. Uwangi, gay in scarlet circles, carried shovels, buckets, and other implements. Either load could scarcely have been managed by a large, strong human being; but the Kooks bore them in their long, stringy arms without apparent effort.

Under Salazar's direction, Kono spread a tarpaulin beside the marked-off rectangle. Uwangi began as-

24

sembling the timbers into a frame, which Salazar secured with nuts and bolts.

"It's one thing we can do better than the Kooks," Salazar remarked. "With only three fingers and a thumb, and claws instead of nails, they're not so handy with nuts and bolts."

When fully assembled, the framework supported the screen horizontally over the tarpaulin. The screen itself hung from four short chains hooked to eyebolts on the framework, so that it could be swung through an arc.

Salazar dismissed the Kooks and picked up an edger. He tested its semicircular blade with his thumb, then set the edge against the ground just inside the bordering strings. Planting his foot on the flange of the edger, he applied his weight and sliced into the olive-green turf. Then he moved the edger and repeated the action.

"Let me try that!" said Kara.

Salazar handed her the edger; but when she put her foot on it, she proved too light to drive it through the root-tangled turf. "At least," remarked Salazar dryly as he took back the tool, "you haven't put on weight."

"What did you think?" she retorted acidly. "That grieving over my single state, I'd gorge until I swelled like a balloon?"

"No, of course not—"

"After all, I might want to catch another husband some day."

"Well—ah—of course, if . . ."

"If I gained a kilo, all I'd have to do is to pedal out here to sweat it off."

With a grunt, Salazar dug in the edger. "Be glad to have you, any old time."

She smiled warily. "If by 'have' you mean you

would put me up, I'll be glad to come whenever my job demands it."

"Now who's evil-minded?" said Salazar with a grin.

When the rectangle had been outlined by cuts, they spent the rest of the day grubbing up vegetation and piling it on the tarpaulin. The three assistants finished their survey and started to clear another test pit. At quitting time, Kara stretched and yawned.

"I'll have some mighty stiff muscles," she said, "But I won't have any problems sleeping tonight."

Kara and Salazar exchanged a pregnant glance. He said: "At least not if—" He bit off the half-formed *double-entendre* when he noticed three pairs of youthful eyeballs swiveling in his direction. The kids, he thought, are eaten with curiosity about our relationship. Let 'em guess! He resolved thenceforth to handle his guest with reticent courtesy, nothing more. That seemed to be her desire anyway.

The following day saw the clearing of more test pits. In the afternoon, Kara said: "Keith, couldn't you do a little actual digging, to help me with my article?"

"Guess so, if we don't go below the surface layer." Salazar raised his voice: "Hey, kids! Will you come here, please?" He turned back. "We divide the preliminary excavation into arbitrary ten-centimeter strata, called from the top down: Surface, A, B, C, and so on. Ito, Marcel, take shovels. Galina, show Miss Sheffield how to work the screen. I'll do the bagging."

Kurita and Frappot began to fill a bucket with freshly-dug earth, which Kurita dumped on the screen. Galina Bartch vigorously rocked the screen, so that brown soil cascaded through the meshes. Presently there were only stones, lumps, and clods spread out across the screen. Galina stirred these with her gloved hands, crushing the clods, until all that remained unsieved was a mass of pebbles and fragments.

"What did we get?" asked Salazar.

Galina held up a piece of rust-red brick. "Shongo work?"

"Probably. Put it here." Salazar spread the mouth of a cloth bag, to which was attached a tag reading: TEST PIT 1, SURFACE.

"Here's something," said Galina, holding up another fingernail-sized fragment in azure and gold. Salazar said:

"Porcelain, glazed. That means it's not Shongo; their technology declined from the days of the Nomoruvian Empire until their recent burst of industrialization. It could be trade goods from the Shongo period, or a piece of old Nomoruvian work grubbed up and redeposited." He held the bag open. "Lend Kara your gloves, Galina."

So it continued for an hour, with Kara sharing the job with Galina. Then Salazar applied his tape to the pit. "Ten centimeters," he said. "Let's take this one down another ten, after I scrape it."

Salazar squatted in the shallow excavation and, with sweeping semicircular strokes of his sharpened trowel, began to shave thin slices of brown earth from the high spots along the edge.

"What are all those dark spots?" asked Kara.

"Burrows of worms and other organisms—that is, the Kukulcanian equivalents—which have filled in again," said Salazar. "This dark area might be a burial, but there's no sign of remains yet. Or it might be a post-Nomoruvian trash pit. When you hit something like this but don't know what it is, you call it a 'feature.' "

"No golden idols?" said Kara.

"Kara! You of all people know better than that!"

"Sorry. I was only teasing."

Salazar continued: "That's like joking about bombs at the spaceport. It's the worst thing that could happen. As soon as the rumor got out, half of Henderson would be here with picks and shovels to dig up the site and ruin the stratigraphy. Next thing, there'd be a fad among rich bastards like Bergen to stick ancient Kookish artifacts on their mantlepieces, so that without exact records of discovery, every such object's scientific value would be destroyed. Get some pictures, Galina."

With her tiny camera, the girl took several shots of the now smooth-bottomed excavation. Digging and sieving resumed. More objects came to light and were meticulously placed in another labeled sack. There was half of a broken, rusted iron door key. There were bits of brick, worked stone, glass, copper, and pottery. Frappot exclaimed:

"Aha, Keith! I think we have a remain."

He held up a length of pearl-gray bone. Salazar fingered the piece, saying: "Part of the leg of a domestic tisai, I think. Liu will have to look it over to make sure; and he'll run a sample through the AMS to give us a date—"

"Through the *what*?" Kara broke in.

"Sorry; the accelerator mass spectrometer. Sometime I'll explain how it works. This bone was cut in two, as with a cleaver, and these nicks were made with the same sort of tool. Evidently from a Kookish butcher shop. This might be the site of such a shop, or again the bone might be from someone's family dinner, or even from a Shongo picnic. I shouldn't expect much Shongo stuff at this level, unless—"

Salazar broke off and straightened up, staring at the far end of the site. There, three Kooks on three copper-scaled jutens paused as they emerged from the scrubby timber beyond. Kara and the assistants rose, looking askance at the newcomers.

"Damn!" muttered Salazar. "Choshas again! That guy we saw yesterday must have gone for reinforcements. Get down, all of you! Take cover!"

"What cover?" asked Frappot. "With all the bushes cleared away . . ."

"Lie down in the test pit!"

"But there is not enough room. . . ."

Salazar threw himself prone between the test pit and the newcomers, who sat their mounts and stared. Craning his neck to observe four human beings trying to fit themselves into a depression only big enough for two, the archaeologist barked:

"Marcel! Go fetch the rifle! Bend low as you run!"

He pointed to the pile of gear at the edge of the field, against which his rifle leaned. As Frappot started on his way, Salazar eased his pistol from its holster.

One of the strange Kooks set its mount into motion. The *thump-thump* of the juten's bipedal gait resounded across the clearing as it trotted towards the same pile of gear. Salazar thought: That nomad's after my gun. As its mount ran, the Kook rider drew out a firearm, a massive object like a Terran horse pistol of the powdered-wig era. The Kook cocked and raised the weapon, taking aim at the running graduate student.

Since the invader was too distant to be picked off with a pistol while on the move, save for a fantastically lucky shot, Salazar aimed just ahead of the running juten and, as the animal's body came into his sights, squeezed the trigger. The juten pitched forward on its beaked head; its rider flew out of the saddle and turned a somersault as it struck the ground.

The Kook staggered to its feet and peered about. The lance in its saddle boot was broken; but the native found the pistol where it had fallen. It hastily aimed the firearm at Salazar and pulled the trigger. The weapon failed to fire. Knocked the priming out of the pan, thought Salazar.

The Kook set out on foot for Salazar, holding its pistol by the barrel and bounding from side to side. Salazar fired at this difficult target and missed. He fired and missed once more. Beside the pile of gear, Marcel Frappot stood holding the rifle. The youth dared not shoot, since Salazar was in the same line of fire as the Kook.

Salazar fired a third shot. The Kook staggered and squawked. The shot had grazed but not seriously wounded the attacker. Then it hurled itself at the archaeologist, swinging the big flintlock pistol like a hammer at the gun in Salazar's right hand. The butt struck Salazar's barrel and sent his weapon spinning away.

The Kook swung its pistol over its head, aiming it at the Terran's skull. Salazar snatched from his boot the sharpened trowel, stepped quickly inside the Kook's swing, and drove the trowel into the native's painted belly.

The beaked mouth opened in a screech as the Kook clapped a clawed hand over the wound. Another blow with the pistol butt sent Salazar's tropical helmet flying, while Salazar, gripping the trowel in both hands, stabbed again and again. On the fourth stab, the Kook sank, bleeding profusely and gasping incoherent sounds in its own raucous tongue.

"Marcel!" Salazar called. "Cover the others!"

As Frappot sighted along the rifle barrel with his finger on the trigger, the two remaining Kooks turned their mounts and jounced away into the brush. Kara, Galina, and Ito climbed out of the test pit, slapping dirt from their hair and clothes and asking questions.

"Keith!" exclaimed Kara. "Thank goodness you're alive! I thought for a second I saw your head bouncing away, but it was only your hat."

"No credit to me," growled Salazar, picking up his helmet. "Must be losing my grip, missing easy shots like that."

"And me," said Frappot, "I dared not shoot with you in line with this one."

"Who is it who tried to kill you, Professor?" asked Ito.

"A Kampairin," said Salazar, studying the painted gold-and-scarlet symbols on the Kook's scales.

"Isn't that a nomad tribe?" asked Galina.

"Yep; one of old Kampai's boys."

"Are we likely to see more of them?" asked Frappot, as if eager for another chance to show his mettle. His face was flushed.

"Can't tell yet," said Salazar. "This is pretty far outside their normal range. Let's get on with the job."

During the evening at camp, Kara said, "I know dirt archaeology includes a lot of tedious drudgery, but—"

"Any profession does, when you get into it," Salazar interjected.

"I wanted to ask, don't you expect to find anything more exciting than little bits of glass and brick and stone? No golden idols, of course; but something I could at least take a publishable picture of."

Salazar shrugged. "We might come on a statue, or a mosaic, or a cache of copper utensils. No way of telling except to dig. What I dream of finding but probably shan't is King Bembogu's fabled library. If I did, you can bet your ballet slippers I'd keep mum about it until I got the stuff out, or the looters and souvenir hunters might beat me to it."

"Was Bembogu that last ruler of Nomoruvia you were telling me about?"

"Yep. Our information about him comes from much later documents and is partly fictionalized; but he's supposed to have been a scholarly king who amassed a library of 4,096 scrolls."

"That's a peculiar number."

"It's the square of sixty-four. Since their number system has a base of eight, it's their equivalent of ten thousand."

"What happened to him?"

"A barbarian invasion caught him without his body paint on; he'd neglected the army in order to raise his subjects' standard of living; so he was routed and slain and the city was sacked. Seems to have been one of those unfortunate rulers who were too humane and enlightened for their own good. It shows what happens when you try to make woolly-minded academics like me into kings or generals."

"Rubbish, Keith! You'd make a fine king or general."

Salazar grinned. "Thanks, but I think I know my limtations. Anyway, there's not the remotest chance of my being asked to fill either rôle."

As Salazar and Kara pedaled along the main street of Neruu, the industrial center of the Shongo nation, the sky was dark with the smoke of a hundred chimneys and the air was clangorous with hammering, sawing, and the whir and clatter of machine tools. Forges glowed redly through open doorways in the plain, boxlike stone buildings.

A few Kooks passed the Terrans, their scales painted with a multitude of symbols in a rainbow of colors. One could read from these symbols a Kook's age, sex, clan, caste, marital status, occupation, and achievements, but to master the complex system required years of study. To his regret, Salazar had only a rudimentary grasp of it.

Beaked heads turned as the Terrans rolled past; but there was no rush to crowd around the aliens. The Kooks gave each a cursory stare, then went incuriously about their business.

"Their industrial development is oddly unbalanced by our standards," Salazar explained. "Excellent time-pieces but no electrical equipment; steam engines and vehicles but no flying machines. Somebody once made a steam-powered dirigible airship, but it blew up. Without petroleum, I suppose they have no way to get started in aeronautics. They make good masonry, pottery, and glassware; but their only cloth is crude stuff for things like tents and curtains. Not wearing clothes, they haven't had the motive to develop high-grade textiles."

"I wonder why they haven't begun to copy our advanced weapons?"

"It's their ultra-conservatism. They invented the muzzle-loading musket a couple of thousand years ago; but they've only just begun to rifle the barrels. They haven't started on breechloaders and repeaters, though they've known about Terran guns for a century."

"Just as well for them. Where's this ceremony?"

"At the athletic field outside the town."

"I thought they had no games or sports?"

"They don't; but they're enthusiasts for athletic drills, if you can call them enthusiastic about anything."

"They sound like bores."

Salazar chuckled. "Their social events make a meeting of the Maravilla Society seem interesting. They're easier to respect than to love. They're cold, rigid, formalistic, and hidebound; but for us that has advantages. Kooks are pretty honest and trustworthy; you can rely more on a Kook's word than on a Terran's. They betray their emotions by moving those bristles on their necks. Since it's an unconscious reaction, which they can't seem to control, each Kook carries a built-in lie detector.

> *"The Kooks may be stolid*
> *And lacking in charm,*
> *But their promises solid*
> *Protect you from harm!"*

The exercise ground was about the size of an American football field, enclosed on three sides by a fence, towards which crowds of Kukulcanians were converging. Salazar said:

"If we move right lively, we can grab places yonder."

They leaned their bicycles against an unoccupied section of fence as more Kooks clustered beside and behind them. The rasping sounds of Kukulcanian speech assailed their ears, and the peculiar fishy smell of Kooks invaded their nostrils. At the base of the square-bottomed U outlined by the fence, a separate little crowd of natives clustered, jabbering and gesticulating. Kara asked:

"Which are those?"

"The loving couples," said Salazar, "about to consummate their union. There are also some couples already mated who haven't succeeded in begetting offspring."

"How do they feed their young? I don't see mammalian characteristics."

Salazar found himself staring at Kara's mammalian characteristics. When she noticed, he averted his gaze. "The primitive tribes regurgitate, like Terran birds that feed their young in the nest."

"Ugh!"

Salazar smiled. "Other species, other customs. These urbanized folk think that custom barbarous, too; they mince and mash the food and spoon-feed their little ones. Some of their physicians condemn this practice as nutritionally unsound. They call for a return to regurgitation, which they say gives the Kooklets some needed enzyme."

"How did they hit on this strange custom?" She nodded toward the clump of Kukulcanians inside the fence.

"Maybe a relic of primitive times, when any male could have any female he could catch. Now the females make sure their chosen mates catch them. It's a puzzle, because Kooks seems to have a strong pair bond—stronger than ours."

"I see what you mean," said Kara with an edge in her voice.

Salazar gulped at the unfortunate allusion to their failed marriage. "Anyway, they—ah—Cabot Firestone thinks this pair bond may be mostly imposed by their culture. Since they're born lawyers who worship precedent, they maintain customs and ceremonies going back hundreds of thousands of years."

"How do you archaeologists know what their customs were so long ago?"

"Because their written records go back more than ten times as far as ours. For instance, it was a major revolution for them to give up trial by ordeal, about thirty thousand years ago."

"You mean like those medieval trials where they threw you in the river and judged you innocent if you drowned?"

"Yep. Had a picturesque kind of ordeal. They tied

you to a—" Salazar glanced away and stiffened. "Quick, down on one knee!"

"What's up?"

"High Chief Miyage is here. He doesn't like me, so be careful. Down!"

The two Terrans knelt, along with the mass of natives, as a small group of Kukulcanians strode through the squatting crowd. One, whose hide was painted in brilliant patterns of scarlet, gold, and azure, wore a golden disk the size of a hand suspended from his neck by a golden chain. With his big golden eyes fixed on Salazar, he strode purposefully towards the archaeologist, croaking:

"Hail, honorable Sarasara!"

"Hail to your Highness!" said Salazar.

"Is all well with your clan?"

"All is well with my clan. Is all well with your Highness's clan?"

"Thanks to the Universal Law, all is well. You may rise, and also the alien with you. We have pondered your excavation of the ruins of Nomuru. We do not wish this to continue, at least for the present."

The words struck Salazar like a blow in the solar plexus. He pulled himself together enough to say: "May I ask your Highness why not?"

"Certain of your fellow aliens have approached us, offering to lease the area. They wish to change the land to attract others of their kind, to perform whatever sinister rites you creatures indulge in. We are negotiating, and we do not wish our proceedings disturbed by your activities."

"Sir, may I ask who these Terrans are?"

"You may not. When and if agreement is reached, these details will become public."

The High Chief began to turn away. Remembering what Dr. Samuel Johnson had said, that when a man knows he is to be hanged in a fortnight, it concentrates his mind wonderfully, Salazar called:

"A moment, Your Highness!"

"Aye?" said the Kook chieftain.

"Permit me to say that, if my excavations continue, they may reveal matters that, in the long run, will prove of more advantage to your federated tribes than any plan of my fellow Terrans to turn the area into a resort."

"How so?"

"Your Highness knows that for centuries, Nomuru was a great and famous capital."

"Aye, but what of that?"

"On my own world, several nations make much of their income from relics of ancient times. People come from afar to see them and freely spend money in the nations displaying these relics."

"We do not understand why anyone should go far from home to see old stones and bricks."

Salazar: "I assure Your Highness that such is the case, and I wager that the same will come to pass here, since your people so revere tradition. The site, when excavated and tidied up, will attract countless visitors, both Terran and of your kind."

"What do you wish of us, O Sarasara?"

"To permit me and my crew to continue our digging, at least until these developers actually begin work at the site."

"Very well, for the time being. We shall consult our council and inform you of our final decision. May you lead a tranquil—"

"One thing more, Your Highness. We have had trouble with stray Choshas." He told of the death of the Kampairin raider. "If you will send your people to Nomuru, they will find the body beneath a tarpaulin on the edge of the field."

The Kook's neck spines rippled in a way that corresponded to a Terran's frown. "That is significant, Sarasara; it is meritorious of you to bring the matter to our attention. The Kampairin are forbidden by treaty to come within thirty-two *itikron* of that place. We shall have our subordinates investigate and send a stern warning to Chief Kampai. May you lead a tranquil life!"

"May Your Highness's life also be tranquil."

"May no obstacles spring up in your path."

"May Your Highness overcome any obstacles that arise. . . ."

The High Chief disappeared into the crowd. Kara asked: "What has Miyage got against you? He seemed polite enough."

"He used the grammatical forms proper to an inferior. As to our mutual dislike, he had a dispute with the Empress. Hey, it's show time!"

At the end of the field where the couples assembled, the rite took shape. An elderly Kook, distinguished by a ribbon about his neck, mounted a stand and embarked upon a rhythmic speech. When he had finished, High Chief Miyage took his place and began an even longer speech. Kara said:

"It sounds as if they were speaking in verse."

"They are," said Salazar, "with end rhymes and all.

> *"The Kooks talk in verse,*
> *And to make matters worse,*
> *The tones of their vowels,*
> *Must agree with their howls!*

"I once got out of a ticklish fix by reciting Macaulay's *Horatius*—or as much of it as I could remember.

They couldn't understand the words, but it convinced them that the Terrans could be cultured beings. Now comes the grand coitus."

Pushing and shouting, the nuptial pairs, gay in their emerald-and-white wedding paint, lined up. The females stood in the first line; the males, distinguished by the small crest of spines on their heads, formed a second line behind them.

An assistant handed High Chief Miyage a double-barreled musket with gold-chased barrels sparkling in the sunshine. The High Chief cocked one hammer, aimed at the azure sky, and pulled one trigger. The musket vomited a puff of gray smoke. At once the female Kooks set off at a run towards the unfenced end of the field.

The chief then cocked and fired the second barrel. The bridegrooms pelted away in determined pursuit. Salazar muttered:

"The girls won't run hard enough to escape."

The runners passed the ends of the fence and continued out into open country. By the time distance shrank their figures, every female runner had been caught by, or let herself be caught by, the male who had been posted behind her. The Terrans could not clearly see because of the churning clouds of dust; but the females seemed to have dropped to hands and knees, while the males approached them from behind.

"Isn't that how Terran birds do it?" asked Kara. "I've seen Conrad's chickens in action."

"Yep. Like birds, they don't waste any time, either," he added, as the couples began to straggle back to the field.

"What next?" asked Kara.

"More speeches. All the couples deliver their own remarks."

"They seem a long-winded race."

"Yep. Oratory is their main art form. Their painting, sculpture, and music are nothing much; but their poetry, drama, and rhetoric are highly developed. A Kookish Michelangelo once made an eight-day nonstop speech."

"All in verse? Wow! I've only heard speeches that *felt* as if they'd been going for eight days. Since I can't understand their croak, do you think we could start back?"

"Yep. Come along." Salazar wheeled his bicycle away from the fence, carefully threading his way among the crowding Kooks. He had a foot on a pedal when a shout brought him round.

"Hey, Salazar!" roared the black-browed Conrad Bergen, emerging from the native crowd and followed by the rest of his hunting party. "What are you—by God, you've got my bitch! I'll—"

Kara gave a small scream as Bergen started toward her, fists swinging. Salazar thrust his bicycle in front of the red-faced, wrathful man; the two antagonists and the bicycle collapsed in a tangle. After they had sorted themselves out and risen, Bergen aimed a furious swing at the archaeologist. Salazar ducked and landed a punch on Bergen's nose; but a second later another swing caught him on the side of the head and sent him sprawling.

"I'll teach you to steal my dame!" screamed Bergen, kicking his recumbent foe in the ribs. Despite the pain that shot through him, Salazar caught Bergen's booted ankle in both hands. A heave toppled the bulky Bergen, who fell with a thud that shook the trampled earth. As Salazar, slowed by the pain in his side, rose more slowly to his feet, he saw Bergen do likewise. Almost at once, a multitude of scaly talons seized upon both, and the black eyes of musket muzzles stared them in the face.

"What is this?" croaked High Chief Miyage. "These animals dare to defile our ancient ceremony? Prepare them for execution!" The forked tongue flicked out.

Scaly hands relieved Salazar and Bergen of their pistols. Bergen asked: "What's he say?"

When Salazar had translated, Bergen cried: "Hey! Do they mean that?"

"Sure."

"But—can they really do that? We're humans!"

"Who's going to stop them? Here they are the human beings; we are just monsters from outer space."

"What will they do? Shoot us?"

"They might. Beheading is their favorite method."

Chief Sambyaku squatted a curtsy to his tribal superior. To the Kooks holding Salazar and Bergen he said: "Do nothing before you receive additional commands." The two chiefs moved away in earnest speech.

Bergen, his arms and legs firmly gripped in Kookish talons, glared at Salazar. Though stunned by the rush of events, Salazar pulled himself together, saying with professional calm:

"I said you had a medical problem. Now, unless Sambyaku can talk Miyage out of it, you'll soon learn how long a head stays conscious after it's cut off. I've always wondered if one sees the ground rushing up at one."

"If that's a joke, you've got a gruesome sense of humor," grated Bergen. "What good would knowing that do you? You couldn't write a book about it afterward."

"That does rather dampen the pleasure of discovery."

"It's all your fault! If you hadn't meddled in my affairs . . ."

"I never meddled," snapped Salazar. "I was going

to Neruu, and the lady asked to come along. Your relations with—"

"Son of a bitch!" screamed Bergen. "When I get loose, I'll beat you into a glob of jelly!"

"Without your head, you might have trouble finding me," said Salazar.

The two chiefs reappeared, and High Chief Miyage said: "Our loyal vassal Sambyaku has persuaded us that it were but fair to give you aliens a chance to fight for your lives. O Justiciar Kanini!"

"Aye, Your Highness?" said the aged, beribboned Kook whose speech had preceded the High Chief's oration.

"What says the law anent the interruption of a sacred rite by aliens from other worlds?"

From one of his pouches, Kanini produced a Kukulcanian book, a scroll mounted in a small glass-fronted frame. This frame was equipped with two little cranks, whereby the tawny scroll of native paper could be unrolled from one spindle and rolled up on the other. Kanini turned one of the cranks, scrutinizing the lines of print. Kara had disappeared.

At last the aged legalist croaked: "May it please Your Highness, there is no precise provision for such a case. Since aliens have been coming to this world for less than two octoquadrates, too few cases have accumulated to furnish precedents.

"The likeliest precedent I can find," continued Kanini, "goes back to the days of barbarism, many octoquadrates ago. When a domestic beast had injured or slain its owner, it was turned loose to be attacked by a beast of prey. If it defeated its attacker, it was pardoned. Since these aliens are lower animals, I propose that we release them in the field with a *porondu* from the town menagerie. The contest will provide an unexpected climax to the ceremony and impart an edifying moral lesson to the onlookers as well."

"A worthy thought," said High Chief Miyage.

"A moment, sire!" said Chief Sambyaku. "Does Your Highness propose that they fight the porondu with bare hands? Such a contest would be too one-sided either to let the aliens redeem their lives or to impart a moral lesson."

"There is something in what you say," mused High Chief Miyage. "We cannot lend them guns, for they would simply slay the beast, or even aim at us! Ah! Let a pair of spears be fetched from the town museum, one for each alien!"

An hour passed while Salazar and Bergen, their wrists and ankles bound with thongs, sat on the ground beneath the vigilant gaze of two musket-armed guards. Bergen roared and cursed, making wild threats and accusations against Salazar. The latter sat mutely until Bergen, too, subsided into sullen silence. From afar came the droning, rhythmic croak of Kookish speech.

"Like a roost of goddam crows," muttered Bergen.

When Kara Sheffield and the three remaining men of Bergen's party approached the captives, the guards warily shifted their guns. Chung, in the lead, broke the news.

"I have tried to convince the High Chief that he should release you two; but when Kooks make up their minds . . ." Chung shrugged. "It is like those laws of the Pedes and Mersians. At least, he agreed not to molest the rest of us. I am sorry."

"Oh, Keith!" wailed Kara. "How I wish I hadn't insisted on coming here!"

"Don't blame yourself," said Salazar. "You couldn't have foreseen this."

Bergen growled at his guide: "What'll you do if this creature kills me?"

"Return to Suvarov," said Chung with a deprecatory shrug. "I do not think your friends will wish to continue the hunt."

"And if we survive—at least, if I do? I'd still want my hunt."

Chung ducked a bow. "In that case, Mr. Bergen, you must find another guide. I fear that travel with one of your ebullient temperament is dangerous to my health."

"Hey, you've got a contract with me!"

The guide gave a *pro forma* smile. "It permits me to withdraw for reasons of health. Fear not; I shall send a replacement, my cousin Ma Qiali—Charley Ma, you could call him."

"When will he get here?"

"Perhaps in a sixtnight. He must come from Gueilin."

"Hell! Am I supposed to sit on my duff—"

The two chiefs, surrounded by eight Kooks, crossed the turf with dignified stride. At their command, scaly hands loosened the captives' bonds, hauled the apprehensive prisoners to their feet, and hustled them back to the now-empty enclosure. Salazar and Bergen were each handed a long spear with a tapering steel head lightly spotted with brownish oxide.

As their escort retired, Salazar and Bergen faced their foe, one of the major predators of the planet Kukulcan. The dinosaurlike porondu stood a few meters off, with four Kooks holding its leashes. Much larger than the domesticated juten, which it otherwise resembled, its huge beak was carried over two meters above the ground. Its body scales were brown splashed with acrid yellow, and its arms, the size of a man's, ended in sharp-clawed talons.

"Professor!" muttered Bergen. "Looks like we've got to be allies, like it or not."

"Yep," said Salazar. "Let's keep three meters apart. When it goes after one of us, the other should try to spear it under the arm."

"Here it comes!"

The handlers simultaneously cast off their leashes and dashed for the gate, which they quickly latched behind them. With a raucous scream, the porondu lumbered towards Salazar, who gripped his spear and lunged for the creature's breast. The point was stopped by a bone.

Before Salazar could withdraw his weapon, the porondu seized the shaft in its saw-toothed beak and snapped it with a powerful jerk of its head. The archaeologist found that he held a meter of shaft without a steel spearhead. The porondu raised its head, opening its beak to show the teeth within.

Bergen ran forward and thrust his spear into the creature's side. With a shriek, the porondu wheeled, swung its head low, and smote Bergen in the ribs. The blow hurled the huge executive sideways. He fell, rolled over, and tried to sit up, but the breath had been knocked out of him. As he lay coughing and gasping, the porondu squatted down on his legs, pinning him to the ground. The porondu, which Salazar realized must weigh at least half a ton, opened its raptorial beak, then hesitated as if pondering which part of Bergen to tear off first.

Half-disarmed, Salazar did the only thing he could think of. He ran behind the squatting porondu, leaped to its back, and slid into a sitting position behind its arms.

"Get up!" he yelled in Shongo, beating the animal over the head with the shaft of his broken spear.

The porondu lurched to its feet and tried to crane

its neck around to the left to seize its tormentor.
Salazar whacked the beak as it approached. When it
swung its head, as large as that of a horse, around to
the right, the archaeologist struck it on the other
side.

The porondu danced about, trying to shake off its
rider; but Salazar seized one of the small arms near
its base and clung precariously to his perch, wishing
for a proper saddle. The beast reached back with its
free arm, trying to claw the archaeologist off its back.
Salazar's bush jacket ripped at the shoulder, and he
felt the sting of a deep scratch on his arm but pounded
the groping member until it gave up trying to seize
him.

The porondu then set off at a jouncing run for the
open end of the field. Soon the enclosure and the
chimneys of Neruu disappeared behind a roll in the
ground.

Still clutching the arm, Salazar gripped the scaly
torso with his legs as best he could, wondering if the
beast would run clear to the Western Ocean, thousands of kilometers away. After a kilometer, however, the monster slowed.

When at last it halted, Salazar wondered what to
do next. If he slid off, he would be devoured on the
spot. Although the creature had tired, it could still
outrun a man on those long, ostrichlike legs.

At last Salazar shouted: "Back to Neruu, you!" and
hit the porondu on the side of its head. As it shied
away from the blows, it gradually turned around.
Relieved, Salazar whacked its rump until it lurched
into motion.

A quarter-hour later, Salazar guided his unruly
mount into Neruu's athletic field. Every time it tried
to turn away or to peck at its rider, Salazar yelled

and struck it. When the pair were within the enclosure, he called out in Shongo:

"You, in charge of the beast! Come and get it!"

The handlers ran out, secured their leashes, and led the cowed monster away, its two slight wounds still oozing crimson blood. Salazar slid off the tail and fell in a heap. The porondu's wide body had spread his legs so far apart that now his hip joints ached and he could barely stand. Bergen helped him to his feet, saying:

"You okay, Professor?"

"Still sore where you kicked me."

"Sorry about that, but you know how it is in a fight. I'm kind of battered myself, where that thing butted me in the ribs. What was it the old Kook with the ribbon said that I couldn't understand? Oh, here he comes!"

The aged justiciar assumed a formal stance before the Terrans and intoned: "His Highness has decreed that you twain have earned acquittal of all charges. You shall go free, on condition that you do the High Chief a small favor."

"What is that?" said Salazar.

"He knows that you aliens must have some ceremony corresponding to our Intromission Day. He wishes to observe it."

"What's he say?" demanded Bergen.

Salazar translated, adding: "I could give him a song and dance about our very different customs; but to keep our heads in place, I'd better offer him something."

"Jesus!" said Bergen. "I can't ask my people to demonstrate for him. I could give him a card to Erika's Place in Suvarov. You know it?"

"I've heard about it," said Salazar. "It wouldn't

do. He might want to take part in the activities, and that's impossible. He would injure the girl terribly."

"Well then, I'll get him a table at Nasr's Club. His floor shows run right up to the whole bit; I've warned Nasr to clean up his act or lose his lease. But for this one time . . ."

Salazar conveyed the promise to Kanini, who nodded and marched off. Bergen exulted: "Say, that was a close call! Where'd you get the idea of jumping on the creature's back?"

"I read adventure stories as a kid," said Salazar. "Where are our people?"

"There!" Bergen pointed to a knot of worried-looking Terrans pressed against the fence.

The justiciar came back with two Kooks, who ceremoniously returned the men's pistols to them. Salazar looked ruefully down at himself. His jacket was tattered from the porondu's claws; his half-bared torso bled from several deep, stinging scratches, while every joint and muscle throbbed like a toothache.

"You okay to walk?" asked Bergen. "We've got to figure out what to do next."

"We!" said Salazar. "If you're going to fly off the handle any minute and start slugging, we—Miss Sheffield and I—intend to get the hell away and stay there."

"Aw, don't worry! We saved each other's lives; that ought to cancel out any grudges. What say?" Bergen thrust out a hairy paw.

"Very well," said Salazar without enthusiasm, taking the proffered hand. "What are you doing here? I thought you were bound for Kinyobi Valley."

"Chung told us about this Intromission Day ceremony, and we wanted a look at it," said Bergen with a naughty-boy grin. "What's intromission, anyway?"

"Literally, insertion; also used as a synonym for copulation."

"Oh, you mean fucking!"

As the crowd of Kooks streamed back into Neruu, Salazar and Bergen rejoined a white-faced Kara clutching her bicycle, and a subdued pair of Bergen's hunting companions guarding Salazar's bike.

"Keith!" cried Kara. "Are you all right?"

"Feel as if I'd just lost a theological argument with the Chief Inquisitor," said Salazar, "but I'm still ambulatory."

"I'd like you to meet Conrad's friends, Derek Travers and Oleg Pokrovskii. Dr. Keith Salazar, the archaeologist."

"I remember you from bridge," said the bearlike Pokrovskii. "You hero! Like Sviatogor in old Russian myth, riding de wild monster."

"Me? Shucks. I just couldn't think what else to do."

Pokrovskii chuckled. "Is old proverb, every dog have wolf inside, trying to get out."

Bergen asked: "Where's Chung?"

Travers answered: "He took off as soon as he saw you were safe. Said he'd send his substitute."

"Slant-eyed son of a bitch!" growled Bergen.

"Well," said Travers, "you did bully and bellow at the little chap. I'm surprised he stuck as long as he did."

"Let me handle the help, Derek. What the hell do we do meanwhile? No one can really talk to the Kooks, though Derek knows a few words. Except . . ." He swiveled around and stared from narrowed eyes at Salazar. "Except you, Professor. You speak their bone-in-the-throat language and know the country. How'd you like a temporary job as guide, to fill in until this guy Ma arrives?"

"Nope," said Salazar.

"Why not?"

"Not my line, and I've got my own work."

"Look. Chung said the Kooks go vacationing after this grand screwarama. So there won't be any around to dig for you. I'll make it well-worth your while. You big-brains are never paid what you should be, because your minds are all clogged up with theories. So you can use some extra cash, and from what I saw today you'd be a good man to have on our side in a pinch. What would you ask?"

"Don't like killing things for fun."

"Oh, one of those! Just show us the way and talk to the Kooks, and we'll do the killing. With the whole planet swarming with animals, we're not endangering any species." Bergen paused. "Five hundred a day?"

Salazar hesitated. The sum equaled the whole daily allowance from his appropriation, including his own modest compensation. "Well—ah—"

"Six hundred," said Bergen. "No more, though."

Salazar took a deep breath. "Okay, but I won't let anyone push me around."

"Fine," said Bergen. "Ask the Kooks where we can camp tonight. It's too late to start for the valley."

"First I shall have to take Miss Sheffield back to my camp, to leave her in charge of my students."

"Oh, bring her with us!" said Bergen. "She'll get a story out of it."

"Good idea," said Kara. "How—"

Salazar interrupted: "Good Lord! I'll have enough to handle without the emotional explosions of a once-engaged couple. Forget it; I wouldn't touch the job."

"Not to worry," said Bergen. "Kara and I will act like—like two old friends."

"I'll believe that when Miyage joins the Maravilla—"

"Keith!" said Kara. "Don't nitpick. You and Conrad can watch each other to make sure neither one gets out of line."

"Eh?" said Bergen, cocking his head and looking sharply at Kara. "What's the professor to you?"

"He's my former husband, that's all."

"*What?*"

Pokrovskii roared with laughter. "Woman, ex-husband, and ex-fiancé all on same trip? *Bozhe moi!* Is makings of big Russian tragedy. If anybody shoot anybody, don't point de gun toward me!"

"Shut up, Oleg," said Bergen. "Everything will be on the up-and-up. I won't make passes at Kara if the professor won't. Okay?"

"Jeepers, what a prospect!" said Salazar. "I'd have to be a damned fool—"

"Oh, come on Keith!" begged Kara. "We need you. I need you."

"But—" Suddenly realizing how much he wanted Kara, the archaeologist felt his resolve melt like a snowflake in May. Kara continued:

"And I'll make you a deal. If you'll fetch my sewing kit along with my pack from your camp, when you get your stuff, I'll sew up the rips in your jacket."

"Come on, sport!" urged Bergen. "I admit I blow my top, but this time I'll be a fucking angel. Scout's honor! If anybody steps out of line, we'll head for home."

"How long d'you figure this trip'll take?" asked Salazar cautiously.

"Depends on the game; eight or ten days ought to do it."

"Okay, then." Salazar sighed with inner forebodings. "We'll have to leave the bikes in Neruu. The way to Kinyobi is merely game trails or open country."

"But, I say!" said Travers. "How do you know the Kooks won't steal them?"

"I've found the Kooks more trustworthy than most human beings. You go gather up your helpers with their loads, while I fetch Kara's and my stuff and give my people their orders." Before he started away, pushing the two bicycles, he flashed Kara a grin and muttered: "Didn't know angels could! Wouldn't those wings get in the way?"

Hours later, as the sun set, Salazar reappeared afoot, followed by Kono and Uwangi, each bearing a duffel bag. He said: "All fixed. I'll show you where you can camp."

"Hey!" said Bergen. "Could those two Kooks of yours come with us? We'll need all the extra hands—or claws—we can get."

"If you'll pay their regular wage, in addition to what you pay me."

Bergen grunted. "Damned New England skinflint! Okay."

When camp had been set up and a fire laid, Bergen said: "We've been eating each other's cooking, and it's a wonder we haven't died of it. But Kara's a good cook. So if she's to come with us . . ."

"Women's work, eh?" sneered Kara. "I get the message. Where are the pots and pans?" With Pokrovskii's help, she began her preparations.

Around the fire, Bergen poured drinks. Travers said: "Doctor Salazar, are you really an American, born on Terra?"

"Ayup. Why?"

"You sound different from the Americans I've known; almost like an Englishman."

Salazar grinned. "I'm a down-east Yankee, and that's how they speak on the coast of Maine."

"But isn't Salazar a Spanish name?"

"Actually it's Portuguese, from an ancestor who caught fish for a living. You're from the English Midlands, aren't you?"

"I was born on Kukulcan; but my grandparents all came from Manchester when my parents were children. How'd you know?"

"Accent."

"My dear fellow, I don't *have* an accent! I merely speak English; it's you Americans who have accents."

Salazar gave his first hearty laugh since his return from Henderson. "There'll always be an England!"

THE
HUNT

Epsilon Eridani raised its fiery eye above the tree-
tops as the hunting party, five Terrans and ten
Kukulcanians, struck camp. Conrad Bergen said:

"Professor, before we go on, I'd like a look at that
turf you're digging into. It's only a little out of our
way. Maybe you could tell us about your work."

Salazar's vanity tingled. "Okay, if you don't mind
backtracking. Follow me."

He led them along the forested trail towards his
camp. A half-hour later they emerged on the site,
where Salazar's three assistants were busily digging
and sieving a test pit.

As his captive audience strolled the area, Salazar
launched into the history and archaeology of Nomuru.
Although normally laconic, he became animated and
even garrulous in speaking of his specialty: ". . . so
the Despotate staggered along for a couple of centuries as a kind of rump empire; then a new wave of
invaders from the south overran the area. . . ."

"Conrad," said Travers, pointing, "look at that little river, the Mozii I think it's called. If there were a dam at the downstream end of the site, we should be standing in a lake two or three meters deep."

Pokrovskii squatted, scooped up a handful of dirt, and fingered it. "Is good alluvial clay. We can ship it to kiln in Henderson, get bricks at reduced price."

Travers pointed an eager finger: "Then your hotel could go over there—"

The import of the words abruptly snatched Salazar away from his account of bygone events. "Hey! Are *you* the people the High Chief is dickering with, about making this area into a resort?"

Bergen shrugged. "Well, yes and no."

"What kind of answer is that?" rasped the archaeologist.

"I'm not working directly with the natives; a packager in Suvarov is putting the deal together. But everyone's a winner. I'll give my guests bathing and boating facilities and a fine view, while Derek's lake will protect the locals' crops against droughts and provide the power for a mill."

"What happens to my buried city?"

"It gets flooded. But we won't start filling the area for at least a year, which'll give you plenty of time to dig your little holes."

"And one can't stop progress, you know," added Travers. "We owe it to these natives not to leave them stuck in eighteenth-century technology."

"But—" Salazar was about to launch into an impassioned speech on the need to preserve Nomuru as it was for scientific excavation. A year's respite was ridiculous, since the material here would keep archaeologists busy for a Terran century.

But Salazar bit back his words. Bergen was only interested, he felt sure, in piling fortune on fortune;

while Travers was an inveterate do-gooder who insisted on helping the natives whether they wanted help or not. Neither would be swayed in the least by arguments about the importance of archaeology in understanding the past.

Suppressing his dismay and resentment, the archaeologist donned a sickly smile. Better, he thought, to keep his eyes and ears open and his mouth shut while he studied his antagonists and pondered ways to derail their plan.

"Tell me about your projected hotel," he said. "I once stayed at a resort of yours, Conrad; the one at Tenabe."

"Have a good time?" asked Bergen, brightening.

"First-rate." Salazar said nothing about his marital troubles with Diane, which had begun to emerge, like blue-black thunderclouds on the distant horizon, during this wedding trip.

"I can see it all now," said Bergen, gesticulating widely. "The main hotel here; a row of love-nests there. That's what I like, to *create* something. The money's nice, but I *got* money. I like to make things move!

"You understand, Professor, we'd let you keep on digging even after our lease becomes effective, until the place is actually flooded. If there's some big golden idol buried here, we could agree to share the proceeds. . . ."

"This is *not* a treasure hunt!" snapped Salazar. "We're looking, not for gold or jewels, but for knowledge of the past. Real archaeology has as much resemblance to the digs in stories and on the screen as a real chess game has to the adventures of Alice in *Through the Looking Glass*."

"Huh? What's that?"

"A fairy tale by a nineteenth-century British writer."

"Never heard of it," said Bergen indifferently.

With a forced grin, Salazar changed the subject. "What happens when some stubborn bastard blocks your plans?"

Bergen slowly closed the fingers of his right hand into a fist. "I take care of *him*, one way or another."

"Hm. We'd better push on, if we want to get to Kinyobi Valley by the nineteenth," said Salazar dryly. Bergen, he thought, had yet to learn what a stubborn bastard he, Keith Adams Salazar, could be.

"There's your valley," said Salazar, as the group reached the crest of a ridge along the northern side of the Kinyobi area. A wide, green plain, hemmed by hills and low mountains, stretched before them. Down the middle of the plain, reflecting the azure of the sky, crawled the lazy Tsugaa River.

Most of the plain was open parkland, with occasional clumps of trees. Salazar pointed. "See those little black dots beneath the trees? In the heat of the day, the local animals cluster under them for the shade."

Binoculars raised, Bergen scanned the view. Excitedly he exclaimed: "Hey, isn't that a herd of tseturen, under that clump yonder—those plants that look like oversized pineapples?"

Salazar raised his own field glasses. "Yep, three or four."

Bergen continued to sweep the landscape. "There's one of those big two-leggers with a beak, like the porondu you rode."

Salazar looked. "That's a *fyunga*, an even bigger predator—the largest on this continent. Notice all the other critters are heading away from it except the tseturens, who are standing in a bunch with their horns toward the fyunga."

Bergen said: "Kind of like one of those flesh-eating dinosaurs they had on Terra long ago, isn't it?"

"Kind of, except for the hooked beak and long arms. We'd better hope it's wandered off by the time we get down to the valley."

"I'm not afraid of it, with this!" Bergen slapped his fourteen-millimeter rifle. "It's only an oversized lizard."

"Maybe so; but I should want a cannon or a ray weapon. You'd be surprised how much damage a fyunga can absorb and still make a snack of you. Actually, it's more of a scavenger and a hijacker of smaller predators' kills. It's too ponderous to catch the little plant eaters. But it'll snap you up quick enough when it can. This fellow seems to be heading away, so let's find a place to camp."

An hour later, under Salazar's supervision, the Kooks were setting up tents beside a small effluent of the Tsugaa. Bergen sat on a camp chair and, speaking to the poignette on his wrist, gave orders to his subordinates in Suvarov. Salazar leaned against a tent pole and held a similar conversation with Galina Bartch at the site.

When Bergen finished, he clicked off and said: "Hey, we've got a couple of hours of daylight yet. Let's go out and pot a tseturen or something!"

"Getting the head of a tseturen back to camp will be an all-day job," said Salazar.

"We could leave the carcass overnight—"

"And come back next day to find it picked clean. A pack of *poöshos* would tear it apart in no time."

"Okay, okay," groaned Bergen. "Any time I want a little fun, you think up some way to nix it. Like that other New Englander, the one who was always burning witches. What was his name? Cotton Wool or something?"

"Cotton Mather. And they didn't burn witches; they hanged them. Conrad, you can do as you damn please. I'm just telling you what'll happen. If you want to shoot a smaller critter for meat, that's reasonable."

"Which is the best eating? The two-legged or the four-legged?"

"Doesn't much matter. A tisai, the quadruped that looks something like a scaly pig, is pretty good."

"You'd better come along and point one out. Coming, boys?"

Footsore, Travers and Pokrovskii begged off. Bergen picked up his heavy rifle, slapped the stock, and said: "This is the medicine for thick-skinned large game: fourteen millimeters and over seven hundred meter-kilos of muzzle energy. It's a real import from Terra, not the junk our local machine shops turn out."

"For the kind of game we're hunting, don't use that cannon; it'd scatter the animal over a hectare." Salazar shrugged. "But bring it along, just in case."

Half an hour later, the archaeologist was pointing out features of the local fauna. "The main distinction among the larger animals is not between mammal and reptile, as on Terra, because there are no mammals. It's between the bipedal and quadrupedal forms, which have evolved separately for millions of years. It's—"

"Save the lecture. Isn't that our dinner?" Bergen pointed.

"Yep." Offended, Salazar clammed up.

Bergen took his light rifle from the Kook who carried his guns, sighted, and fired. As the bullet hurled the tisai over and over, Bergen gave a triumphant whoop. But the tisai regained its feet and started away, hopping on three legs. Bergen fired again and missed; then Salazar fired. This time the animal dropped and lay still.

Bergen grunted. "Where'd you learn to shoot like that?"

"On the police range in Henderson."

They returned to camp with the Kook shouldering the carcass and toting one of Bergen's rifles with his free arm. As the smell of roasting tisai filled the camp, Kara Sheffield took Salazar aside.

"Keith, are you getting along all right with Conrad?"

"No explosions so far, though my geniality's worn so thin you can read a newspaper through it."

"Watch out for that terrible temper of his. Knowing you, I can't believe you approve of his resort plan."

Salazar smiled. "Ask me no questions and I'll utter no prevarications. Have any of our heroic hunters been stalking you?"

"So far, we've all been too tired after a day's hike. But stand by for the next installment."

"I shall, my dear. It's not really my business; but I can't help taking an interest."

Where the ten Kooks squatted in a circle, one of them began to play an instrument, which it blew and strummed at the same time. Although rhythmic, the music resembled no Terran tune. When several other Kooks sang a wailing song to it, Kara commented:

"Isn't that weird? Do you know what it says?"

Salazar replied: "It's a herder of domesticated tisais, calling to another herder: 'Bring your animals over to my side of the mountain to graze; the herbage is thicker here.'"

"Oh. It sounds better when you don't know what the words mean."

"Like most operas," added Salazar.

* * *

Next morning, when Bergen finished another long-distance conference with his workers in Suvarov, the hunters, with four of the Kooks as gun bearers, set out for the grove where they had seen the tseturens. They passed a herd of medium-sized quadrupeds, grazing. The animals raised their heads and, as the party approached, bounded away. Salazar said:

"Their flight distance is pretty short, because this area hasn't yet been hunted by Terrans."

"I presumed the natives would have hunted them," said Travers. "They have guns."

"The Shongos are satisfied with their crops and herds and manufactures. They consider hunting one's meat a barbarous practice."

"Don't they take time for sport?"

Salazar shook his head. "Except for some juten racing, the idea of fun and games is foreign to them. When one saw a tennis match in Henderson, he asked: 'Why don't they hire servants to play it for them?' Besides, their social system is so compartmented that nobody does much outside his hereditary occupations."

Another half-hour brought them in sight of the copse. Looking through his field glasses, Salazar reported: "They're still there, Conrad. Four."

"There isn't much cover. What'll they do if we just walk up to them?"

"Probably stare stupidly." Salazar moistened a finger and held it up. "We'd better circle around to the left, to keep downwind of them."

Bergen took from his bearer the fourteen-millimeter rifle. "Okay," he said in an authoritative tone. "Here we go. The rest of you, stay behind me. Don't shoot unless I tell you to."

He tramped off across the plain. His booted feet swished through the green, grassy vegetation and met the ground with solid thumps. Clouds of pseudo-insects rose on iridescent, glassy wings.

Salazar started to caution him: "Watch where you put your feet—" when Bergen leaped aside with a curse as something reared up and struck at him. The archaeologist ran forward in time to see a slender, black-and-white-striped, ribbonlike shape slither away and vanish.

"Did it bite you?" he said. "Where did it hit?"

"Just my boot," said Bergen. "What was it?"

"A *boshiya;* something like a Terran lizard, except its bite is venomous. A few centimeters higher, we'd have had to amputate and carry you back."

"Good God! Why the hell didn't you warn me?"

"You didn't ask, and you get itchy when I try to tell you about the local biota. Besides, you insisted on going first."

"Okay, okay, Professor. Go ahead and lecture."

"You'd better let me lead," said Salazar, striding out ahead as he launched into one of his regular classroom discourses. "Tens of thousands of years ago, the Kooks were civilized when our slope-headed ancestors were still whacking at one another with clubs. But the Kooks used a trial by ordeal with boshiyas. They tied you to a stake in a pit and dumped the critters in with you. If one bit you and you died, that proved your guilt and saved the expense of the executioner. There's a Terran legend about some hero that happened to; he held some snakes off for a while by playing his harp with his toes. Better detour around that bluish patch. That's filegrass. It'll cut up your boots."

The march continued more slowly, with Salazar in the lead, looking cautiously down and about before each step. As they neared the grove, the bulky forms of the tseturens grew from distant slate-gray blobs to ponderous quadrupeds munching peacefully on the fresh, pale-green leaves of the lush, low herbage.

The tseturens were barrel-bodied, pillar-legged animals with massive hindquarters and short, bowed forelegs. Their gray hides were warty instead of scaly. The huge heads each bore four horns, one pair set side by side on the nose and another, longer pair protruding from above the eyes.

At fifty meters, the massive beasts raised their heads, peering nearsightedly about. Salazar halted, saying: "Better not go closer. Want to shoot, Conrad?"

Bergen clanked the bolt of his heavy rifle, raised it, and pulled the trigger. The gun roared, and its recoil rocked the burly land developer back on his heels.

The largest tseturen toppled over, moving its legs in a feeble, uncoordinated way. Snorting, the other three lined up along the fallen one's back and thrust their horned muzzles between it and the ground. After much heaving and grunting, with the help of its herd mates, the huge beast rolled shakily to its feet. As it started to stagger away, Bergen fired again.

This time the tseturen went down for good, and Bergen gave a yell of triumph before Salazar could restrain him. One of the other tseturens, the second largest, swung its head, sniffing. It located the hunting party and, with a thunderous snort, advanced at an earthshaking trot.

"Aim between its eyes!" barked Salazar.

Bergen fired. Salazar heard the smack of the bullet distinct from the roar of the gun. The tseturen shook its head as if irritated and kept coming.

Bergen fired again, with no more success. Keeping his voice unruffled, Salazar admonished: "You're shooting high. Aim below the eye level."

Salazar heard the crack of one of the lighter rifles in the hands of Travers or Pokrovskii. The tseturen was a mere fifteen yards away and moving fast. Over his shoulder, Salazar, shouted:

"Run, Kara!"

Bergen fired again, completely missing. He worked his bolt and found his magazine empty.

"Run, all of you! Scatter!" shouted Salazar.

Bergen reversed his weapon, holding it by the barrel, preparing to bash the animal with the butt.

"You, too, Conrad!" yelled Salazar. But Bergen continued to stand his ground. In the seconds remaining, Salazar sprang to one side, knelt and sighted on the tseturen's neck. His face was twisted with concentration. His rifle cracked, and the tseturen pitched forward on its belly.

Simultaneously, Salazar felt a sharp blow on the head, and his tropical helmet went flying. He staggered, then spun around to see Pokrovskii lowering his rifle. The tubby Suvarovian dropped his gun into the lime-green grass and rushed forward, crying:

"Keit'! Keit'! You are not dead? I stupid ass! I did not mean to shooted you!"

"Just parted my hair," said Salazar, running a hand across his skull. "One centimeter lower and you'd have needed another guide."

"So glad, so happy you are all right! I am world's biggest fool! I would have killed myself if I had murdered you! I will never make a hunter!"

Pokrovskii, face wet with tears, locked Salazar in a bear hug and kissed his cheeks. Kara and Travers added their more restrained expressions of relief at Salazar's survival.

Salazar ruefully examined the remains of his helmet. The bullet had nearly split it in two. With a sigh, he tossed it away.

"I get you odder hat," said Pokrovskii.

"They don't make these on Kukulcan," said Salazar. "I got it in Bombay, on Terra. It would take decades to get another. But . . ." He shrugged.

Bergen asked: "Keith, how come you brought down that animal with one shot from your pea shooter, when I couldn't stop it with three from my cannon?"

"I cut the spinal column. Using your gun as a club would have been as futile as hitting it with a flyswatter."

"For a guy who doesn't like hunting, you're sure a killer," said Bergen with grudging admiration. "Those things move pretty fast, in spite of their build."

"Yep; but they run out of wind pretty quickly. I once got away from one by outrunning it."

"You *did*? Well, you skinny guys have an advantage there. Now we'll start collecting a head. I'll take the other one; it's bigger. Will you tell the Kooks what to do? We ought to get some of the meat, too."

"We shall have all the steaks we can carry—until they get too high," said Salazar as he motioned to the two natives.

Insects had already begun to buzz around the two carcasses in thickening swarms. The rest of the day, Salazar directed five bloodsmeared Kooks as they hacked, sawed, and chopped their way through the tseturen's thick neck. Meanwhile five other Kooks went back to the ridge, felled several small trees, and built a crude sled.

All around the great carcasses, the planet's arthropodal organisms circled in a glittering, buzzing cloud. Most did not molest the Terrans; but one large blackwinged buzzer alighted on Bergen's bull neck. Bergen leaped into the air, slapping. The blow crushed the attacker, but a thread of scarlet blood trickled down Bergen's neck.

"What the hell was that, Keith?" growled Bergen, studying the remains of his assailant.

"Forget the scientific name," said Salazar. "Most of these bugs hunt by smell, and our scent is strange to them. But that kind hunts by heat-seeking."

"Is it liable to give me sleeping sickness, or something?"

Salazar shrugged, "Don't rightly know; but it seems unlikely. Few Kukulcanian microorganisms can live in a Terran body."

Salazar thought that his first reaction to Bergen's offer, to refuse it, had been right. It was not impossible that Pokrovskii had shot at Salazar on Bergen's order, to get him out of the way as a possible rival for Kara. In any case, the archaeologist resolved to cut the hunt as short as he could.

Before the sun settled down on the tops of the distant hills, the tseturen's head had been separated and, along with enough steaks to feed a platoon, hauled back to camp, salted, and put into huge plastic bags. As they sat around the fire in the gloaming, Salazar asked:

"Seeing as how you got what you came for, Conrad, shall we start back tomorrow?"

Bergen took a deep draft, then pursed his lips. At last he said:

"Look, Keith. I didn't expect to get my main trophy the first day in the field. It would be a waste of opportunity not to pot a few more."

"Where would you put them all?" asked Salazar.

"Let me worry about that. Now, I made some mistakes today; but with practice bagging a tseturen should be no harder than shooting fish in a bathtub. So there's really no sport in it.

"I want to kill something that'll give me a run for

my money—like that porondu thing we fought at Neruu." He gulped another draft. "Do they have 'em around here?"

"I suppose so," said Salazar, "though I haven't seen one."

Bergen swallowed another gulp. "I like the big flesh eaters. They can kill you just as quick as the plant eaters; and besides, they're smarter."

"They have to be," said the archaeologist. "The food of the plant eaters doesn't hide, run away, or fight back."

"Damn, damn," muttered Bergen, getting to his feet and striding back and forth, his face crimson in the firelight. "I want one of those what-you-call-'ems—fyungas."

Travers ventured mildly: "I—I should like to get back to my family. . . ."

Kara cut in with an urgent whisper: "Keith, watch out! When he's drunk he gets really wild."

Bergen tossed off another glass and scowled down on the seated Salazar. "I'm on pins and needles. Must be that damned bug. Keith, wouldn't the smell of those carcasses attract porondus and other predators?"

"It might."

"Well, look, I want to go back with some lights and see. If there's a porondu or a fyunga there, I'll bag him."

"Not practical; those species are diurnal. Some predators are nocturnal; they spot you in the dark when you can't see them. One of those could pull you down before you could raise your rifle."

"So what? I've got an I. R. viewer."

"Still too risky. I know some—"

"Scared?"

"Just trying to use sense."

"Then come along! I gotta have some real action!"

"No," said Salazar.

"What d'you mean, no? This is my safari; what I say goes."

"You go get yourself killed by a pack of poöshos if you like. I won't."

"Coward! Yellow-belly!" roared Bergen, waving his fists.

Travers and Pokrovskii traded looks of alarm. Kara said sharply: "Conrad! Pull yourself together! You're ill!"

"Hell I am! Never felt better! I could kill that tseturen with my bare hands, if this sniveling wimp—"

Salazar stood up. "You can get yourself another guide, starting tomorrow. I'm not staying to listen to this sort or crap."

"The hell you're not! You agreed to guide me for the whole hunt, or until that guy Ma shows up. You can't quit in the middle."

"And you agreed not to push me around. I was a fool to take this job, and I'm leaving with dawn's first light."

"I'll go with you," said Travers eagerly.

"But you can't leave me out here!" shouted Bergen. "Since I can't talk Kook, I'd be helpless."

"Tough luck," said Salazar. "The rest of you can come with me or stay, whichever you like. Kara, you'd better come with me."

"I think I've got my story," began Kara.

"But I'm giving you an *order*!" yelled Bergen.

"Shove your order!" said Salazar. "I'm—"

"Think I'll let you ruin my hunt and make off with my dame?" screamed Bergen. "I'll show you, you son of a bitch!" Bergen launched himself at Salazar with fists swinging.

The other three Terrans all spoke at once. Kara

cried: "Derek! Oleg! Stop him! He's out of his head!"
Travers called: "You're being ridiculous, Conrad!"
Pokrovskii said: "Calm down! Calm down!"

Paying no attention, Bergen closed with Salazar,
who belatedly rose and got his fists up. He thought
he landed one good punch, but Bergen's swing sent
him sprawling. Bergen stood over him, bawling:

"Get up, you goddam sissy! Where's your manhood? Too dainty to hunt, eh? Get up and fight, or
I'll kick you again!"

Kara screamed: "Conrad, you're the coward, beating up a man half your size!"

Salazar rolled to his feet and made a futile attack
on Bergen, who blocked the smaller man's punches
and knocked him down again. The difference in size
was too great to overcome, even if the archaeologist
had been a trained boxer.

Urged on by Kara Sheffield, Travers and Pokrovskii
at last seized Bergen's arms and pulled him back,
though his struggles made them stagger.

Dizzily, Salazar got to his feet, licking the blood
that ran from a cut lip down into his beard. His left
eye was nearly closed, and a punch in the chest had
winded him.

"We'd better tie him up," gasped Salazar, dabbing
at his cut lip. "At least until he quiets down. He
might kill one of us."

There was a sudden outburst of Kukulcanian croaks
and guttural cries. The ten natives who had accompanied the hunting party sprang to their feet with
shrieks of alarm and raced off into the darkness.
Almost at once, the firelit circle was filled with a host
of other Kukulcanians, armed with muskets, pistols,
and sabers. The Terrans had no chance to go for
their firearms; before they could do more than cry
out, the newcomers had seized them all in scale-
mailed talons.

Salazar found himself being carried off in a horizontal position, with four Kooks clutching wrists and ankles. The others received the same treatment, despite Bergen's bellows of protest.

"What is, Keit'?" came the voice of Oleg Pokrovskii in the dark.

"Choshas, if I read their painted symbols right," mumbled Salazar.

"De wild tribes?"

"Yep. I'll try to find out what's up." He spoke to his captors in Shongo, but they did not reply.

The quintet of Terrans was bundled into a large two-wheeled cart and stood upright. Their wrists were lashed to wooden bars, which rose from all sides of the vehicle and supported the roof. The raucous sounds of Kookish verbiage filled the night air.

"Terrible talkers," murmured Travers. "What'll they do to us?"

"No idea," replied Salazar.

A whip cracked, and the vehicle lurched into motion. Sounds and smells convinced Salazar that the cart was pulled by a pair of *kyuumeis*, smaller and slenderer relatives of the tseturen, which were domesticated by the Kooks as meat and draft animals and often called "buffalo-lizards" by Terrans.

Salazar checked the time by his poignette; but since his hands were tied to bars a meter apart, he could not reach the little buttons to call his assistants at Nomuru. Through the bars, he tried to track their direction by the stars that diamonded the clear night sky. But fatigue, discouragement, and self-contempt at his inability to vanquish Bergen at fisticuffs made concentration difficult.

In the end, he simply stood with eyes half-shut, clutching the bars against the sway and jolt of the springless wagon. Around the vehicle, dimly-seen Choshas jounced along on their jutens.

Hours later, the cart stopped at a cluster of yurtlike structures, black domes against the starlight. Kooks untied the Terrans and hustled them out of the wagon, two of the creatures gripping the arms of each captive.

"Hey, Keith!" growled Conrad Bergen. "What's this all about?"

Salazar shook his head. "I don't speak Chosha."

"Why not, if you're such an old Kookish hand?"

"Shongo's hard enough, with more complications even than Russian."

"What about noble Russian language?" said Pokrovskii. "Is language for heroes—"

"Oh, shut up, Oleg!" exclaimed Bergen. "Now of all times to argue over languages!"

Before this dispute could be carried further, their captors marched the Terrans into a large central tent, dimly lit by smoking, oil-burning lamps. On a heap of ornate, gold-embroidered cushions lounged a Kook distinguished by a skin completely bare of painted symbols, save for a large red cross on the chest. Salazar knew that, to most Kooks, to appear in public without one's painted symbols was considered indecent or at least uncouth.

Before the chief, on a rug bearing a checkerboard pattern of red, white, and black squares, lay an assortment of weapons: a musket, two pistols, a long curved saber, and a large knife that was almost a half-sword, all agleam in the lamplight. Four Choshas carried in the Terrans' firearms and dumped them unceremoniously before the seated Kook.

The Kook opened its mouth to speak, and Salazar hoped the creature would use a language he could understand. To his surprise, the Kook chose a

Kukulcanian attempt at English. The words were at least partly intelligible. Pointing a clawed hand at Salazar, he began:

"Thou ay-yen from outer space with spines on face. Who art thou?"

Puzzled by the archaic English, Salazar replied: "Keith Salazar."

"Who he? I ask, what dost thou?"

"Work at the University."

"Aye, but how? Annoy me not, ay-yen!"

Beside him, Kara whispered: "Don't play the Maine storekeeper, Keith!"

"I am head of the Archaeology Department," said Salazar, "and Curator of the Archaeological Section of the Museum."

"Ah. It was thou who slew one of my tribe, few days ago. Have interesting prans for thee."

"I acted in self-defense," said Salazar.

"That thy story. Next one. Thou must needs be ay-yen femay, because of ugry budges in front. Who thou?"

The interrogation went down the line. When Travers, the last captive, had identified himself, Salazar asked: "Are you Chief Kampai?"

"Not chief. Prophet of true religion. Put you in pen for night. Lord Jesus come to me in dream, tell me what to do with you." He added a sentence in Chosha.

Taking a firmer grip on the Terrans, the Kooks silently marched them out of the Prophet's presence. The party zigzagged among the smaller tents and approached an open enclosure. Holding lanterns high, the Kooks, gripping alien arms to forestall resistance, searched each Terran in turn and confiscated every metallic object. Salazar's and Bergen's poignettes were removed from their wrists. This done, their captors released them and hastened out, bearing the loot and the lanterns. They slammed and secured a gate behind them. By the dim starlight, supplemented by feel, Salazar ascertained that the Terrans were shut up in a wooden cage, about four meters long by three wide.

"Is outrage," muttered Pokrovskii.

"Yep," said Salazar. "Question is, what do we do about it?"

"Is your fault, Conrad," grumbled Pokrovskii, "for starting fight, so we did not hear nomads coming."

"Shut up or I'll fire you!" growled Bergen. "The professor's right. Sorry I went off my rocker, Keith. That bug bite must have given me some sort of fever."

"How are you now?"

"Fit as a double bass."

What a pity, Salazar thought, that Bergen's indisposition had not proved fatal! He suspected that the insectoid bite had nothing to do with Bergen's explosion; that it had been triggered by a combination of liquor, sexual jealousy, and the developer's volcanic temper. But he said only:

"Try to find some clean, dry spots and get some sleep. We shall need all our wits in the morning."

THE
CAGE

Salazar awoke before dawn, stretching cramped muscles. Looking around the cage, he saw Pokrovskii snoring peacefully, while the others began to stir. A young Kook with a musket stood guard outside the gate.

Sudden motion at the other end of the coop caught Salazar's eye. What looked like a heap of rags sat up. In the growing light, a craggy, middle-aged Terran face appeared. A pair of pale eyes locked on Salazar's, and a thin-lipped mouth uttered:

"*Hvem er De?* Who are you?"

"Keith Salazar, from the university." When Travers shook Pokrovskii's shoulder, the Suvarovian looked up; and Salazar completed introductions, adding: "Aren't you the Reverend Hjalmar Ragnarsen, who recently disappeared?"

"I am that miserable sinner. I know who you are. Why are you people here?"

Salazar summarized the hunting trip and their unceremonious capture. "And you?"

The man sighed. "Professor Salazar, I have learned that the forces of evil can pervert the best intentions. I came among the Choshas to bring them a message of Christian love and peace; and what happens?"

The missionary paused until Salazar was forced to ask: "What did happen?"

"My first discovery was that Chief Kampai speaks English, at least better than I expected. He also reads the language. I gave him a Bible and found that he is an extremely fast, perceptive reader with an eidetic memory. In a sixtnight he had gone through the whole of the Old and New Testaments, including all the minor prophets, and could quote a passage anywhere from that enormous work."

"Oh!" said the archaeologist. "So that's why he talks Jacobean English!"

"Yes; he believes that is the language of Jesus. He is actually convinced that Jesus appears in dreams and gives him orders to exterminate all the sedentary Kukulcanians on this continent. When this has been done, he thinks Jesus will tell him what to do next. The worst is that, however outrageous his intentions, he can always quote a line of Scripture to justify them.

"For instance, because God favored Abel's offerings of lamb over Cain's of grain, he is sure that God prefers the pastoral life of the Choshas over the agricultural ways of the settled nations.

"He lured the other Chosha chiefs to a parley and killed the lot, making himself the Grand Khan of the nomadic tribes. For justification, he cites the killings of Uriah, Joab, and so forth by David and Solomon."

Salazar commented: "Such treachery is un-Kookish."

"Oh, Kampai cites Samuel's butchering of his prisoner, King Agag."

"Lucky you didn't bring a copy of Machiavelli's *Il Principe*," said Salazar dryly. "How about this extermination of sedentary peoples?"

"He quotes Deuteronomy twenty, where the Lord tells the Israelites that in the land of Canaan, 'which the Lord thy God doth give thee for an inheritance, thou shalt leave alive nothing that breatheth, but thou shalt utterly destroy them.' He also mentions First Samuel twenty-seven, how David as a bandit chieftain raided towns and 'left neither man nor woman alive.' "

"Well," said Salazar, "how would *you* interpret these passages?"

"My dear professor! I am no simpleminded Biblical literalist. We must understand these things in the light of the conditions in those ancient times. It is my business to separate the divinely-inspired parts from the accretions, the myths and legends—"

"Hey!" said Bergen, finally wide awake. "You guys can argue theology all day; but I want to know, first, what these stinkers are going to do with us; and second, how the hell do we get out?"

"I know no more than you," said Ragnarsen. "Have you seen that pole in front of the big tent, on which Kampai hangs the heads of his enemies?"

"God, no," said Bergen. "It was dark when we got here. Does it include human heads?"

"I believe there are a couple, along with those of the rival chiefs. Kampai cites David's taking Goliath's head for a trophy."

"Goddam natives!" fumed Bergen. "If we could only get in touch with our people in the settlements, we could wipe the bloodthirsty vermin out!"

Salazar said: "After all, Conrad, you collect the heads of other species for trophies. So what's the difference between you and Kampai?"

"Because I'm human, that's what! I got a soul, or at least people like the Reverend here tell me so. They don't."

"They have a similar belief in a spirit that survives the body. Their evidence is about as good as yours."

"You can treat 'em like they was human; but I know what species I belong to. We ought to show 'em who's boss! The way you old Kookish hands bow and scrape to their chiefs and kings disgusts me. I won't kneel down to any fucking animal! If it wasn't for that pack of spineless, do-gooding, time-serving bureaucrats—"

"I say!" interrupted Travers. "That's unfair. I'm one of those civil servants. In my department, at least, we try to do the right thing. We know we can't please everybody."

"You know the history of the policy, Mr. Bergen," said Ragnarsen. "There are reasons—"

"Bullshit!" roared Bergen. "Now you see what damage meddling by you parsons does. The natives weren't bothering us until you came all the way from Terra to fill them with ideology, which they turn to their own purposes."

"You are unyust—I mean unjust!" cried Ragnarsen. "I—"

Salazar shouted, in the authoritative tone he used on refractory students: "Quiet, all of you! We can't afford to quarrel. Tell me, Reverend, how is it that, if you brought Kampai his new creed, he's thrown you in the clink?"

"I noted the direction his Biblical studies were taking and tried to show him the error of his ways. He did not take kindly to criticism."

"Who does?" said the archaeologist. "What does he intend to do with you?"

"He has not decided."

Motion outside the cage interrupted the colloquy. A group of Choshas appeared at the gate and began untying the rope-lashing that held it closed. When the rope was removed, one Kook slipped through the doorway and beckoned Salazar. As the archaeologist reached the gate, two others seized his arms and marched him off.

The group proceeded to the principal tent, before which rose the malodorous pole that Ragnarsen had mentioned. It had a dozen crossarms, whence hung heads, Kookish and Terran, like ornaments on a Christmas tree.

Inside, Salazar found Prophet Kampai squatting on his gold-embroidered cushions. The Terrans' rifles and cartridge belts were now laid out neatly on either side of the chief, along with the Kookish weapons. Salazar said:

"Good morning, Your Reverence. Is all well with you?"

"Good morning, Sarasara. All is well with me; is all well with thy clan?" (It sounded like ". . .is aw way with thy cran?")

"All is well with my clan. Have you led a tranquil life?" And so through the litany of Kukulcanian greetings. Between the thick Kookish accent, the erratic grammar, and the Biblical phraseology, Salazar had to pay close attention to follow the Prophet's words. At last Kampai said:

"Thou art Terran scientist, yes?"

"Yes."

The prophet picked up one of the hunters' rifles. "Canst thou make guns like this?"

"No sir. I am not an engineer or a machinist. Even if I were, I should need a machine shop and raw material."

"If thou hadst all the machine shops of Neruu, couldst thou make guns there?"

"No, sir."

"Wherefore not? Ye Terrans call yourselves wise; and thou art scientist, wiser than others."

Salazar sighed. "It is true, Your Reverence, that much knowledge has come into the possession of Terrans on their own world. But the amount is so great that a single Terran can learn only a small fraction of it in his lifetime, even though science has greatly lengthened our life spans. My fraction is knowledge of the remains of people of former times: their houses, utensils, and works of art. I have never even seen how a gun is made.

"Now I understand that you intend to kill all the Shongorin, along with all the other sedentary peoples of this world. If you kill them all, there will be no one with the knowledge of how to operate their machines."

Kampai grunted. "Something in what thou sayest, Sarasara. Perchance we must needs keep some alive long enough to show my people how to work machines. But machinists of Neruu hate aught new. Make guns as they did long time past, when people fought with swords.

"I desire guns like unto yours, that shoot bam-bam-bam. Terrans in Henderson and other Terran cities have laws, not to permit us these good guns. Sometimes can bribe Terran to give anyway, but need regular supply. Besides, Terran guns not fit us. Need different stocks." After a pause, Kampai continued: "Cannot see how thou canst be useful, Sarasara. I wait for Jesus to command me what to do with thee. Take him back!"

"A moment, Your Reverence! It would be a great favor to us if, in addition to our food and water, you furnished us with a place where we can answer the call of nature in privacy. We are fussy about such things."

"Call of nature? What that?"

Salazar explained, until Kampai said: "Funny ay-yens. Orright, I give order."

When his escort had delivered Salazar back to the cage, the leading Kook pointed to Bergen and beckoned. While he was gone, other Choshas came in and handed each Terran a wooden bowl of porridge and a horn spoon. To Salazar the food was completely tasteless, but he was inured to such things. While Kara and Travers obviously had to force theirs down, Ragnarsen ate his without emotion and Pokrovskii attacked his as if it were a gourmet feast.

"Is proverb," he said. "Hunger is sauce that make tripe better than caviar."

An hour later, Bergen returned. With a self-satisfied smirk, he said: "It's all fixed. They'll free us as soon as Oleg goes back to Suvarov and returns with a ransom."

"How come?" asked Salazar.

"Simple. Kampai has no particular use for us, now that he's got our guns. He asked me if I could make more rifles like ours at Neruu, and I told him no. Naturally, these creatures have no idea of checks or other commercial paper; so it'll have to be bullion from the Henderson branch of the Suvarov Bank. I suppose he'll use it to buy war materials."

"From gun runners, most like," said Salazar. "Then what's to stop them from wiping out the settlements?"

"We've still got the zappers. Would you rather have your head dangling from that pole?"

"But why Oleg?"

"Because he works for me. They wouldn't let me go; I was too big a fish to turn loose. Kara, haven't you got a notebook and a pen?"

"Yes; I happened to—" she began.

"Give 'em here, so I can write out an authorization."

Salazar asked: "Kara, how come the Kooks didn't take your pen when they searched us?"

She shrugged. "It was in a little pocket in the cover of the notebook. Besides, they're not much used to Terran things."

As Bergen finished his letter, another squad of Choshas, leading three saddled jutens, approached the cage. Pokrovskii cried: "*Chort!* I won't ride those things!"

"You will," growled Bergen, glowering. "It'll cut the time in half, and we'd better fetch that gold before Himself changes his mind and hangs our heads on his tree."

Pokrovskii sighed. "Hokay, if you raise my salary. Be good reducing exercise."

Soon the construction supervisor, clutching fearfully at his saddle, jounced away with his escort.

Days dragged by on wounded legs. The five in the cage found temperatures mild enough; but when a shower blew up, they had no shelter. After the storm passed, they stripped to underwear and hung their soaking khakis on the cage poles to dry. The Kooks gathered, pointing and croaking. Wearing no clothes and indifferent to weather, they appeared to find the human reaction to rain a source of wonder.

The food was adequately nourishing but routinely tasteless. When Bergen cursed its monotony, Salazar said: "Be glad they're not serving their gourmet delicacy, called yoekan."

"What's wrong with it?" grumbled Bergen.

"You'd call it a compote of mashed bugs."

Bergen clapped a hand to his mouth and half rose before he regained control of his stomach.

To pass the time, the five captives talked in turn

about their specialties. Bergen elaborated on grandiose plans for hotels and other enterprises. Ragnarsen gave sermons. Kara told of journalistic triumphs. Travers described the plans of his department for improving the lives of the "natives."

Salazar lectured on archaeology. He hoped to arouse in Bergen some spark of interest in the drama of the rise and fall of civilizations. But, while Kara and Ragnarsen followed his words with active interest, and Travers gave at least polite attention, Bergen's fidgeting and wandering gaze betrayed his boredom. He made his ennui so obvious that, after giving a second talk, Salazar took him aside and said:

"I guess these matters don't interest you much, eh, Conrad?"

Bergen shrugged. "To tell the truth, they don't. There's no money in 'em; and anyway, who cares whether some old guy ate with a knife and fork or chopsticks? What's past is dead and gone. I'm more interested in the future."

Bergen glanced toward Kara who, curled up in a corner of the cage, was napping. He stepped in the opposite direction, beckoned Salazar with a finger to follow, and lowered his voice. "Now listen, Keith. I know we've got to stick together here. But I saw how, at the camp, you'd have walked off with Kara and left the rest of us to cash in our checks in the wilderness."

"Well?"

"I just want you to understand. No matter what she says, she's my woman. If I see you making time with her—well, when you get back to civilization, you'd better have your insurance paid up."

A younger Keith Salazar might have told Bergen to go to hell; but by now he had learned to take the long view. If he and Bergen quarreled openly, or if he gave the developer an excuse to beat him up again, the Kooks would merely gather about to enjoy the spectacle. Besides, Bergen might kill him, in which case there would be nobody to oppose Bergen's aggressions towards Kara. So Salazar's first duty, for the present, was to stay alive and able-bodied. He said evenly:

"My dear Conrad, you seem to think I'm your rival for Kara."

"Well, aren't you? I've seen the way you look at her when you don't think she's watching. You get as horny as those tseturens I shot."

"Whatever my private feelings, she's made it plain she wants nothing from me but a business relationship. As for you, that's up to her."

"Okay; but don't say I didn't warn you," growled Bergen, turning away.

Late on the sixth day, a stir among the Kooks announced Pokrovskii's return. The three jutens and their riders stalked up to the cage. On a lead, one of the escort towed a kudzai, heavy-laden with a pair of large saddle bags. At a Chosha's command, Pokrovskii's mount squatted; and the man, now visibly less fat, slid off the juten's tail.

"Damned beast shake me to pieces," he groaned. "But I got your stuff, Conrad. Now we go give it to prophet."

Pokrovskii disappeared with the escort and the beast of burden. An hour later he came back with a crowd of Kooks. The captives eagerly crowded towards the gate.

"No, no!" said Pokrovskii. "Not all at once. Stand back; got to do this right, say Prophet."

A Chosha untied the rope-lashing. When he opened the gate just wide enough for the passage of one person, Pokrovskii ordered: "You first, Conrad."

Bergen slid through. Pokrovskii cried: "Now you, Kara!"

As soon as Travers had made his exit, the Kook slammed the gate and began to tie the lashing back in place.

"Hey!" cried Salazar. "What about us?"

"You stay," grinned Bergen. "Himself has so ordered."

"The hell you say! You fixed it this way—" Salazar leaped to the gate and tried to undo the lashing. But the Chosha on guard punched his knuckles with its scaly fists until he gave up, his hands lacerated and bleeding.

The four freed captives walked off. Salazar saw Kara arguing vehemently with Bergen as they disappeared among the tents. He turned back to Ragnarsen.

"You weren't much help, Hjalmar!"

The minister shrugged. "What could I do? I did not expect to be freed with the rest of you, unless the Prophet had another nocturnal visit from Jesus. I was not surprised, observing how Bergen hates you."

"You figured that out? He and I have been acting fairly civil here."

"I know; but I have some small skill in reading human emotions. I suspect that this animosity arises from your common interest in Miss Sheffield. I understand that she was once married to you and later affianced—"

"And as far as I know," said Salazar, "she wants nothing from either her former husband or her former fiancé."

"Bergen is a man of great force, unused to having his wishes thwarted. He will not give up easily, and I should not wager on Miss Sheffield's ability to restrain him on their present journey." Ragnarsen sighed. "What chance have two simple idealists like us, caught between a visionary fanatic and a selfish, unscrupulous plutocrat? Sometimes one wonders whether the good God knew what he was doing when he designed the universe."

Next morning, using sign language and the few words of Chosha that he had picked up, Salazar indicated that he wished to see Prophet Kampai. An hour's wait later, claw-locked to a pair of guards, he was led to the Prophet's tent. Kampai was judging disputes, so Salazar had to wait for hours more. When at last he was admitted to the revered one's presence, he said:

"Your Holiness, has there not been some mistake? I am sure the ransom arrangement was meant to include me and the Reverend Ragnarsen as well."

"Thou art mistaken, Sarasara," said the Prophet. "Mr. Bergen hath made it plain that payment should be for him and other three alone. Whereas he will be useful to me when I have spread the blessings of my divinely directed rule around this world, I yielded his desires unto him. As for thee, I await instructions from Jesus, as do for thy holy man. Thou mayst go; may thy life be tranquil!"

Salazar spent the rest of the day conferring with Ragnarsen, discussing ideas for escape. The minister, however, took a fatalistic view and lacked enthusiasm for any plan. Extending his hands palms up, he said:

"In addition, it is my duty to undo the harm I have unwittingly done. I must attempt to convince Kampai that the true God is not the bloodthirsty tribal chieftain of the Pentateuch. . . ."

"Hjalmar," said Salazar, "you haven't learned that in one way, the minds of the Kooks work much like ours."

"What do you mean?"

"They use their brains for thinking up plausible reasons for doing whatever they want to do. Kampai wants to rule the world. If he couldn't find pretexts in the Bible, he'd find them elsewhere or make them up in his own scaly head."

On the third night after Bergen's departure, as Salazar was sleeping fitfully with his back against a corner of the cage, something poked his spine.

"Keith!" Kara whispered. "Get ready to leave. When I shoot the sentry, grab his knife and cut the lashing; there won't be time to untie it."

"What—how—"

"Don't talk; just do as I say!"

Salazar rolled to his feet. He paused to shake Ragnarsen, whispering: "Get up, Hjalmar! We're leaving!"

"Huh? *Hva er dette?* Oh, it is you—"

"Hush! Come with me!"

Silently the two approached the gate. Salazar dimly glimpsed Kara, flitting ghostlike outside. The sentry stood stolidly; Salazar knew that, in addition to poor night vision, Kooks found it hard to stay awake at night. A flash and the crack of a Terran rifle, and the sentry fell.

"Here!" whispered Kara, thrusting the hilt of the sentry's knife through the bars. Salazar grasped the heavy, broad-bladed weapon in both hands and slashed at the half-seen rope. At the second blow, the lashing parted; and the gate creaked open.

Then the velvet blanket of darkness was rent by the raucous voices of Choshas, aroused by the shot. While gunfire was familiar, since the nomads practiced at targets and fired muskets to celebrate, the sound of a Terran rifle at night in that place called for explanation.

Salazar felt his way through the opening, then turned. "Aren't you coming, Hjalmar?" he whispered.

"No. I must remain to set this misguided chieftain's feet on the path of grace."

"But your head will grace his pole!"

"As God wishes."

"Hurry, Keith!" whispered Kara. "Take the gun."

The pair zigzagged among the tents, whence came a babble of Kookish voices raised in inquiry. As the fugitives rounded a tent, Kara tripped over a tent rope and fell. As Salazar paused to help her up, a musket-bearing Chosha appeared. The Kook shouted and, when the Terrans continued their flight, fired. Salazar heard the whistle of the ball close above his head.

"This way!" gasped Kara as the clamor grew.

Then they were out of the camp. Salazar in turn took a tumble in the darkness. "Goddamn! Bashed my knee," he mumbled as he scrambled up. He ran on, limping.

Two more muskets barked. Kara said: "They've seen us. Let's duck off to the side."

"Okay. To the right!"

They changed direction abruptly. There were more musket shots, but the Choshas seemed to be firing at random.

"Down!" breathed Salazar. "Let 'em go past."

The fugitives threw themselves flat and lay motionless while a group of Choshas ran past them in the darkness, heading in the wrong direction.

For half an hour, Salazar and Kara lay still, taking only shallow breaths, until the search party straggled back to the encampment. Salazar whispered: "Think we can crawl away now."

When they had worked their way on hands and knees beyond the lights of the camp, they rose and began to walk, Salazar painfully.

Kara said, "Unless I've gotten turned around, there's a little stream across our path. I left supplies somewhere along its bank."

They slogged on. Eventually the grassy herbs and low shrubbery of the plain gave way to plants of increasing size, until Salazar nearly bumped into a tree.

"I think this is it," said Kara. "Trees grow along the banks."

"Gallery forest," said Salazar. "Which way is your cache?"

"I don't know. Let's rest here until we can see better."

They sat down wearily, their backs against the tree, and listened for the footsteps of pursuers. At length, Salazar murmured: "Last I saw you, you were going off with Bergen. How did you get the gun? Why did—"

Kara cut him off: "One question at a time! I tried to talk Conrad out of abandoning you, but I might as well have argued with a lamppost. Derek and Oleg had the decency to agree with me, but not to the point of forcing the issue."

"Naturally; he smells of money to them."

"Well, I kept at Conrad, but I only got him to thinking about me. He wanted to revive our engagement; even joked about getting me pregnant, so I'd have to marry him. I didn't find that very funny; even less so when he boasted that, before we reached home, he'd show me what a real man could do, whether I liked it or not. In other words, a good, old-fashioned rape."

Salazar's fists clenched as Kara continued: "So I watched for a chance to get away. The first night, Conrad kept a sharp eye on me; I think he suspected. He's awfully smart, you know. By the second night, we'd fallen into a routine; so I left while the others slept—even the Kook guiding us, whose turn it was to stand watch. I stole some food they'd been given. When I found this stream, I hid my loot and went on to the camp."

"Go on!" said Salazar. "How did you get in?"

"I walked into the camp and, with three words of Chosha and signs, got them to take me to Prophet Kampai. I explained to him about journalism and convinced him that he owed it to posterity to let me proclaim his triumphs, virtues, and ideals. So for hours I interviewed him."

"Flattery will get you everywhere. So?"

"At last I brought the subject around to music. He confessed that he plays an instrument, one where you hit strings with little hammers. He sent his guards away—I suppose he didn't want to lose face before them—and gave me a demonstration. Then I sang some Terran songs. I worked around to lullabies, and presently I had him sleeping soundly. So I picked up your rifle—at least, I hope it's yours—and this bandoleer or whatever you call it."

"Did you think of shooting him?" asked Salazar.

"Yes; but if I had, they'd have been all over me. Even if I'd spoiled his plans of conquest, it wouldn't have gotten you out; and I don't think our heads would have profited from the view atop that pole.

"So I walked out of the tent, as bold as brass. I told the sentries it was Kampai's orders. They couldn't understand the English, but they got the drift and didn't stop me. The rest you know."

"You're simply incredible!" said Salazar. "And now that it's light enough to go on, which way?"

An hour of wading along the stream bed, squelching through mud banks and hopping from one rounded boulder to another, brought them to Kara's cache in the gully. This consisted of a bag of native meal, an iron pot, and a folding tripod to hang it from.

The light was now strong enough to give the fugitives a chance to survey each other. Kara suppressed a giggle at Salazar's appearance, and he smiled wryly at hers. Both were covered with dirt and had twigs in their hair. The knee of Salazar's right trouser leg gaped to show a barely-scabbed wound from his recent fall. The legs of both were mud-caked to the calf. Kara still had the well-filled cartridge belt slung over one shoulder. She said:

"Remember that camping trip on Mount Nezumi, when the storm blew our tent away?"

"Shall I ever forget! You were an absolute brick." Salazar hefted the rifle. "This looks like my gun, or at least it's one of the same model."

"I hoped so." Kara collected twigs and sticks and laid a fire on a patch of dry sand beside the stream. Salazar helped, cutting some larger pieces with the Chosha knife.

"How do we start it? Rubbing sticks?" he asked.

"No; I stole a box of matches."

Presently she had a brisk fire going. She scooped stream water into the pot and hung it from the tripod. Salazar asked:

"Did you leave any of this porridge for them?"

"No; why should I? It won't kill them to ride a few days on empty stomachs; it'll serve them right. What'll happen to poor Ragnarsen?"

Salazar shrugged. "Probably have his head dangled from the pole. It was bad enough on Terra, when preachers and politicians went around trying to impose their customs and ideals on peoples of different cultures. Attempting that with another species is a sure way to disaster."

As a ruddy sun peered between the trees on the

far side of the stream, Salazar ventured: "Kara darling, you've been an angel and, I admit, I've been an utter louse. But in spite of all, could we ever get together again?"

She poured a handful of meal into the boiling water and stirred. "No, Keith. I admit a lingering fondness for you, like the feeling one has for an old coat. But as for anything closer, forget it. This is either a friendly, businesslike relationship or nothing."

"Then why did you take such a hideous risk?"

"I couldn't let Conrad get away with that monstrous double cross at the expense of someone I'd known so w-well. . . ." She angrily wiped an eye.

Salazar sighed. "If you ever feel like changing your mind . . ."

"I think this mush is about ready," she said. "There's only one spoon; so we'll have to take turns."

When the pot was nearly empty, Salazar paused with the spoon halfway to his mouth. "Kara, let me ask you something."

"Well?"

"Wait! What's that?"

Before Kara could answer, Salazar's attention was snatched away by the croak of Kookish voices and the creak and rattle of equipment. He warily rose and peered through the shielding vegetation that grew on top of the chest-high bank of the stream.

"Oh, God!" he muttered. "It's the Choshas."

"How did they ever trail us?" whispered Kara.

"They've got a breed of tisai, trained to hunt by smell, like bloodhounds or those pigs the French use to sniff for truffles."

Salazar checked his rifle. "Ten rounds. Let's see that bandoleer!"

When Kara handed him the cartridge belt, he

swore under his breath. "Damn! You picked the one with cartridges for Bergen's cannon."

"How stupid of me!"

"Not at all; you wouldn't have known."

"Aren't they compatible?"

"Lord, no! It would be like mating a woman with an elephant."

"Horrible idea—"

"Put the fire out. Oh, oh, too late!"

The approaching Kooks were mounted on jutens, with several of the foremost riders leading tisais on long leashes. Now they all dismounted and, holding their muskets in both clawed hands, like Terran soldiers executing "Port arms!" they advanced briskly, shouting to one another and pointing to the curling thread of smoke. They spread out as they came.

"Maybe they don't know we're armed," muttered Salazar. "Eleven rounds aren't many; but we'll do what we can. They'll have the sun in their eyes."

The nearest Choshas came closer. Kara whispered: "Aren't you going to shoot?"

"Hush! I've got to make every shot count."

When the nearest Kook was scarcely a stone's throw away, Salazar, resting his elbows on the top of the bank, sighted on that particular Chosha and carefully squeezed off a round. The gun banged, and the Chosha fell instantly.

Muskets boomed all up and down the line, emitting cotton-ball puffs of black-powder smoke. Unable to locate their adversaries in the thick brush, Salazar's cartridges being smokeless, the Choshas fired blindly. Salazar shifted his aim to the next attacker and fired; down it went without a squawk. A third fell likewise.

With an outburst of cawing and croaking, the other Choshas in the skirmish line ran back to the safer place where their comrades held their mounts. There were somewhere between a dozen and a score of them. Salazar could see them conferring while they recharged their muzzle-loaders. Some excited tisais ran round and round their handlers, entangling them in their leashes.

Kara said: "Over there to the left, Keith, I think one is crawling toward us on his belly."

"Amerind tactics," muttered Salazar. "A smart Kook." He held his fire until he thought he saw the Chosha's head. "Damn! I pulled too quick and missed. That leaves us—let me think—six rounds."

The Choshas were still conferring in a distant clump. Kara said: "Couldn't you shoot into them from here?"

"The gun would carry easily enough; but I couldn't pick off individuals. Now they're starting to spread out more widely. I see what they're planning to do—go up and down stream, cross over out of range on both sides of us, and come at us from all sides." He chewed his lip, then said: "Kara, quick, stoke up the fire! Then pull those cartridges out of Bergen's bandoleer and pile 'em near the fire; not too close. And first take the pot and the tripod off!"

Kara stoked the fire with the rest of the collected firewood and then set to work on the bandoleer. Salazar aimed toward the creeping Kook. Waiting until the Chosha half rose and brought up its musket, Salazar fired. The Kook disappeared, but there was a thrashing in the shrubbery.

"Winged that one, anyway," he growled. "Five rounds left. How're you coming?"

Kara had removed all the cartridges from their sleeves and was trying to move the pot. But the additional fuel had caused the fire to blaze up, so that it was hard to lift the vessel without getting burned.

"Ouch! That thing's hot!"

"Should have told you to move it first. Use the belt to handle it, dunk the ironware in the stream to cool it, and start downstream, taking all our stuff. Keep your head below the level of the banks."

"But—"

"Don't argue; I know what I'm doing!"

Kara set off, bending low. Salazar poked up the fire, added a couple of branches, and picked up a double handful of the big-gun cartridges. He dumped them on the fire and quickly added the rest of the pile to the flames. Then, snatching up the rifle, he ran crouching after Kara.

Downstream they went with reckless speed, leaping obstacles, stumbling, recovering, and pushing on. Behind them, one of the fourteen-millimeter cartridges exploded, then another, then a whole fusillade. The Choshas' muskets answered, firing in the direction of the sound.

When Salazar and Kara stopped to catch a belated breath, half a kilometer beyond the fire, they could still hear an occasional boom of Bergen's huge cartridges and the answering reports from the Choshas' muskets.

At length they resumed their flight, though at a more moderate pace. But of the Choshas they saw no more.

THE
MUSEUM

Salazar said: "Kara, if I remember the local maps, this stream is the Yukke. It flows into the Tsugaa, which joins the Sappari. If we go downstream to the Sappari, we can follow it up to its junction with the Mozii, and then we shall be home."

"Won't that mean a big detour?"

"Maybe; but I don't know any more direct route to Nomuru from here. We should hike even farther if we get lost and wander in circles."

"I hope our food holds out," said Kara with a sigh of exhaustion.

Painfully, they picked up their packs and continued downstream. They no longer tried to scramble through the stream bed, alternately sandy and rocky. Instead, they walked along the edge of the gallery forest, now and then pushing through the vegetation to make sure they were still paralleling the brook.

As the sun clung to the western horizon, they

stopped. At this point, the stream had carved out a mirror-still pool, reflecting the overarching greenery. As they came out on the bank, a red-spotted brown thing half a meter long scuttled on four webbed fins or stumpy limbs—it moved too fast to tell which—into the water and vanished with a plop.

"What's that?" asked Kara.

"The locals call it a *nazikuna,* and it has a scientific name as long as your arm. You could call it a fish in the process of evolving into a salamander—or rather, the Kukulcanian equivalents of those organisms—like some of the Terran Gobiidae."

"Huh?"

Salazar chuckled. "Professorial lecturing is a hard habit to break. I mean those little critters called mud skippers. Now, how about a bath? We can wash ourselves and rinse out our clothes here, and our ancestral spirits know we could use it. Come on, take 'em off!" He began to unzip.

She looked at him with her level, greenish-gray-eyed gaze. "No, Keith."

"It's only a friendly suggestion, nothing more. After all, we—"

"That's just it. Your intentions may be as pure as the snows of Mount Nezumi; but once we were splashing around together, your mind would be fighting the pubic wars."

"Well, could you blame me? You're such a ravishable—"

Kara frowned. "No! And I really mean it."

"Afraid you might yield to my lecherous advances?" Clowning, Salazar twisted one end of his mustache.

"If you really want to know, I'm afraid I might snatch up a rock and cave in your skull. That would leave me alone in this wilderness, to be eaten by some exotic creature."

"At least the beast would show good taste."

She interrupted. "We can wash separately. Would that thing we saw bite us?"

"No; it lives on bugs and worms, not gorgeous Terran women."

"All right, then; you go back to the edge of the forest and start our supper. Take the matches, and don't waste any. And don't come to see how I'm doing!"

"Oh, all right," said Salazar.

He was stirring the porridge when Kara reappeared in her underwear and boots, carrying her khakis. She hung the wet garments on branches near the fire, saying: "I'll take over the cooking now, Keith."

"Okay. I'm afraid this is all we have to eat until we get home. I don't dare spend our few remaining cartridges on hunting game." He quoted:

"And we all fell ill as mariners will,
On a diet that's cheap and rude;
And we shivered and shook as we dipped the cook
In a tub of his gluesome food."

Salazar went back to the stream, stripped, plunged, shivered, and set about scrubbing what mud he could from his ragged clothing. From force of habit, he kept an eye out for ancient artifacts. A fragment of pale stone caught his eye; he picked it up and found it a piece of worked flint. He was tucking his find into the pocket of his bush jacket when he heard a scream.

"Keith! Help!"

He threw the garment on the bank and bolted through the brush, to view an appalling spectacle. Kara stood with her back to a tree on the edge of the gallery forest, holding Salazar's rifle by the barrel like a club. Before her, hopping and dodging about, stood a huge porondu, like the one that Salazar had ridden. The predator was lunging at Kara with its raptorial yellow beak, which gaped periodically to show big shearing teeth in the back of a rapacious mouth. Each time, as the beak approached, Kara whacked it with the gun butt.

"Why don't you shoot?" yelled Salazar.

"Won't—fire!" she gasped.

"Give it here!" He sprang forward and snatched the rifle. As the porondu stepped back a pace to consider the new arrival, a glance at the rifle showed Salazar that the safety was on. A flick of his thumb armed the gun, and he smoothly lifted the weapon to his shoulder and fired at the beaked head. The crack of the rifle was followed by the thudding fall of the beast.

Rescuer and rescued stood for a few seconds, breathing hard and staring at the recumbent animal. In a small voice, Kara asked: "How did you do it, Keith?"

"Took the safety off. Always keep it on until I'm ready to shoot. We should have four rounds left."

"When I shot the sentry," she said, "There wasn't any such complication."

"Kampai must have taken the safety off when he was fooling with the gun."

"Guess I've got to learn more about guns. Anyway, thanks—thanks a million."

"You saved my life when you got me out of that cage," said Salazar. "So now we're even. What's so funny?" he added, looking puzzled.

Kara tried to stifle a laugh, without complete success. "It's just that a stark-naked man with a high-powered rifle—well, it's a bit incongruous. Please don't be hurt."

"I'm not," said Salazar with a rueful smile. "Guess I do look kind of ridiculous. Me Tarzan, you—"

"At least, you've kept your shape."

Salazar's smile became vulpine. "Wish I could say the same for you."

"Why, what's the matter with my shape?"

"Nothing that I know of; but I shall have to see it to judge."

"Keith! You're just a dirty middle-aged man!"

Salazar gave her a satyresque smirk, reciting:

> "Oh, be not amazed
> When a beautiful lass
> Elicits a pass
> From a partner bedazed!"

"Stop it, Keith! You and your poems!"

"They're not poems with a capital P," he said. "Mere jingles."

"You're just turning on the charm to soften me up. Go put your clothes on!"

"Woman, I practically flayed my poor bare feet getting here when you yelled, and I won't go—"

"Oh, all right; I'll fetch your things. Take over the stirring."

When she returned with Salazar's wet garments, she put on her own, now nearly dry, and hung her companion's across the bushes. When the porridge bowl was empty, Salazar said:

"Let's have the knife. I'll see if I can cut us a couple of porondu steaks."

"Could we smoke them or something? They'd last longer."

"Have to cut thin strips, but it's a good idea." He struggled into damp garments.

With strips of porondu sizzling over the fire and

little zutas flitting overhead, they improvised beds of leafy branches. Salazar said: "Better put your boots on. Otherwise, bugs might crawl into them and sting you when you put them on in the morning."

As they stretched out, Kara asked: "Where's the knife, Keith?"

"Here." He sneezed.

"May I have it, please?"

"Here it is; but why?"

"Thanks. Just in case you might crawl in your sleep."

"Look!" he protested. "I'm no Conrad Bergen, to fling a woman down and—"

"Of course not; but I also know the tricks the biological urge can play on even an upright, civilized fellow like one I used to know, by the name of Keith."

"Thanks for the flattery; but after a day on the run, even my natural urges are laxating. Of course, give me a few days' rest . . ."

"And then I'll be back in Henderson, out of reach of your tentacles."

"So now I'm an octopus! You know, they have a fascinating system of reproduction. Like Kooks they seem emotionally cold; but the male develops a process on one arm—"

"Good night, Keith."

"But seriously, Kara, when you urged me to take this guiding job, I thought you might still have a teeny bit of feeling for me."

"I let you think so, I confess, because I had to. I needed Conrad's story, but I didn't dare put myself in Conrad's power without you along as a counter-weight."

"To balance that bastard, you needed someone like Blackbeard the pirate. Sorry I didn't measure up."

"Oh, Keith, you did just fine. But what's got into you, after all your heroic—"

"It's not what's gotten into me; it's what hasn't—"

"That's enough! Good-night again, and I mean it!"

"Good-night, Miss Sheffield."

Next morning, Salazar slept later than usual. The sun was already high when a snuffling, rending sound aroused him. He sat up, looked around, and gave a piercing yell. At the same time he reached out to shake Kara's shoulder.

"What—what—" she mumbled.

"It's a fyunga! Run like hell!"

They scrambled up, still only half awake. A dozen meters away, where lay the body of the porondu that Salazar had shot, crouched a maroon fyunga, big enough to swallow a man at a gulp. The predator was tearing with its vast hooked beak at the carcass of the porondu. Aroused by the outcries and motion, it lurched to its two massive legs, like tree trunks with claws, and started towards the fugitive pair.

"This way!" said Salazar, clasping Kara's hand and pulling her along. After them came the snorting fyunga with earthshaking strides.

Salazar ran out of the gallery forest and into the plain, which afforded better footing. Kara allowed herself a brief glance back.

"It's gaining on us!" she gasped, speeding up.

"Don't sprint!" called Salazar. "Save your wind."

They ran and ran. The thud of the great, taloned feet shook the very earth behind the fugitives as the pursuer's pace increased for a time, then leveled off. In his turn, Salazar took a quick look backward.

"It's slowing," he panted. "Run—a little farther."

They settled down to a steady jog. At last Salazar said: "It's stopped. We can take it easy."

They trotted another fifty paces and halted, fighting for breath. For a few minutes the fyunga stood staring; its sides heaved, and it shook its head as if in angry frustration. Then it turned and plodded back towards its interrupted meal.

"I knew it would run out of breath before we did," said Salazar. "Provided we were in shape. Good thing we had our boots on! Oh, oh, look what's happening!"

Standing knee-deep in the grasslike herbage, they had an uninterrupted view across the plain to the edge of the gallery forest, half a kilometer away. There, a smaller fyunga was now feasting on the porondu carcass. The beast that had chased them gave a loud cry, between a scream and a roar, and lumbered toward the interloper like an angry ostrich. The other fyunga looked up, opened its beaked, tooth-lined maw, and replied with an even louder trumpet.

A battle of titans seemed inevitable. Before actual contact, however, the larger fyunga paused to issue an earth-shaking bellow. It lunged at the other, which drew back just far enough so that the attacking beak clashed on air. The second fyunga snapped in turn, also failing to draw blood.

The combatants circled each other, roaring and snapping but doing no damage. Then the smaller creature broke away and jogged off, pursued by the larger with bellows of triumph.

"Mostly bluff," said Salazar. "Quick, let's get our stuff while they're still at each other!"

They returned to the campsite as fast as exhaustion allowed. Salazar snatched up his rifle and the bag of meal; Kara collected the spoon, the tripod, and the pot, into which she flung the strips of half-smoked porondu.

*   *   *

When they halted at midday for a snack, Salazar said: "Kara, if I bend over, will you give me a swift kick?"

"Whatever for?"

"Stupidity. Should have remembered that the smell of carrion would draw other predators. And I shouldn't have yelled when I woke up, but roused you quietly. We might have slithered away without that jabberwock's noticing us."

"Could you have shot the beast?"

"With this popgun? I'd only have annoyed the critter." He struck his forehead with the heel of his hand. "Seems as how I can't do anything right."

She put an arm around him and squeezed. "Nonsense, Keith! You're a fine, brave man, so pull yourself together! If it had been anyone else, *we'd* be the carrion by now. No, don't try to kiss me! You're only a friend, but the best friend a woman could have."

Salazar sighed and turned his eyes skyward like a martyred saint. Instead of an angel, he saw a hurato swinging down from a branch by its prehensile tail, with the evident intention of stealing the bundle of meat.

Salazar rose and shouted: "Get away!" and the arboreal carnivore retreated. Picking up his burdens, the archaeologist helped Kara to her feet, saying: "Let's go!"

When Keith Salazar and Kara Sheffield entered the big tent at Nomuru, Galina Bartch and Marcel Frappot were at work in the laboratory, washing fragments of stone, brick, and metal in large metal trays. Hearing the gentle splash of their labors, Salazar led Kara to the laboratory. Galina, a fragment of brick in one hand and a toothbrush in the other, screamed.

"*Prividyeniye!*" she shrieked.

Smiling, Salazar shook his head. "No, not ghosts."

"*Grand Dieu!*" echoed Frappot. "We were told that you were dead!"

"The report is somewhat exaggerated," said Salazar. "We're alive and hungry enough to eat a kyuumei, horns and all. Who told you we were dead?"

Frappot said, "First, Kono and Uwangi came in, saying that you had all been captured by the Choshas while they fled. Then that man Bergen, the developer, came through four or five days ago, with Pokrovskii and a Kook guide, all of them half-starved. He told us that his whole hunting party had been seized by the Choshas and condemned to death. All of you had managed to escape, but the natives recaptured you and Miss Sheffield."

"One of his lies," said Salazar. "He bought his way out, with his pals. Kara came back and helped me escape. Why wasn't Travers with them?"

"Bergen said that Travers was killed during the flight. When they pitched camp, he took a bucket to fetch water, and a fyunga got him. Bergen heard him scream and ran out with his heavy rifle; but the fyunga was disappearing with Travers in its jaws. Bergen fired but could not stop it. He seemed much upset, since Travers had a wife and child back in Suvarov."

"Travers mentioned a family," said Salazar. "He seemed like a kindhearted young man, if full of impractical ideas for turning the Kooks into twenty-third-century Terrans with scales. Tell me, what's been going on here? Where's Ito?"

"Ito went to Henderson to get supplies and to report to Doctor Patel that Bergen's survey crew had chased us off the dig."

"Chased you off? How come?"

"A couple of days after Bergen's visit," said Frappot,

"this gang arrived with transits and tapes and ordered us off. They said Mr. Bergen had obtained a lease from High Chief Miyage, and they wanted to get started on the development. They had the—how do you say it—the muscle of us."

"Are they out there now?"

"I suppose so. That is why Ito, he went to the museum. Galina and me, we have been working on the specimens until Ito comes back with instructions. But what of your adventures?"

"I want to go see these alleged surveyors first," said Salazar.

Galina frowned. "Please, Keith! You and Miss Sheffield look as if you would drop dead if you took another step. Had you not better rest?"

"After I've spoken to these people," said Salazar. "You go lie down, Kara."

"May I have a bath and a bite to eat first?" said Kara in a weak voice.

"Sure; I'll have Kono fix you a bath and Uwangi rustle you some grub. You'll have hot water, no twigs under your bare feet, and no hungry porondu waiting to pounce." Both gave the ghost of a laugh.

"Refer you to some incident of your escape?" asked Frappot.

"Yep. Come on, Kara; let's find Kono and Uwangi."

On the site, Salazar discovered a crew of five men and one woman. The men were squinting through a transit, driving stakes, and stretching strings along the ground. The woman held a clipboard from which she read off numbers and made notations. Aching at every step, Salazar strolled as casually as he could to the group, saying:

"Excuse me, but who's in charge here?"

"I am," said the woman, a massive, leathery brunette. "Who are you?"

"Doctor Salazar, from the University," Salazar did not ordinarily introduce himself by title, but in this case he would need all the prestige he could command. "And you, madam?"

"I'm Selina Kovacs, working for Mr. Bergen. What do you want?"

"Do I understand correctly that you drove my archaeologists off the site?"

"We couldn't have 'em futzing around and getting in our way. After we finish the survey, you can dig all the silly holes you want, until the bulldozer arrives."

"Did you tell my people that Bergen had closed a lease on this site?"

"Yeah, or at least it's so near to closing it might as well be. And Mr. Bergen wants to get going here."

"I think you've been misinformed. Bergen got back from his hunting trip only a few days ago, and it takes the Kooks longer than that to agree to any deal with Terrans."

"Says you. All I know is, we got our orders, and we're going to carry them out. And nobody better try to stop us!"

The five men had lined up, scowling grimly, behind Kovacs. Three were about Salazar's size, but the remaining two were egregiously large and powerful. Moreover, a couple of the men wore pistols in holsters. Salazar was glad that he still had his rifle slung across his back. Something about having a gun in evidence tends to restrain unfriendly folk who might otherwise make trouble.

"We shall see," Salazar answered, turning away.

Salazar borrowed Galina's poignette, his own having been lost to the Choshas. He called his boss, Dr. Skanda Patel, the director of the Museum, to report his survival. He and Kara decided that a day of rest was in order before she returned to Henderson to file her story and he accompanied her to report to Patel at the Museum. So they spent most of the next day sleeping while their clothes were being washed and repaired. When Salazar left his room for a bite of lunch, Frappot remarked:

"*Separate* beds? *Juste ciel!* After being alone with her so long in the wilds, I should think that you and she, you would have made some other arrangement." The graduate student seemed genuinely upset.

Salazar grinned. "*Mêlez-vous de vos affaires donc, mon petit!*"

The next day still found both Kara and Salazar too worn and footsore to leave the camp; but early the following day they set out for Henderson on their bicycles. The third time that the rough trail forced them to dismount and push their vehicles, Salazar muttered: "Damn it, I think I'll learn to ride a juten after all; an animal is more practical in this country. I've been meaning to learn, but there always seemed to be something more urgent to do. I think I'll ask Sambyaku to find me a mount and a teacher."

When they remounted on a smoother stretch, they observed another cyclist coming towards them. Salazar cried: "Ito!"

The stocky Kurita hurried forward, saying: "*Taihen da!* Keith! And Miss Sheffield! Why are you not dead?"

"Because we beat the odds and escaped from the Choshas. I've had more close calls in the last sixnight than in the preceding decade on Kukulcan. Galina and Marcel will tell you. What's Patel doing about Bergen's resort plan?"

"I could not get a definite answer from Doctor Patel. He is full of ideals and good intentions, but as for carrying them out . . ." Kurita spread his hands.

Salazar sighed. "I know Skanda. Let me think. . . . Ito, how's your Shongo?"

"I can make myself understood."

"All right. Pick up supplies at the camp and go find High Chief Miyage; he's probably at Biitso. Try to learn whether Bergen's lease on the site is now in effect. If it isn't, tell him that Bergen has already sent surveyors there, and hint that it's likely to start a lot of litigation. Kooks are afraid of getting caught in the Terran legal system, which they think of as a conspiracy to steal their lands. Then come back to the camp and report to me; or, if I'm not there, wait for me."

Kurita rode off. Salazar and Kara continued towards Henderson. As other trails joined theirs from right and left, like streams uniting to form a river, they no longer needed to dismount and wheel their bicycles past stretches of mud or rocks. The trail by stages became a genuine road, flanked by the farmlands whence Henderson's citizens drew their comestibles.

Salazar and Kara pedaled past other Terrans, afoot, on bicycles, or riding jutens. An occasional Kookish steam car, with a Kook or a Terran at the wheel, lofted a plume of gray-and-white smoke from its tall, slender stack. These vehicles, of native manufacture, had been modified for the Terran trade by the addition of upholstered seats and other amenities of indifferent interest to Kookish riders.

"Why haven't you bought a car, Keith?" asked Kara. "We used to own one."

"What happened to it?"

"It finally gave up its mechanical ghost, soon after you left."

"Well, that's why. The roads around here soon shake these steamers to pieces. The Kooks haven't yet faced up to the need for paved, all-weather roads; and in my present work I haven't really needed a car."

"When are we going to start building our own cars?" asked Kara. "With us so far ahead technologically, one would think we could design a car far ahead of these native contraptions."

Salazar shrugged. "The market's too small to make it pay. The Kooks wouldn't want our cars unless built to their own body specifications. When our Terran population grows big enough, I daresay someone will try it. Without liquid hydrocarbons, though, I doubt this planet will ever see an automobile age like the one we once had on Earth."

"If Terrans ever become so numerous," said Kara thoughtfully, "they'll encroach on the Kooks' lands. Then we can expect *real* trouble."

"I know," said Salazar. "There's a faction here—perhaps you know about them—that would like to treat the Kooks as Europeans once treated the peoples of other Terran continents. Their attitude was: since we have guns against their bows and spears, what do we care for the rights of the backward barbarians, without even title deeds to back their claims? And can you imagine the legislature of the United Settlements ratifying a treaty limiting Terran births?"

They rolled through a suburb of Henderson and into the city itself. Eventually they passed under an arch in the old city wall. This rampart of stone had replaced the wooden stockade that the first settlers, arriving on the *Maravilla,* had erected for protection. Now the city had expanded well beyond the wall; nobody guarded the gates, the valves of which had long since vanished.

Salazar said: "There was a movement years ago,

before I met you, to tear down the wall, since it restricts travel in and out of the city. I was new to Kukulcan then; but with the rashness of youth, I started a counter-movement to preserve it."

"I never knew that!" said Kara.

"Yep. My party carried the day, but it was a mighty close thing."

"Really!" said Kara. "You always have a surprise up your sleeve. I wonder that you won, since most of the early settlers didn't give a damn for historic preservation."

"Like Bergen." Salazar chuckled. "I turned my knowledge of history to account; I dangled the prospect of money. I pointed out that in nineteenth-century Europe, many cities tore down their medieval walls, thinking themselves modern or progressive. A century later the few towns that had kept theirs, like Chester and Carcassonne, found their walls a mighty tourist attraction and a hefty source of revenue. Of course, they had to cut passages here for some avenues and the railroad."

Salazar waved towards the terminal of the Imperial Feënzun Railroad. On one of the tracks alongside the modest terminal building, a train was made up. The little locomotive, with a vertical boiler, was getting up steam as a Kookish fireman shoveled in coal. Attached to the engine were three small, four-wheeled flat cars, each with a railing around its edge. Here the Kooks were satisfied to ride standing, clutching the rail. A fourth flat car, in deference to Terran tastes, had benches and an overhead frame on which canvas could be spread in wet weather.

"You know they could have much bigger, more efficient trains," said Kara. "I've seen pictures of the huge locomotives they have on Earth, which would make that little thing look like a toy."

Salazar smiled. "They know about our monster engines but don't want them. Those engines are much too heavy for their tracks, so they'd have to roll new rails and lay new tracks; and they think electrical machinery harms their ancestral spirits."

"What a mulish lot of stick-in-the-muds!"

"Absolutely; it makes them exasperating to deal with. No sense of humor to speak of, and an insanely complex family, clan, and caste organization. But it also has advantages."

"Such as?" she countered.

"Compared to us, they have a pretty stable history, without many of the social pathologies we've developed on Terra. They have little crime, and they're pretty honest and trustworthy. When they say they'll do something, expect them to do it or perish trying. They think we are a frivolous, treacherous lot and have a saying: Trust a dry river bed before a fyunga, and a fyunga before a Terran."

"Serves us right, I suppose," said Kara. "I contributed to our troubles by urging you to take that guiding job with Conrad."

"And I was just as dumb, showing off the dig to those guys and not guessing they were the ones planning to develop it. I should have known they didn't give a damn for science."

"Don't blame yourself. You were marvelous after we got out of the cage."

"So were you. Are you quite sure—?"

Kara stopped. "I turn off here, Keith."

She held out a hand, which Salazar clasped. He would have kissed her, but she forestalled that by holding her arm rigidly extended. Salazar said: "Tell me, would you have really stabbed me if I had, as you put it, 'crawled in my sleep'?"

"N-no; but I'd have still fought you off. You'd have looked the way you did after your bout with Conrad."

*   *   *

The University of Henderson Museum was housed in a large red-brick building of vaguely Romanesque design. Salazar said to the small, brown, anxious-looking Patel, the director:

"But don't you see, Skanda, this dig is the Museum's opportunity of a lifetime! Horenso, where I worked last, is all dug and consolidated, and it was mostly standing anyway. No mystery. Nomuru's much older and a virgin site. There's no limit to what it may tell us about the decline and fall of the Nomoruvian Empire. It's as if we had an unplundered Pompeii, or as if Rome had been buried by a natural catastrophe in the principate of Nero and never dug up!"

"Yes, yes, my dear colleague," said Patel, making a steeple of his fingers. "But we must consider all angles. This Bergen is truly dangerous. Rumors say that he is not above hiring criminals to take extreme measures against those who stand in his way. And he has enough influence in the legislature . . . He might be able to have our appropriation cut to nothing at the next session."

Privately, Salazar groused that Patel should be called Skanda the Unready for his ingenuity in finding reasons for inaction. "I should think the story of his treatment of me would cause some reaction."

Patel wagged his head right and left. "Perhaps it would; but even if you got your story into print, he would have a different tale, and his companions on the hunt would confirm his words."

"I might," growled Salazar, "go to some extreme measures myself to save this dig."

Patel smiled. "You are one of those stubborn New England Yankees. Formally, I forbid you to do anything of the sort. But," he said, winking, "if you should undertake such a wicked course of action, be sure that I know nothing about it. Then I can deny all knowledge with a clear conscience."

"I read you," said Salazar. "And here's my bill for expenses. I hope you can put it through right away, because I lost a lot of personal things and I need cash to replace them."

"Wait a minute!" said Patel, staring at the paper. "Are these the things you lost when the Kampairin captured you?"

"Yep."

"But I cannot authorize this payment! You incurred the loss, not on the site, but while off on this shikar. I have no objection to your taking a few days off; but during that time your effects are not the Museum's responsibility."

"Hey!" cried Salazar. "You mean you won't repay me?"

"I mean exactly that, Keith. If anyone other than Chief Kampai is liable, it would be your then employer, Mr. Conrad Bergen."

"Hell! I doubt if that bastard'll pay me the three thousand he owes me for guiding them before the Choshas grabbed us."

"You could sue."

"Without a written contract? More likely he'll sue me, claiming I deliberately led the party into ambush. Besides, he can afford more lawyers and appeals than I ever could. Now look here, Skanda, I've given the goddam Museum my heart and soul for more years . . ."

A bitter argument raged until Patel said: "Keith, here is a possible way out. In the course of this hunting trip, did you do anything that could be classed as an archaeological reconnaissance?"

"Hm, let me think. Yep, I did."

"With what results?"

Salazar pulled from his pocket the piece of chipped flint he had picked up on the banks of the Yukke. "Wouldn't you call that a tanged projectile point?"

Patel held a magnifying glass to his eye. "It certainly looks like one. Where did you find it?"

Salazar told him, adding: "It's just a surface find, without stratigraphical context; but we know practically nothing about the Kookish Stone Age. This isn't much, but we've got to start somewhere."

Patel smiled. "Good! It may be years before we can do serious work in the Chosha territory. Meanwhile, I suppose I'll countersign your expense account."

Salazar went to his office in the museum. From a drawer in his desk he took out a set of plans to the building. After studying these, he reached into another drawer full of tools and withdrew a flashlight, a hammer, and a screwdriver.

He went down to the sub-basement and picked his way along dusty, little-used corridors until he came to a room with a locked door. He let himself in with his passkey and examined the interior.

The room was crowded with large wooden crates, stacked two deep. Salazar pried up a corner of one crate and, peering in with his flashlight, confirmed that it held a dozen rifles. There were twelve crates of this kind and twelve of another shape, which proved to contain boxes of ammunition. Salazar hammered the corners of the crates closed and returned to his office.

On his way out, he looked in on Patel, hard at work amid a hodgepodge of papers. He said: "Quitting time for honest men, Skanda! Or are you going to work half the night?"

The small brown man smiled. "I am what you call the night owl. You go on to whatever dissolute revelries you like."

*   *   *

Salazar's friend Cabot Firestone had invited Salazar to dinner, so sundown found them drinking in Firestone's small apartment. The psychologist was about Salazar's age, but tall and broad with a big, square-cut red beard flecked with gray. A widower, Firestone lived alone in Henderson, as did Salazar. The latter told Firestone of the recent events.

"Zeus almighty!" said Firestone. "You always seemed a quiet, self-contained chap. I wouldn't have expected swashbuckling adventures on your part."

"Didn't have much choice," said Salazar.

Firestone said thoughtfully: "It looks as if Ragnarsen and other missionaries, with the best intentions, have brought religious fanaticism to a world that had been free of it. Ragnarsen's a mild, benevolent guy, but you see what destructive uses his teachings can be put to."

Salazar grunted assent. "The Kooks' only religion is veneration of their ancestors, and nobody tries to convert an outsider to that. If Kampai isn't scragged soon, we may have wars of religion like the Terran ones: crusades, jihads, extermination of minor sects, and so forth."

"And if you point that out to missionaries, they say: 'Better they should die and be saved than live and be damned!'" Firestone changed the subject. "By the way, how's Kara now?"

"Far as I know, okay. She came back to Henderson for her newspaper job."

"A splendid woman. Are you and she contemplating anything?"

Salazar almost told Firestone, as he had young Frappot, to mind his own business; but Firestone was his best friend. They had gone to college together. In addition, Firestone was the only other downeaster Salazar knew on Kukulcan. So he merely said: "No. At least, not right now. I hadn't seen her since our poor little Rodney's funeral, and that time she refused to speak to me."

Firestone said, "I took her out to dinner, just before she went on your dig. Hope you don't mind."

"Jeepers cripus, why should I? She's her own boss."

"Sure, but people do retain feelings toward former spouses. I thought—there wasn't any—I mean, it was just a restaurant dinner."

Salazar waved aside Firestone's excuses. "Whose bed she ends up in is no business of mine."

"How about you, Keith? I mean, have you got your sights on another woman? I wouldn't ask, except that such things are a matter of professional interest."

Salazar grinned sardonically. "I know; you like to gossip and then pretend it's psychological research. The answer is no. I've struck out in that game and figure I'd better stay on the bench. Besides, all the women I could stand seem to be already hitched, or else they're community-chest types I don't care for."

"That's due to the surplus of men here," said Firestone. "It gives the women an unfair advantage in picking and choosing; just the opposite of Terra, where the surplus is of women."

"I know." Salazar gazed at the wall as if looking afar. "That's why most Terran nations allow a limited legal bigamy, to take care of the surplus. We're not so enlightened here."

Firestone smiled quietly. "You'd be surprised how much informal polyandry we have here—*ménages à trois* with husband, wife, and her lover cohabiting more or less peacefully."

Salazar shrugged. "I've heard of such broad-minded husbands, but I don't know any."

"Had you and Kara been quarreling before you broke up?"

"No; so I don't even have the excuse that people in my position give, that the marriage had 'broken down' or 'fallen apart' like a piece of defective machinery. I first learned what the Bible means by 'a contentious woman' when I married Diane.

"Let's face it: I was a copper-riveted fool to run out on Kara. It was like demonic possession, if I believed in that sort of thing. Down underneath I knew it was impossible and that some day I should be sorry; but so strong was the urge that I went ahead anyway. Diane's not even better-looking than Kara, aside from being younger."

"I come upon such cases all the time," said Firestone. "Men call themselves reasoning animals; but that's true only part of the time."

"Diane appealed to my sympathies. Sort of got me on my blind side, by a song-and-dance about the dreadful things her family and her ex-husband had done."

"Did you ever ask the family or the ex for their side of the story?"

"No, but I learned enough so I should have been warned. Diane's family is the most quarrelsome this side of Donnybrook Fair. Their get-togethers are one long wrangle, with everybody trying to put down, or take advantage of, or pry something out of everyone else. Such attitudes carry over into the married lives of the younger members; all of Diane's siblings have had turbulent domestic histories. They're takers, not givers. I suppose Diane's more to be pitied than blamed; but that doesn't excuse me. What happened to me, Cabot? Had my brain turned to mush?"

Firestone said: "Your brain wasn't the organ in charge at the time. People have been falling in love with unsuitable mates ever since Helen ran off with Paris of Troy and I daresay long before that. These urges come upon most people, more often on men—nature's way of spreading their genes through the species."

"How could I do that when all the time I never had a hostile thought about Kara? She still attracts me."

"One can love two women at once, being attracted to one while still attached to the other. Could you have subconsciously resented the fact that she was the dominant one of the pair of you?"

Salazar shrugged. "Maybe. I should be glad to have that dominance back; but she's dead set against it. Why?"

"To most," said Firestone, fingering his beard, "abandonment by a loved one is a major trauma; and most have a deep, visceral fear of it. When the abandonee sees a former spouse, he or she is torn. A lingering attachment pulls the ex-mate one way, while a lasting resentment pulls the other. As to which wins, I couldn't predict."

"I see," said Salazar, staring moodily. "Guess I did give her cause for hard feelings. I used to think I was a pretty good guy, but I find I had feet of clay clear up to my knees."

"Couldn't you have had just a quiet affair, without upsetting your marriage?"

Salazar shook his head. "For one thing, Diane's a blabbermouth; a clandestine affair with her would stay clandestine for no more than ten minutes. For another, I felt I had to be honest with Kara; my damned scientific training."

"No matter how it hurt?" Firestone sighed. "A little hypocrisy isn't always bad. Hypocrisy, like liquor and religion, is one of the lubricants that make civilized life possible."

"Wish I'd asked you before things had gone too far."

"You'd have paid as much attention as the tide did to King Canute in the legend. But don't give up. If you two can still stand each other after weeks of camping out in the bush, it just might be love. You've got plenty of time, with modern longevity."

"I know. The myths promised eternal youth, and medicine has given us eternal middle age instead."

Firestone: "What do you do for temporary relief?"

"Nothing. You know what happens to professors who fool with students."

"Having a hard time?"

Salazar shrugged. "Chastity may not be the most fun in the world; but nobody ever died of it. One gorgeous redhead politely propositioned me last term. She'll be back as a graduate next fall, after the same thing."

"Grades of A?"

"No; she's an all-A student who doesn't need to offer her alabaster body. She just likes it—and me. She hasn't said so in plain Anglo-Saxon, but stick around."

"Some would envy you."

"Let 'em. My real concern is not assuaging unrequited lust but saving the Nomuru site. Bergen's going ahead with his resort, despite threats of a Kookish war."

Firestone said: "I hear he's made a deal with the Choshas, to protect his resort area."

"He might have, at that." Salazar frowned in concentration. "I shall pay a call on High Chief Miyage, to alert him to Bergen's double-dealing. But Miyage's had it in for me ever since my work last year on the boundary-stone dispute. . . .

"You see, Cabot, the independence of Shongosi is

guaranteed by a treaty between the High Chief of the Choshas and the then Emperor of Feënzun. Evidently Prophet Kampai won't pay the treaty any mind. So if Miyage scorns my warnings against Bergen and the Choshas, my next step, to save the site, will be to go see Empress Gariko. She's friendly to me for the same reason Miyage isn't: my boundary findings were in her favor. Maybe I can convince her to prepare for war with the Choshas."

Salazar stood up. "Thanks for the chow, Cabot; and also for stirring up a brain cell or two."

Firestone said: "I'd better walk you back to your place."

"Why?"

"If you're in Conrad Bergen's black book, it's not a good idea to wander around town alone at night."

"Not quite alone. I'm packing my in-town pistol, the little one."

"And what good would that do if someone shot you in the back? Let's go."

THE
FREEMARTIN

Shortly after Salazar returned to Nomuru, Ito Kurita came back from his visit to High Chief Miyage. Kurita reported that the contract with Bergen was not yet final, and that he hoped he had sown enough seeds of doubt to delay the proceedings.

"I did not see the High Chief himself," said Kurita unhappily. "He is most discourteous. He sent word that he had no time for aliens but would let me speak to an underling. It was most humiliating."

After the surveyors departed, the site of Nomuru saw the three assistants diligently shoveling and sieving at one of the test pits, while Salazar struggled to master the art of riding a juten. When he picked himself up from the ground for the second time, he said in Shongo to his riding instructor:

"Sensao, I shall never be able to ride this creature without what we call stirrups."

"Sati—" said the Kook, neck spines indicating puz-

121

zlement. "What is the Terran word again, honorable sir?"

"Stirrups."

"Satrapsa? And what be those?"

Salazar explained. The instructor commented: "Strange. We ride without these satrapsa and never fall off."

"I do not, like you, have claws on my feet to hold on with."

"Unfortunate creature! You must order these things in Neruu. Meanwhile, you must try again. Get back in the saddle and tell the juten: 'Go forward; turn left; turn right; halt!' "

"Very well." Mounted again, Salazar said to his mount: "*Katai!*"

The juten obediently paced forward. A riding juten bore a lead rope looped about its neck, but the rider controlled it entirely by vocal commands.

"*Mai shida!*" said Salazar, meaning "Turn left!"

The juten promptly turned right. Salazar, who had leaned to the left to brace himself for the turn, rolled off the juten's back again.

"*Tomai!*" he yelled after the departing beast, which stopped at the command. Bruised and battered, Salazar faced his instructor. "Sensao, what did I do wrong this time?"

"You said *mai shida* when you should have said *mai shida.*" The Kook pronounced the two commands with different tones.

"But I used the low-rising tone in *shida!*"

"But, honorable sir, you forgot that, in that combination, the low-rising tone changes to high-level."

Salazar sighed. "I thought my Shongo good enough for most purposes."

"It is, honorable sir, for talking with us Shongorin. When you barbarians misplace the tones, we are intelligent enough to guess your true meaning. When you use the wrong status forms, we know that you do not mean to insult us and make allowances for your ignorance. Now mount again!"

Cursing a language that distinguished the words for "right" and "left" only by a complex system of tones, Salazar once more heaved himself into the saddle. This time he went through the drill without mishap. He had just halted his mount when he heard a cry of "Hurrah!" and saw Oleg Pokrovskii standing at the edge of the site, clapping. A cylindrical box reposed at his feet, and behind him stood another Terran.

"Keit'l!" called Pokrovskii, beckoning. "I got something for you!"

Salazar called, "Wait here, Sensao!" and guided his mount to the place where Bergen's fat construction superintendent stood. Pokrovskii opened the box and, with a flourish, whisked out a broad-brimmed straw hat. Handing it up to Salazar he said, "I owed you hat, because I ruined other. Try it on; had to guess size. This my assistant, Bill Kovelenko." He indicated his youthful companion.

Salazar acknowledged the introduction and donned the hat.

"Thanks, Oleg. When I dug in Mexico, before coming out here, they wore hats like this. Did you come all the way from Suvarov just to give me this hat?"

"Not exact. I wanted to see how dig was coming, because my boss in terrible hurry to get started."

"Has he a firm agreement with High Chief Miyage yet?"

Pokrovskii spread his hands. "Always he say, is so close as not to matter. Now let me see diggings. I admire de science."

Warily, Salazar, still mounted and guiding his juten by voice, led Pokrovskii across the site, detouring around test pits and explaining his work. "Here's the surviving top course of a Nomoruvian stone wall; notice the rusticated ashlars. . . ."

As they neared the pit on which the assistants were working, Pokrovskii suddenly cried: "Hey, who that?"

Salazar looked. "Another goddam Chosha!" he breathed. "Where the hell did I put the rifle? Better get off the site, Oleg, in case this fellow wants to take a head. Marcel! Fetch the rifle!"

"I left it back in the tent!" came Frappot's wail.

Pokrovskii and Kovelenko were trotting away toward Salazar's camp. Kovelenko, younger and spryer, had sprinted far ahead. The Chosha set its juten toward the lumbering Pokrovskii. As Salazar watched, the Kook raised its huge pistol and fired, without effect. It holstered the firearm and drew a long, curved saber.

Salazar shouted: *"Mai shida!"* to his juten, hoping he had used the correct tone. To his relief, the dinosaurlike mount turned left. Salazar cried "Faster!" in Shongo and fumbled with his own holster.

The Chosha, bearing down on Pokrovskii, swung the saber high. Coming up behind, Salazar fired his pistol, but the jouncing gait of his mount caused him to miss. He fired again, this time at the Chosha's juten.

The animal tottered and pitched forward, throwing its rider head over heels. When Salazar halted his own bipedal beast with a shout of *"Tomai!"*, the fallen juten was feebly moving its limbs and the Chosha was beginning to stir and sit up. Its saber stood upright in the turf, driven in half the length of the blade.

"Oleg!" called Salazar. Pokrovskii had already paused in his flight. Seeing the Chosha sitting on the ground, he started back toward it.

The Chosha staggered to its feet, saw Pokrovskii nearing with murder in his eye, and turned to flee. Pokrovskii grasped the hilt of the upright saber, pulled it free, and ran after the Kook, waving the weapon and shouting: "*Iditye syuda!* Come here!"

The Chosha had run but a little way when it blundered into a test pit a meter deep. Pursuing it, Pokrovskii, propelled by momentum, tumbled into the pit on top of the Kook.

The others rushed to the pit. Salazar and Kurita hauled Pokrovskii out, while Kovelenko and Sensao, the Shongo riding teacher, gripped the arms of the Chosha and hoisted it out in turn. When the marauding nomad got its breath back, it set up a loud, discordant outcry. Salazar realized, from the captive's lack of a crest of small spines, that it was a female.

"Do you understand her?" Salazar asked Sensao.

"Aye. She protests our cruelty in nearly crushing her to death beneath that great fat Terran. She thinks her ribs are broken."

"Well, she was after Mr. Pokrovskii's head."

After translation, Sensao said: "She admits this but says that death would have been so quick that the fat Terran would have felt no pain. Besides, it would be an honor to lose one's head to so mighty a warrior as she."

After more speech from the Chosha, Sensao continued: "She asks what you mean to do with her? She says that she was supposed only to scout; but the sight of you aliens aroused her battle lust. If she goes back to Prophet Kampai, he will order her head cut off for disobeying orders and letting herself be captured."

"Tell her we shall have to consider the matter." Salazar added in English: "The rest of you, take her back to camp and tie her up. Don't leave her near anything she could use to get free, and take turns guarding her."

He turned to the instructor. "Sensao, please tie the jutens up and see to their food and water. Then join us in the tent; I shall want your services as a translator."

He started after the others, but Pokrovskii touched his arm. "Keit'l!" he cried, seizing Salazar and kissing his cheeks. "I got to tell you something. Can I trust you tell nobody? Is important."

"Yep," said Salazar.

"Hokay, First, I work for Conrad, so I got to do what he says, like when we left you in cage. Was awful. I tried to change his mind but could not. Now, you good man and I like you, as well as saving my life."

"So?"

"So I got to warn you. Conrad not going to wait for signing contract with High Chief. Will soon send crew with bulldozer, to shape terrain for resort."

"If he does that before the contract is final," said Salazar, "Miyage may tell him where to shove his agreement. Kooks are sticklers for protocol."

"I know. But Conrad very impatient man. Says business with Kooks worse than with Suvarov government. Committees, administrators, procedures, appeals, delays. He not appreciate efficiency of our government."

"That's your damned Russian influence in Suvarov," said Salazar. "You think everybody should be cogs in a vast machine, with all the little wheels turning in mesh."

"Of course! Is price of civilization!"

"Sure, but you carry it to the point of lunacy. You got the idea from the Byzantine Empire and have followed it ever since, under the Tsars and under the Communists and under the Constitutionalists. Over-organization is the Russian national vice."

"Well, de supersalesmanship is American national vice."

"Maybe you've got something there, Oleg. And another thing. Tell Bergen the next time he sends a gang to interfere with my work, they won't chase my people off the site, like last time. If I have to shoot a few, I will."

"Oh!" said Pokrovskii, looking solemn. "Then I got to tell you one more thing. The construction crew have order, if you interfere with them, to kill you; and boss don't mean it as how-you-say number of speech. He say, never mind laws of Terran Federation. Don't apply in Kook lands; and Kooks, if one Earthman kill another, won't interfere. You interfere if you saw two porondus fighting?"

"Thanks for the warning," said Salazar. "I've never killed a fellow Terran, but I daresay I could learn. Now we'd better question the prisoner."

As they followed the others toward the camp, Pokrovskii swished the Chosha saber through the morning air. "Is like Cossack *shashka*. Fine souvenir!"

The Chosha, wrists bound, stood in the center of a circle of seated Terrans. Sensao interpreted for the prisoner, and Salazar translated from Shongo for the other Terrans. Sensao reported:

"She says that, if you kill her, she hopes it will be

quick. If you wish to cut her head off now, she is ready."

The prisoner bowed her head low, presenting the back of her scaly neck. Despite her brave words, Salazar saw from the rippling patterns of the spines on her neck that she was frightened.

"Is tempting," said Pokrovskii, fingering the saber.

"Waste not, want not," said Salazar. "Perhaps we can find a better use for her." He switched to Shongo. "Sensao, ask her if, since her fellow tribesmen now regard her as dead, she would like to change her allegiance."

"She says she would, if you will become her new chief. She said you must be a great chief, from the way the other aliens obey you."

"Good thing she didn't see me after my fights with Bergen," muttered Salazar. "Do you know the rituals, Sensao?"

"Well enough, honorable sir. The Kampairin can correct any errors."

"What is her name?"

"She is Oikisha, daughter of Kussiti, granddaughter of Danjan. She is an *onnifa*—a barren female leading a warrior's life."

"Ask her if she will swear by the spirits of her ancestors and by her immortal honor to take me as her liege lord and be my faithful liege man?"

"She say she will, honorable sir." Salazar noted that the pattern of the Chosha's moving neck spines now betrayed feelings of hope.

"She must understand, first, that she will have to learn Shongo. She cannot serve me if we must communicate through an interpreter."

"She will do that, honorable sir. If you hire me for my present pay, I will teach her."

"Also," added Salazar, "I want her on my visit to the Empress, as servant and bodyguard."

"She will faithfully perform those duties, assuming that you will likewise meet your obligations toward her."

Salazar said to the others: "This will be a tedious business, taking at least an hour. We have to mix drops of each other's blood and all that sort of thing. Why don't you go eat your lunch while Sensao and I struggle through the ritual?"

The other Terrans assured Salazar that they would be interested in the ceremony; but, after listening for a while to the archaeologist and the two Kukulcanians exchanging groans and gasps and shrieks, they drifted away to the mess.

After lunch, Pokrovskii and Kovelenko set out on the hike back to Henderson, from where they would take the railroad to Suvarov. Salazar spent the afternoon on the dig, leaving Sensao and Oikisha in the camp. While the onnifa scrubbed the painted symbols from her scaly hide and painted on a new set, mostly white and yellow stars and sunbursts to symbolize her new allegiance, Sensao drilled her in the rudiments of Shongo.

When Salazar returned to the camp, he told Sensao: "One more day of riding practice must suffice. The day after that, Oikisha and I shall set out for Machura to see the Empress. Can you buy Oikisha a cheap but serviceable riding juten in Neruu, and another for baggage?"

"I can, honorable sir; but what about your satrapsas?"

"I shall order them; but until our return from Machura I must rely upon my saddle."

After dinner, Salazar wrote up the day's results and composed a work schedule for his assistants over the next few days. When he entered his sleeping compartment, he found Sensao sitting on his folding chair. The Shongorin rose, saying:

"Honorable Doctor Sarasara, Oikisha has asked me to learn when you wish to copulate. What may I tell her?"

Salazar's jaw sagged. "God in Heaven!" he exclaimed before changing to Shongo. "What makes her think that I want any such thing?"

"Oh, sir, it is a rigid custom among the Choshas. It is part of the mutual obligations between an onnifa and her liege lord; they copulate as often as desired whenever the liege lord is without his lawful mate. Oikisha asked me if you had a lawful mate. I told her that I understood you did not; so Oikisha stands ready to perform her duty."

"I evidently did not know native customs so well as I thought," said Salazar. "But Sensao, such copulation is impossible, because of the physical differences between our species. If I tried to meet Oikisha's expectations, the result would be no pleasure for her and severe pains to me."

"I am sorry, honorable sir," said Sensao. "If you cannot meet your part of this obligation, she will consider her oath to you cancelled and resume her allegiance to Prophet Kampai. Since you are Kampai's foe, for having escaped from him and killed some of his people, she must try to slay you. If she succeeds, she must then return to her tribe, although she knows that they will kill her forthwith."

Salazar pounded his forehead with the heel of his hand. "What in the name of your ancestral spirits shall I do?"

"Sir, the most practical course would be to take your pistol and shoot Oikisha."

"Ugh! I don't like that course, either. Let me think."

For some moments Salazar sat, staring. Sensao stood immobile. At last, looking at the new poignette on his wrist, Salazar felt the stirring of an idea. He glanced at the time, looked up Kara's home number, and pressed the buttons to call her. Kara's voice came thinly out of the little instrument: "Hello?"

"It's Keith," said Salazar. After amenities, he asked: "Has your story on the hunting trip appeared?"

"Would you believe it, McHugh refused to run it? He wants me to rewrite the piece to make Conrad Bergen look like a hero, instead of the rat I showed him to be. Several of Conrad's enterprises advertise in the *News*, and McHugh's afraid of losing the revenue."

"I should have shot Bergen during the hunt and called it an accident. But that's not what I called about."

"Well?"

"I'm leaving in two days for Machura, to beard the Empress Gariko—that is, I would if she had a beard. Could you come along? It'll be a great story for your paper if I pull it off; I don't think even McHugh could bottle that up."

"Why—I don't know, Keith. You've taken me by surprise. I need time to think. . . ."

"Sorry, but I've got to leave the day after tomorrow. You'd have to start for Nomuru in the morning."

"Why me? Phil Reiner actually speaks their croak, and native affairs are his job."

"No, Kara; this has to be you."

"Why? If you've got any romantic notions, forget—"

"No, no! This is an emergency. . . ." He told of the capture of the female Chosha scout, her change of allegiance, and the duty unexpectedly thrust upon him. "Do you know what a freemartin is? It's a sterile, physically abnormal cow. The Kooks have the equivalent."

The poignette snickered. "Why not give her a try? The Reverend Ragnarsen would disapprove, but the poor man is probably dead."

"Kara, aren't you familiar with the Kooks' anatomy? You know what happens to a pencil in a pencil sharpener. The long and the short of it is that I've got to have a nominal mate for a few days; or else I have to shoot Oikisha. She's only trying to do her duty."

"Why don't you shoot her? You didn't mind killing some of those Kooks who pursued us."

"A battle is one thing; but shooting a captive in cold blood, and a female at that, is another. You know I'll kill when I must, but my heart's not in it. And if I fool around long enough, trying to figure a way out, she says she'll have to kill me."

"Why not make Galina your 'nominal mate'?"

"God! Do you think those biddies on the University's Committee on Coercion and Harassment would believe it was nominal? Besides, Galina might get ideas of her own. One very-much-younger girlfriend will last me a lifetime."

"Who else is going with you?" she asked.

"Just Oikisha. I can't take Marcel or Ito away from the dig."

"In other words, we'll be by ourselves for all practical purposes. Look here, Keith, is this a ploy to get me into bed with you? Because if it is, you can go jump—"

"No, no, Kara! I don't do things like that."

"You didn't use to; but I can think of other things you didn't use to do, either."

"Oh, please, Kara! I've paid my penalty. I promise

not to lay a finger on you—at least, not without permission."

"You mean, a finger or any other organ!"

"Okay, a finger, toe, ear, or any other part. I need you, just as you needed me on that hunt."

After a long pause, the poignette said: "All right, I'll come."

"Good! Can you get here tomorrow?"

"Unless I break a leg or fall into the Sappari."

"And don't forget to bring a gun!" Salazar turned to Sensao, saying, "Tell Oikisha that she is misinformed. I have a lawful mate, who will arrive tomorrow to accompany us to Machura."

"What about tonight, honorable sir?" said the Shongorin.

"I am too fatigued to perform my tribal duty tonight, and thereafter there will be no occasion for it. Good-night!"

THE
EMPRESS

Kara arrived the following evening. Over a late dinner, she asked: "Keith, why are we riding these junior dinosaurs? Why don't we go to Henderson and take trains to Suvarov and Machura? It's not much more roundabout and would be lots more comfortable."

"Bergen's passed the word that he'd like the planet better without me. So, until I see how my talks with Miyage and Gariko turn out, I don't care to let Bergen draw a bead on me."

Salazar had intended to leave the day after Kara's arrival, but delays in collecting supplies and buying extra jutens held them up for another day. In the afternoon, Kara tried out her new juten. She teetered uncertainly in the saddle.

"Oh, dear!" she said. "If this thing ever starts or stops suddenly, I'll fall off on my head like the White Knight. If only I had stirrups!"

"I've ordered some in Neruu," said Salazar, standing beside her mount, "but they'll take at least an eight-day. Hey, I just had an idea!"

He stepped in front of the juten, grasped one of its short, clawed forelimbs, and wrapped the digits around Kara's booted ankle. To the juten he said: *"Tettai!"* meaning "hold."

After several trials, he persuaded the beast to retain its grip on the ankle. He rewarded it with a salt tablet and went to work on the other forelimb. At the end of an hour, at the command *"Tettai!"* the juten would obediently grasp its rider's ankles.

"Now how do I get loose?" said Kara.

"That's another lesson." Salazar commanded *"Guuchai!"* and unpeeled the juten's fingers.

After another hour the animal, seduced by salt tablets, would grasp and release its rider's ankles on command. Salazar said: "If we can train the other jutens to do this, we shan't need stirrups! I suppose the Kooks never thought of it because, with those talons on their feet, they've never needed to. Let's see if you can train my Daffodil to do likewise!"

During the extra day, Sesao continued Oikisha's Shongo lessons. Salazar reported to Kara: "Sensao will go with us as far as Shongaro, where Chief Sambyaku hangs out."

"How are the language lessons doing?"

"First-rate; Kooks have marvelous memories. Tell Oikisha that 'water' in Shongo is *mudai*, and she's got it permanently. Wish I were so good."

"On the other hand," said Kara, "such good memories might account for their ultra-conservatism. That can be a disadvantage."

"Especially," added Salazar, "in conflict with a

technologically more advanced species. Oh, well, any virtue overdone becomes a vice."

The next morning saw the departure of Salazar, Kara, Oikisha, and Sensao, each on a juten with a fifth beast to carry baggage. They dropped Sensao off at Shongaro and briefly paid their respects to Chief Sambyaku. As they continued on toward Biitso, the capital of High Chief Miyage, Salazar said to Kara:

"It's hard to work up warmth of feeling for Kooks, with their robotic personalities; but I guess Sambyaku's the closest to a friend that I have among them. I can't help being prejudiced toward him, after he saved my life in that brouhaha with Bergen at Neruu."

Oikisha pulled her mount up beside Salazar's to continue her linguistic exercises. Salazar, whose own Shongo was far from perfect, was hard put to it to act as teacher. Moreover, as Oikisha's vocabulary expanded, she began asking questions.

Was it true that they came from another world? Was it true that the world was round? If so, why did people not fall off it? Why was Salazar digging holes in the ground? Why was he interested in old ruins? How long had Kara been his mate? How many offspring did they have? When Salazar said none, she asked: Was the female Terran an onnifa like Oikisha? How could she be a lawful mate if barren?

When the questions became painful, Salazar said: "Enough, Oikisha. I must rest my voice."

"Never saw such curiosity," he told Kara. "Most Kooks show little interest in Terran affairs."

"She must be exceptionally bright," replied Kara. "Cabot says they vary over as wide a spectrum in intelligence, from genius to moron, as Terrans do."

Nightfall found the party on the road. The country through which they passed was pleasant, with cultivated fields neatly separated by orderly strips of woodland. Salazar said: "Here's a nice little grove, and I'm sure the draw ahead has a creek at the bottom. Let's send Oikisha to fetch water and then pitch the tent here."

Later, fed and relaxed, Salazar and Kara were stretched out in their sleeping bags on the floor of the tent. Salazar said:

"Good-night; sleep—Hey!"

A Kookish head was thrust through the flap into the tent. Salazar switched on his flashlight and reached for his pistol before he saw that it was Oikisha, her big yellow eyes aglow in the beam. He said in Shongo:

"What is it, Oikisha?"

The onnifa replied in halting Shongo.

"What's she saying?" asked Kara sleepily.

Salazar gulped. "I'll be dammed."

"Doubtless you will be, according to the Reverend Ragnarsen; but what is she saying?"

"She wants to see how we do it."

"Do what?"

"Oh, come on! To be precise, she wishes to observe us in copulation."

"Keith! Is this some low scheme of yours—"

"Absolutely not!" he exclaimed hotly. "I promised I wouldn't make a pass. I wouldn't touch you if you stripped naked and wriggled into my bag with me!"

"You'd have a tough time not doing so, considering how narrow these bags are. But I have no intention of giving a demonstration."

"Let me think. If I say we just don't do it before witnesses, she might pop in unexpectedly in hopes of catching us *in flagrante*—I have it!" He spoke at length to Oikisha, who stared and said in Shongo:

"Honorable sir, do you swear by the spirits of your ancestors?"

"Yes. Now please leave us to sleep."

The beaked, reptilian head reluctantly withdrew. Kara asked: "What did you tell her?"

"I said we did it without physical contact, by telepathy. I impregnated you by thinking beautiful thoughts at you. I'm not sure how much she understood, and she didn't seem fully convinced. They think all Terrans are liars anyway."

Kara sputtered with laughter. "I'm sure some of the men at the *News* have thought beautiful thoughts at me; but none has impregnated me yet!"

"I think beautiful thoughts at you all the time," said Salazar. "What's wrong with a little harmless pleasure?"

"Keith! Get your mind above my waist!"

"But darling, you used to love our love-making. Remember—"

"I used to like filegrass rum, too, until I found it disagreed with me. I'm sure I haven't given you any encouragement!"

"Your mere presence is encouragement enough."

"Nonsense! You were never so sex-mad when we were married."

"Does a fish in the river think about water? Whether you mean to be or not, to me you're more seductive than Eve ever was to Ad—"

"Good-night, Keith!"

A little grumpily, he replied:

> *My inscrutable ex*
> *Wants nothing of sex*
> *And puts it to flight*
> *With a frigid good-night!"*

Next morning, Kara was aroused by faint grunts. She opened her eyes to see Salazar in his underwear doing push-ups on the canvas floor of the tent. He finally gave up and lay panting. When he recovered his breath, he said:

"Damn! Can't get past ten; must be getting soft. Will you hold down my ankles while I do sit-ups?"

She gripped his ankles. "You're certainly fit enough, with the hard work you do on the dig. Why do you need these calisthenics?"

He grinned impishly. "Best way I know to make sure I shan't crawl in my sleep."

Biitso was larger than Neruu but less industrialized. The houses were simple blocks of wood and stone, without external ornament save for painted symbols in a kaleidoscope of colors, like those with which the dwellers embellished their own scaly hides.

Salazar found his way to the house of High Chief Miyage, a "palace" only by virtue of being slightly larger than those of its neighbors. Salazar gave his name to the spear-armed guards at the door, requesting speech with the High Chief.

The guard returned, saying: "The High Chief refuses to admit you."

"Now what the hell?" exclaimed Salazar. He explained to Kara.

"Has he," she wondered, "a grudge against Terrans in general? Or you in particular?"

"I suspect it's me, on account of a boundary dispute I was called into last year." He spoke again to the guard: "Tell the High Chief that I have weighty news concerning his chieftainship: that he faces a Chosha invasion!"

Again the guard departed and returned. "The High

Chief will not hear you. Furthermore, he commands you to go away and cease disturbing him."

"Well, he can't say I didn't try to warn him—" began Salazar, when High Chief Miyage himself appeared in the portal with an escort of spearmen and musketeers.

Sighting Salazar and his companion, he rasped: "I sent orders for you to depart, Terran!" His tongue flicked out.

"But, Your Highness, you are betrayed! Conrad Bergen has a secret deal with Prophet Kampai—"

"Away with you! You are a liar and a trouble-maker, as you showed by assaulting my friend Bergen. He has told me about your plots and perfidies. Will you go, or must I have you whipped out of town?"

Salazar had quietly unsnapped the flap of his pistol holster and placed his hand on the butt. The guards and some of the escort brought their spears up to port, while a couple of musketeers cocked their weapons.

"Careful, Keith!" breathed Kara, also fingering her pistol.

"I know," he muttered. "I could take a couple with me, but then we'd be dead. Let's go!"

The two walked away to where Oikisha held their jutens. As they mounted and rode off, Salazar said: "I was tempted to tell him off; but somehow 'Copulate Your Highness!' doesn't have the same clout that it has in the English equivalent."

"Besides," added Kara, "he might have simply said: 'Shoot them!' I believe that once happened to a journalist on Terra, who got sassy with a Latin American dictator."

Leaving Biitso behind, the travelers set up their next camp under threatening gray skies streaked with lightning. Kara Sheffield, sitting on the floor of the tent while rain drummed on the canvas, said: "Keith, you've got to teach me the elements of Shongo. If we got separated in this country . . ."

"I'll try," said Salazar. "First, forget the Indo-European categories: nouns, verbs, and so forth, with their usual inflections. The Shongorin have substantives, predicatives, and operatives. . . ."

An hour later, she said: "If I try to make those horrible sounds any more, I'll have a sore throat."

"Enough for one night." After a roll of thunder died, he went on: "I started to ask you something when the Choshas interrupted. Are you thinking of getting married again?"

"I've considered it. I've had plenty of propositions and a couple of real proposals. But I guess I'm too fussy. I'd want a man with all your good qualities, but one I could absolutely depend upon. There aren't many such paragons around."

Salazar sighed. "If you insist on a faultless man, you'll have to wait for the Second Coming; and Jesus never promised to reappear here as well as on Terra."

"I try to be realistic," said Kara, adding: "Why hasn't Cabot Firestone remarried?"

The warmth of her tone aroused a pang of jealousy in Salazar. "I suppose he's too wrapped up in memories of his wife. They were an exceptional couple, almost obscenely happy with each other."

"Oh? That's sad. When you do find one of those rare perfect couples . . . Anyway, that puts him out of the running, at least for now." She sounded disappointed.

"Why?" asked Salazar.

"I could never compete with the ghost of a perfect wife." She slid into her bag. "Good-night, Keith."

"Good-night, Kara." A little spring of hope began

to bubble. If I just keep after her, he thought, she might yet come around. . . .

In Machura, the streets were noisy and polluted by the smoke of steam cars and trucks. The palace of Empress Gariko was simply a larger version of the modest home of High Chief Miyage in Biitso. When Salazar requested one of the door guards for an audience with Her Imperial Majesty, the guard went in and returned half an hour later, saying that Her Majesty's secretary had made an appointment for a meeting eleven days hence. He spoke in Feënzuo, of which Shongo was a dialect; the Shongorin, however, insisted the opposite: that Feënzuo was a dialect of Shongo. In any case, Salazar could, with difficulty, follow his speech.

When Salazar had translated the message, Kara said: "Good heavens! It seems that Kookish bureaucracies are even harder to deal with than ours."

"You have to know the tricks," said Salazar. To the guards he said: "Kindly inform Her Imperial Majesty that the matter concerns the boundary stones of the Emperor Hamashti."

This time, the guard returned to say: "Pray, honorable sir and madam, follow me!"

The guard led them into a small chamber adjacent to the portal, empty save for a number of cushions scattered about the floor. The guard said: "Honorable sir, Her Majesty commands that you wait here until called for, and that you request aught needed for your comfort."

"Thank you; we shall be comfortable," said Salazar.

When the guard had gone, Kara asked: "What was it you said? 'Open sesame!'?"

Salazar explained: "Last year, Gariko called me in to see if I could settle a nasty dispute between her and High Chief Miyage over the Shongosi-Feënzun boundary. Emperor Hamashti set up boundary stones over a century ago; but where these ran across a flood plain, they'd been buried in silt. Miyage, who's an aggressive bastard, claimed land half a kilometer northwest of the line where the Empress thought the boundary was established."

"What did you do?"

"We couldn't dig up the whole valley; but I black-mailed Skanda Patel into letting me take out our precious GPR—"

"What's that?"

"Ground-penetrating radar. Skanda hangs onto it like a drowning man to an oar, since it's the only one on Kukulcan and at our stage of development irreplaceable. With the help of a professor from the engineering department, I made a hot-air balloon. We took it to the border and inflated it, and I went up with the GPR. One of Gariko's troopers, mounted on his juten, held the anchor rope and towed the contraption back and forth across the valley.

"That was one hairy trip! I had to fiddle with the GPR controls with one hand and pump the bellows with the other, to keep the fire up. If I let it die a little, I started down. The job called for two people, but we didn't have enough lift. Then, just as I finished noting my data, the trooper's juten happened to look up. I guess it took the balloon for some sort of fire-breathing dragon, because it let out a screech and bolted.

"The Kook soldier let go of the rope to clutch his saddle, leaving me gaining altitude. I pulled the valve cord to release hot air, but without first checking wind speed and direction and calculating where I'd come down. As a result, the basket plopped down right in the middle of a nice little bog. I had quite a time, wading in slime up to my knees and keeping the GPR out of the mud."

"Did you find what you were looking for?"

"Yep. We dug up three of Hamashti's stones, right where Gariko claimed the boundary was. They were inscribed, roughly speaking: 'I am the great and glorious Hamashti, Emperor of Feënzun. I am the strongest of the strong, the bravest of the brave, the wisest of the wise, and the purest of the pure.' He forgot to add 'the most modest of the modest,' but went on: 'I have caused these stones to be set up on the line between my Empire and the Shongosi Chieftainship. If any person should deface or remove them, may the spirits of his ancestors disown him!' So you see why Miyage, aside from being a nasty fellow to begin with, doesn't love me."

"I hope this Empress isn't such a megalomaniac."

"That was just the customary style in Hamashti's time. Gariko's less toplofty and formal. Many Feënzurin don't like the change; they grumble that she's been corrupted by Terran discourtesy and is betraying the sacred customs of her ancestors."

"What did you mean about blackmailing Doctor Patel?"

Salazar chuckled. "You know how self-righteous he is? But I learned of certain irregularities in his domestic affairs. I didn't threaten him or anything so crude, just gentle hints."

"What irregularities?"

"Ask me no questions—well, I don't mind saying that Skanda has a large, fat, domineering wife named Toinette and four children. I don't know whether her bullying causes him to stray or his straying leads her to bully. That's for Cabot Firestone to figure out."

"Cabot took me out to dinner—" began Kara.

The guard reappeared. "You may come now, sir and madam."

Squatting on a cushion on a dais, Empress Gariko was larger than High Chief Miyage, and the symbols that embellished her scales were of painted gold. Several golden chains were draped around her neck. Her reptilian head bore a tiara, shaped like those metal bands that held Terran earmuffs in place. This head band was skillfully crafted of gold filigree set with precious stones—rubies, emeralds, and sapphires—which winked in the lamplight.

Salazar approached the Empress and bowed; Kara, watching him for clues, did likewise. In Shongo, Salazar said: "Good day to you! Is Your Imperial Majesty in good health?"

"Thank the Universal Law," she replied, "we are in good health. Is the learned Terran in good health?"

"Thank the Universal Law, my health is good. Is all well with Your Majesty's clan?"

"Thanks to our ancestral spirits, all is well. . . ."

The ritual exchange went on for over five minutes. Salazar muttered out of the side of his mouth: "With one of her rank, strict formality is essential." Then Salazar was nearly startled out of his skin as the Empress, in the midst of the courtly phrases, interjected in accented but understandable English:

"You are quite right, Sarasara; this is a penalty of my lofty station."

When the formalities ended, Gariko picked up one of her little glass-paned boxes with cranks for rolling the scroll within and studied the printing to refresh her memory. Then, looking at her visitors, she said in Shongo: "We are glad to see you again, honorable Sarasara. Are we correct in thinking that the female with you was formerly your mate? We find it difficult to be sure with Terrans; you all look so much alike. One cannot even rely upon your outer coverings to distinguish you, because you are ever changing them. Are we right about the female?"

"How did Your Majesty know?" said Salazar in ill-concealed amazement.

Salazar had a feeling that if Gariko had been physically capable of smiling, she would have smiled. She said: "How could we protect our realm without many sources of information at our command? Am I to believe that you twain have again become mates?"

Salazar winced at the question. Beside him, Kara whispered:

"What's she saying?"

Salazar waved her query aside. "No, Your Majesty. We are merely friends, and Miss Sheffield comes to obtain information for the newspaper on which she works."

"Send us a copy of her story when it appears. And now let us to business." Gariko called to the guards, "Go outside, all of you, and close the door."

When the guards had vanished, Gariko said in her parrotlike English: "I prefer that they do not hear me speaking Terran; they think that it violates tradition and demeans my high office. Sarasara, unless I can crack the crust of custom and precedent, which imprisons my people, I fear trouble from you aliens. But I must move cautiously, lest they accuse me of being un-Feënzish."

"Your Majesty's English astonishes me," said Salazar. "Last time you professed ignorance of the speech."

"I try to learn what I think I shall need for all contingencies. I am now working on Russian. *Kak vi pozhivayetye?*"

Salazar, whose Russian was rudimentary, thought furiously and stammered: "*Khorosho*—uh—*spasibo!*"

"Good! When I have mastered Russian, I shall begin on Chinese, to deal with the Terrans of Gueilin. Now to work. What is this about Hamashti's boundary markers?"

"Your Majesty, your boundary with Shongosi is menaced by a much greater threat than Miyage." Salazar told of his capture by the Choshas and of Prophet Kampai's plans for conquest and extermination. "Miyage has spurned my attempt to warn him, being under the influence of Conrad Bergen—"

"I have a file on Mr. Bergen," said Gariko. "It is reported that he intends to plow up the site of Nomuru for a construction project of his own."

Salazar opened his mouth to speak, but the Empress briskly continued: "I know something of your science of archaeology. With their reverence for tradition, perhaps my people could come to appreciate it. In fact, I wish to send a few likely youths to the Terrans to study the science, which our savants should have developed on their own long ago.

"Let us now review our respective aims, to ascertain how we can help one another. You wish to forestall Mr. Bergen, whereas my paramount duty is to safeguard my borders. The logical course for me is to strengthen the defenses, to refurbish the border fortresses and build others. My spies do not tell me that the Prophet is making cannon, without which he cannot capture the forts."

"A purely defensive strategy, Your Majesty?"

"It is the best that I can envisage. The Choshas are formidable foes, having the hardiness that nomadic life requires. Since their warriors are all mounted, they move faster than our foot soldiers. Therefore we always need an advantage of numbers at the point of contact."

"But, Your Majesty!" said Salazar. "What's to stop the Choshas from pouring into the Empire through the gaps between the forts and ravaging the country behind them?"

"As each band enters, we shall try to assemble enough troops from the fortresses and from the reserve units to outnumber them."

"Wouldn't it be better to occupy Shongosi and attack the Choshas in the Shongo lands?"

"I do not think that I could assemble a large enough force to give us an advantage in Shongosi," said Gariko. "You have not seen a mounted Chosha onset. Our musketeers can mow down the first rank of the attackers, but those behind keep coming and are upon our soldiers before they can reload."

The Feënzurin, it developed, did not have the bayonet. They were armed with long knives and tomahawks for hand-to-hand combat, but these were ineffectual against mounted Choshas.

"Affixing a knife to the end of a musket is a clever Terran idea," said Gariko. "I must command the army to investigate the matter; but that could not be done in time for this impending conflict. Some of our military people have always maintained that it was a mistake to give up the pike."

"Your Majesty," said Salazar, "are you familiar with Terran repeating firearms?"

"I have heard of them. One of our engineers undertook to invent one, although our officers scorned such guns as un-Feënzish. When he tested his device, it blew up and killed him, confirming the officers in their view."

"If I could get you repeating rifles to arm a company, would you then occupy Shongosi?"

"To what purpose? The Shongorin would resist, and we should be fighting them as well as the Choshas."

"If you could destroy the Chosha army afar, you would save much loss of life and property in Feënzun."

"If, if!" said Gariko impatiently. "Even if this Terran-armed company defeated the Choshas, how would that benefit your archaeological project? Unless he were slain in the fighting, your Mr. Bergen would then resume his development after we left Shongosi."

"Why not, Your Majesty, extend a permanent rule over Shongosi?"

"But," said Gariko, "the independence of Shongosi is guaranteed by the treaty with my predecessor Hamashti. It is entirely un-Feënzish to march in and conquer a neighbor without a valid reason. Now that the boundary dispute has been settled through your good efforts, Miyage has avoided provocation."

"Once the Choshas have crossed the Shongo border," said Salazar, "you can rush to their aid, whether they ask for it or not. Afterward I am sure your legalists can find a pretext for staying. They could cite Miyage's stubborn refusal to prepare, despite warnings."

Gariko gave a hiss that was the equivalent of a Terran sigh. "Sarasara, you Terrans are too subtle for us simple, honest human beings. How would all this help your archaeological project? Unless he were killed, Mr. Bergen would continue his work. I should have to honor his contract with the Shongo chiefs. We take such agreements more seriously than, I fear, your fellow Terrans do."

"Does Your Majesty know about national parks?"

"What is a national park?"

Salazar told of the great Terran parks for the protection of scenic wonders, wild life, and relics of antiquity; places like Yellowstone, Serengeti, and the Summer Palace at Beijing. "If you enable me to continue my work at Nomuru, it will not only solve historical problems but also furnish your people with an object lesson. My work will show how great a nation can become and how far it can fall. A park, with guards and attendants, would be a national show place, glorifying Feënzun, inspiring the young, and adding to the Empire's revenue."

"You have given me much food for thought, Sarasara. I shall have to consider your proposals. I must now dismiss you to receive a trading mission. You and your traveling companion shall be accommodated in the palace. I regret that I cannot invite you to dine. My people regard eating with Terrans as a shocking departure from custom. I dare not upset too many ancient traditions at one time."

The Empress cried a command in her own tongue. The guards returned, and a pair of palace servants led Salazar and Kara to a suite. When these attendants explained that they were there to serve the Terrans during their stay, Salazar arranged to have the lighter baggage brought in, his servant Oikisha accommodated, and the jutens fed and stabled.

The spacious suite was lit by several torchères, whence protruded wavering yellow-white flames fueled by a plant oil. Like most Kookish dwellings, the apartment reeked with the dead-fish smell of Kooks plus the sour-sweet odor of this household illuminant.

Since there was not a chair in the palace, the attendants fetched two cushions and placed a stump-legged table between them. When Salazar and Kara were seated with as much comfort as they could manage, the servants brought an unopened bottle of Henderson's best "whiskey," a pitcher of water, and two mugs, which they set on the table. The senior attendant asked:

"When do you wish dinner, honorable sir?"

"In about an hour," Salazar replied, pouring two drinks. When he told Kara what he had ordered, she protested:

"Keith! I hope you're not planning to get drunk in all that time!"

He smiled. "No, my dear; to relax to that extent in Kookland I should have to be certifiably insane." He swallowed a gulp. "But this should wash out the taste of the advice I gave the Empress."

"What do you mean?"

"I recommended the pretexts for naked aggression that European imperialists employed in conquering other continents, in the four hundred years that began with Columbus. If somebody else did it, I should call him a scoundrel; but it was the only way I could see to save the site. Now I shall call my people. Do take a sip; the stuff's not bad."

Salazar pressed buttons on his poignette and presently heard Galina's voice, tiny and tinny with distance. "*Allo?* Hello?"

"Keith speaking," said Salazar. "How's the dig?"

"Splendid! Sambyaku's workers arrived the day before yesterday. We have uncovered that wall down to the footing for a length of four meters. We have come upon the remains of an earlier brick wall at right angles to it, and evidently older; the stone wall cuts through the upper courses of the brick. The stone wall must have been built when the ground level had risen to—"

"Please!" said Salazar. "Conclusions can wait until we have all the data. What else have you found?"

"I am trying to tell you. At the end of the four meters we have uncovered, the stone wall turns at a right angle; and in the angle of the wall we have found a lot of ceramic cylinders, about ten centimeters in diameter and sixty or seventy long. We pulled one out, and Marcel pried off the cap. Inside was a scroll of some sort of leather, tanned by that Kook process which preserves it for centuries—"

"I hope you didn't try to unroll it!" cried Salazar. "It'll crumble into fragments unless treated in the laboratory first."

"No, we did not, although I had to slap Marcel's hands to stop him."

"How many cylinders are there?"

"We don't know. We uncovered the tops of perhaps ten or twelve more."

"Listen carefully, Galina. Cover the exposed cylinders with dirt, and make sure none of you says a word of this to anyone—"

"You think this might be the library of King Bembogu?"

"Can't tell yet."

"When are you coming back?"

"In a few days, I hope," said Salazar. "Any trouble with Bergen's crew?"

"No. The machines have not arrived. He has a man out here every few days to see how we're doing, but nobody has tried to stop us. Mr. Pokrovskii came by yesterday to say that the contract has been signed and the bulldozer will soon be here."

Salazar grunted. "That changes things. Hold on. Let me think." After a silence he said: "Take pits A1, A3, and A5 along the northern side. You and the Kooks dig all three down to a depth of two meters."

"But we cannot do that and keep a record of the finds, stratum by stratum!"

"I know, but we're in a hurry. Have them pile the dirt from each ten-centimeter layer in a separate pile near the pit. Put stakes in the piles, labeled so we can tell which is which. We'll sieve the piles later. Sloppy archaeology, but it can't be helped.

"Then lay a tarp over each of those three pits. Hold it down with rocks around the edge—use ones from the ancient wall if you have to, but paint numbers on them—and spread a coat of dirt over the canvas, so it looks like undisturbed soil."

"You mean to make pitfalls, the way the primitive Kook tribes catch big game?"

"Yep. Don't do it while Bergen's men are there. If they give trouble, don't do anything rash. I'd rather lose the site than my team."

Salazar exchanged greetings with Frappot and Kurita and clicked off. He next called Firestone's apartment. After greetings he said:

"Oh, about as well as could be expected. Her Imperial Majesty has a soft place for me in whatever Kooks have for a heart, as a result of that boundary business. We're working up a deal, but I can't tell you now."

"May I speak with him?" asked Kara.

"Sure." Salazar unstrapped and handed over the poignette. Kara and Firestone went through a simple, banal set of greetings and inquiries; but Salazar noted a warmth in Kara's tone that he had not heard from her since her first arrival at Nomuru.

He thought, does this mean that my best friend and I are rivals for my ex-wife? That would be a sticky one, worthy of an Italian opera! Salazar did not worry about competition from Bergen, since Kara was not one to forgive a black eye. But Cabot . . .

Kara handed back the poignette. As he strapped the instrument on his wrist, Salazar noted the date it showed in the calendar that Terrans had devised for Kukulcan. The familiarity of the date nagged his mind until it burst upon him that it was exactly ten years, Kukulcanian time, since he and Kara had first been married.

A little shaken, he said: "I think we can drink, now." He raised his mug. "Kara, do you know what day this is?"

"Why . . . Fourteen Quintilis, isn't it?"

"Yep. But doesn't the day *mean* something to you?"

The green-gray eyes under the dark curls gave him a level stare that pierced him like a sword of ice. "No."

"But—but it's—"

"I know what you mean. Let's say the date meant something to me once, but it doesn't any more."

Feeling like a deflated balloon, Salazar slumped, took a gulp, and stared at the floor. Anger, sorrow, and self-reproach struggled for command of his psyche. He suddenly felt old, although with modern medicine he could look forward to a century or more of active life.

Kara's voice came as if from afar. "Sorry, Keith; but you asked."

As Salazar continued to stare morosely, she said: "The Empress doesn't seem like a typical Kook."

The archaeologist roused himself. "She's a superior Kookess; her outlook is closer to ours than the rest of her species. That's one of her problems. She sees the need for change, but the inertia of Kookish culture makes Terran conservatism look wildly radical. So whenever Gariko plans to introduce some departure from established ways, she's skating on thin ice."

Kara asked: "Is there an Emperor? A Mr. Gariko?"

"Gariko has a consort, named Aobu or something. I understand he's a minor civil servant in her department of commerce."

"They don't make the consort a prince or a duke?"

"No; it's not a feudal system, but an impenetrable bureaucracy. All they give Aobu is an extra honorific, which could be translated as 'super-honorable' or 'honorable squared.' Otherwise he shuffles his papers, writes his reports, and goes to service the Empress when she sends for him."

With a light laugh, she said: "Now *that's* the kind of husband a girl needs!"

"I suppose I could study up for the rôle."

"No; I had in mind someone like poor Derek Travers."

"That kid!"

"I know he was young; but for a job like this consort's—"

"Bilge, Kara! What a mature man lacks in speed he more than makes up for by—"

Salazar broke off as the attendants arrived with dinner, which they set on the table. The archaeologist ate a spoonful of mush, made a face, and complained: "I suppose it's better than the bark of the rubagub tree; but that's all you can say for it." He poured another mug of quasi-whiskey.

> "This food has the taste
> Of library paste,
> But with enough liquor
> We'll get it down quicker."

Kara laughed. "I've always wondered how you manage to whip out those jingles on the spur of the moment. It would take me an hour with a rhyming dictionary."

Salazar shrugged. "Don't rightly know; they seem to pop into my head."

> "Who'd woo a fair maid
> Must summon the aid
> Of meter and rhyme
> And couplets that chime,
> Or never his love he'll persuade!"

Kara laughed again, then looked sharply at Salazar and changed the subject. "Tell me about some of the nutty characters you've known since we separated."

"Well, there was this dame from the Maravilla Society, who wanted to know where Earthmen stood in the Kooks' social scale of castes. When I explained that we were near the bottom, somewhere between migrant farm workers and collectors of fertilizer, she said: 'Well, we first human families on this planet obviously belong higher on the scale. Please find out, Professor, just where we should place ourselves.'

"The worst of it is, the woman likes me. She corners me for interminable talk, wasting my working time. She makes the Kooks' day-long speeches seem entertaining. I don't dare insult her, because her society furnishes a significant part of our funds." He paused, and then it was his turn to change the subject. "You heard the talk between Galina and me, about those cylinders they've unearthed."

"Yes, I did; and I'm eaten with curiosity. Do you think they've found the Bembogu library?"

"They've certainly found something; but it'll take months of treatment before we can unroll the scrolls, and more months to decipher and read them. It just could be as important for Kukulcanian history as Rassam's discovery of Ashurbanipal's library at Nineveh was for Terran history. Or again it may be a disappointment, like those countless Babylonian clay tablets that turn out, when translated, to say something like: 'Dear Sargon: When are you going to pay me for those fifty sheep?'

"Meanwhile, can I trust you to say absolutely nothing about the find until I give the word? You know why."

"You have my promise, Keith. But then, will you give me an exclusive?"

"Sure; glad to." He yawned. "Excuse me; but isn't it time we crawled into our cocoons?"

Since the palace had no beds, the travelers blew up their pneumatic pillows and inserted themselves into their sleeping bags. Kara said, "These folk seem amazingly indifferent to comfort."

"They're physically tough," said Salazar, "or maybe just insensitive. They think us self-indulgent sissies. Good-night, Kara dear."

Next morning, Empress Gariko leaned forward on her cushions and said in English: "Sarasara, tell me about these repeating guns."

"They are hidden in the University of Henderson Museum. If I can make certain arrangements, I could get them out and send them to you—provided that, when they have served their purpose, they shall be returned to the Museum; no one need know where they came from. And that when you rule Shongosi, you will set up a national park at Nomuru to enable me to continue my work there. I shall also need help in geting these munitions to Machura."

"What help would you need?"

Salazar pressed the calculating switch on his poignette and fed numbers into it. He said: "I shall need at least twelve kyuumeis—make that sixteen, in case some get sick or die on the road. There are twenty-four crates, and each kyuumei can bear two.

That means at least sixteen kyuumei herds. With such a party, there must be a captain or overseer."

"How about getting the guns out of the Museum? Must we break in with explosives? That calls for soldiers."

"No, Your Imperial Majesty. I have a key, and with able-bodied Feënzurin we can carry the stuff out at night and load it. Be sure your people are sworn to secrecy and bring plenty of rope."

"Will you stay here to lead the men and beasts to their destination?"

"I can't, Your Majesty," said Salazar. "I must return to Henderson to assure that we shall not be disturbed while loading."

"Then how shall we coordinate? How many days' travel is it to Henderson?"

"Six or seven, depending on how hard one pushes. The kyuumeis are slower; one should allow them at least twelve days."

"We have enough steam trucks in Machura to carry that load, and the road to Neruu would take them."

"I know, Your Majesty. But your trucks are noisy and conspicuous, with their great clouds of steam and smoke. Even if they crossed the Sappari by the ford without getting stuck, I could never get them in and out of Henderson without waking half the city and causing a stir among the Shongorin through whose lands they would pass. But strings of laden kyuumeis are common enough so that nobody would pay much attention to one more such caravan; and the trucks are not very much faster."

Gariko asked: "Do you seriously propose to return to Henderson to 'make arrangements,' come back here to lead your train of kyuumeis to Henderson, and then return to Machura? The war may be over by then."

"No, Your Majesty. If you'll appoint a caravan leader, I shall explain where to bring his train. Then I shall leave for Henderson, with him and his caravan following. I shall get in touch with your captain as soon as he arrives. When we return to Machura, I must instruct your picked company in the new weapons or they'll waste all their ammunition to no purpose. And now, I should like to ask a favor of Your Majesty."

"What favor?."

"You know my servant Oikisha, formerly a Chosha onnifa?"

"What about her?"

"I should like you to accept the transfer of her allegiance to Your Majesty."

"For what reason?"

Salazar explained the difficulty with the Chosha belief in the proper duty of an onnifa toward her master. "To still Oikisha's importunities, Miss Sheffield and I have had to pretend to be still mated. Since we are not, this is a nuisance."

Thoughtfully, Gariko said: "When a Terran speaks of 'pretending to be mates' with another, does this pretense extend to copulation?"

Flushing, Salazar said: "In this case, no. Our sexual customs are too complicated to explain here."

Gariko's neck spines rippled in a way that implied amusement. "I see that my questions cause that peculiar Terran emotion called 'embarrassment'; so I shall return to our previous subject. Why can you not simply dismiss Oikisha?"

Salazar explained the rules whereby Oikisha lived. "Since I wish neither to kill or be killed by her, I thought a transfer of allegiance would solve the problem. She is intelligent and a hard worker. Perhaps you could lend me one of your people to do our camp chores on the road to Henderson."

"Oh, very well," said Gariko. "I suppose I can find a use for her. Now I must choose your caravan leader. I shall give him a letter to High Chief Miyage, asking permission to send this train through his chieftainship. But—Sarasara, if I say the load on the return trip consists of Terran guns, he will never let it pass. He will on some pretext seize them for his own use."

"Tell him the crates contain agricultural implements," said Salazar, hiding a smile.

The Empress hissed again. "Ah, you tricky Terrans! But what if Miyage pries open a box to inspect the contents?"

"Doesn't Your Majesty have an imperial seal for personal property?"

"Excellent! I shall send with the kyuumeis a supply of seals and wire for attaching them. If you will return in two hours, I shall introduce you to your captain."

THE
BULLDOZER

Salazar, Kara, and Baasu, the Feënzurin native whom
Gariko had sent along as helper and guide, jogged
briskly along the road to Shongaro. Salazar had left
the letter from the Empress to Miyage with a flunky
at the palace at Biitso, without waiting to confront
the hostile High Chief himself. When Baasu got used
to his Terran charges, he became quite voluble:

"Honorable Sarasara, I am pleased to accompany
you and your female. It is a welcome change from
my usual duties."

"What is your regular line of work?" asked Salazar.

"I am a tax collector."

"Persons in your occupation are never popular, are
they?"

"You are more than right, honorable sir! The office
is important, indeed necessary if a nation is to func-
tion in a civilized manner. Yet no matter how honest

and competent he be, the poor tax collector is despised, feared, and relegated to a low caste."

"It is the same with us Terrans," murmured Salazar sympathetically.

"The trouble," continued the Kook, "is that everybody demands a free handout from the government; but nobody wants to pay his share when the tax collector comes around!"

"That, too, sounds familiar," said the archaeologist.

They jogged into Shongaro. Chief Sambyaku was not at home, but questions discovered him in the marketplace, checking merchants' weights. At the sight of the Terrans, Sambyaku said: "Hail, honorable Sarasara! Hail, honorable Sheffira! Is all well with you?"

Salazar replied: "Thanks to the Universal Law, all is well. Is all well with you?"

After the formal greetings were properly concluded, Sambyaku said: "I must complete what I am doing; then we shall talk. Please wait in the shade."

"Neither snow nor rain nor heat nor gloom of night shall stay . . ." muttered Salazar in English. "If you find a Kook painting his house and tell him a gang of nomad raiders will appear any minute, he'll say: 'I must finish what I am doing; then I shall flee.'" Kara giggled.

A mere half-hour sufficed to complete the chief's inspection of weights. Sambyaku said: "Let us walk thither, where few will overhear."

They strolled down the side street where Baasu stood holding the jutens. Sambyaku came right to the point. "Sarasara, granting the concession to Bergen was not my doing. High Chief Miyage overruled me, and under our customs I was compelled to accede."

"I thank Your Honor for your gracious explanation," said Salazar. "What is the present state of Bergen's project?"

"The tractor that Bergen had made to order in Biitso passed through Shongaro this afternoon. The Terrans had attached a huge blade, like a plowshare turned sideways, to the front. I compelled them to remove from the wheels of the vehicle the cleats, which would have severely damaged our streets. The High Chief had sent with the Terrans an escort of musketeers, and for a while an open conflict between his soldiers and mine appeared imminent; but, thank the Universal Law, the Terrans decided that it were better to accede to my demands than to risk a battle."

"I thank Your Honor for this news," said Salazar. "I don't wish a conflict at Nomuru; but under these circumstances anything may happen."

"I understand, honorable Sarasara. I cannot help you with armed force; but neither am I obliged to join Miyage's troop against you. Be in good health!"

"And may Your Honor enjoy good health!"

"May your clan flourish!"

The travelers jogged on. Next day, as the sun sank low, they neared Nomuru, where the road to Salazar's camp skirted the northern end of the site. On a slight rise, Salazar halted his mount and drew out a small brass telescope.

"Kookish work," he explained to Kara. "I lost my good binoculars on Bergen's hunt, haven't had time to buy another, and found this quaint object in a drawer."

He put the telescope to an eye and said: "The tractor's on the edge of the site, with a couple of Terrans working on it and four or five Kooks standing around. I think the Terrans are bolting the cleats back on the wheels."

"Should we ride past?" asked Kara.

Salazar glanced toward the sun, just disappearing behind the scattered vegetation to westward. "The machine's forty or fifty meters from the road. I think we're safe, but just in case . . ."

Salazar pulled his rifle from the saddle boot, checked the magazine, and rode on, saying: "Move briskly and confidently, and don't talk."

The northern end of the site was dotted with little conical piles of dirt, like oversized anthills, each one flagged by a tag attached to a small stake. As they passed the tractor, one Kook unslung his musket; otherwise the group merely glanced stolidly at the riders. When they were out of earshot, Salazar said:

"Whew! Maybe they weren't sure who we were in the twilight. Let's hope Uwangi cooks us a decent meal!"

Over dinner, Galina explained: "Mr. Pokrovskii tipped us off that Bergen's men were nearby. He warned us to keep out of sight. We have been washing and boxing specimens and going out from time to time to see if they had come. A couple of hours ago, the tractor appeared with the Terrans riding it and the Kooks marching beside it."

"Are they camping at the site?" asked Salazar.

Frappot and Kurita spoke in unison. "No. Mr. Pokrovskii said they had arranged to stay in Neruu."

"You three had better stand watches through the night, with my rifle handy. Kara and I would spell you if we weren't dead tired."

After an early breakfast, Salazar and his people crept into a patch of heavy foliage to watch the site. For an hour the tractor stood alone and silent. Then Bergen's men and the Kookish soldiers straggled in. One Terran lit a fire in the firebox and shoveled in coal. Soon a plume of black smoke issued from the stack. Like a monster breathing, the machine began to emit puffs of pearly vapor with a rhythmic hiss. One Terran climbed into the driver's seat and worked levers. The bulldozer blade dipped and rose.

A Terran shouted, thicker puffs of vapor curled skyward from the tractor's stack, and the machine began to move. As it clattered across the site at the pace of a leisurely walk, Salazar whispered: "Where are those pitfalls?"

"It seems to be heading right between two of the open pits," breathed Frappot. "It should soon encounter —Ah! Ah! There it goes!" Frappot's voice had risen.

"Hush up, idiot!" snarled Salazar. The archaeologist kept his eyes on the tractor, which abruptly pitched forward so that the front end, bulldozer blade and all, disappeared, leaving only the after end and the huge rear wheels exposed.

The Terrans surrounding the machine set up a yell; but their voices were drowned by a roar as a cloud of vapor boiled up from the pit into which the tractor had fallen. Salazar glimpsed two Terrans dragging out the driver before the group was hidden by the cloud.

"By God, we won that one!" whispered Salazar. "Their boiler must have burst."

The party on the site clustered at a safe distance from the steaming tractor. Presently they all set out along the road to Neruu, two Kooks carrying the inert form of the driver between them.

"Must have scalded the poor devil," said Salazar.

"Is he dead, do you think?" asked Kara.

"Can't tell yet. Now they're out of sight, let's see the machine."

Holding his rifle ready, Salazar led his people out.

The two unsprung pitfalls had been decorated with clumps of pseudo-grass to look like natural ground.

"They won't get that out in a hurry," said Salazar. "Split a welded seam, just as I thought. Take weeks to repair that boiler."

"Monsieur Bergen, will he give up his project now?" asked Frappot.

"Not likely! If he can't get his bulldozer going again, he'll do the same thing with teams of kyuumeis and draglines; or if need be by Kooks with shovels and wheelbarrows. After all, that's how Qin Shi Huang-di built the Great Wall of China."

"What shall we do next, while Bergen's people are away?" asked Galina.

"Start sieving those little piles from the deep pits and bagging the finds. Keep the rifle handy at all times. When Bergen's gang shows up again, beat it back to the camp and stand watches. Kara and I must go back to Henderson."

Baasu spoke up in Feënzuo: "Honorable sir, I must return to Machura. Could you please pay me now?"

On the road to Henderson, Kara Sheffield rode her bicycle while Salazar jogged along on his juten, leading the beast that Kara had ridden. She said: "Keith, I was just getting used to the motion of that animal. I may get one for myself, if you'll teach it the trick of holding my ankles. It must be something like riding a Terran horse. Have you ever done that?"

"Quite a lot, years ago," said Salazar. "Sometimes I've wished for horses on Kukulcan. These critters are smarter, though."

After a pause, she asked: "How much of what I've seen may I put into my story?"

"Nothing about the gun deal! Some people in Henderson, if they knew, would throw me in jail and lose the key. Okay to say we told the Empress about Kampai and his Choshas." After a moment of silence, he looked sharply at her. "You realize, Kara, that I'm trusting you entirely. You could ruin a lot of things, including me; and I never asked you for an oath of secrecy."

With a small smile of satisfaction, she said: "Don't worry. Even if you weren't my—weren't who you are—I always protect my journalistic sources."

A little embarrassed, Salazar returned to the previous subject. "You could also mention the wreck of Bergen's tractor, without revealing my part in the event. Hey, Kara, slow down a bit. I'm looking for the path into di Pasquale's farm."

"We're stopping there?"

"Just long enough to make arrangements with Vittorio. When the train of kyuumeis arrives, they'll need a place to wait until they come to the museum for the big heist."

"Why must they wait?" she asked.

"Because Skanda Patel's a night owl. Sometimes he doesn't even go home but stretches out on his couch in the office. So I've got to think up a sure way to get him out of the Museum before the caravan comes to town. Here we are!"

Salazar and Kara turned in at the side road leading to di Pasquale's farm. In a nearby field, the farmer looked up from the task in which he and two Kook laborers were engaged. He called:

"Hey, Keith! You want to dig up my crops to look for some damned piece of brick or stone?"

"Not this time, Vittorio," said Salazar. "Can we go back to your house for some talk? It's business."

An hour later, di Pasquale, Salazar, and Kara emerged, looking pleased. The caravan would occupy a field that had not yet been plowed. Salazar said:

"Vittorio, may I board my jutens with you? I don't know of any place in Henderson I could stable them."

"City folk," said di Pasquale with a touch of rustic superiority, "don't know how to ride the things. They buy steam cars and then find damned few roads that'll take them. I'll put the creatures in the barn with mine and tie them up so they can't fight."

"Fine; I'll pay for their fodder."

Kara said: "Does that mean you have to walk to the city?"

"Yep. Let's go!"

In Henderson their paths diverged. In a street uncluttered with passersby, Kara said: "Good-bye for now. Let me know when you leave for Machura again. I want to go, too."

"Why?" asked Salazar warily. "I shall be in enough trouble when the story of the guns leaks out, not to mention that the trip would risk your pretty neck."

"But I do want to see your project through. Please, Keith!"

"Oh, all right," said Salazar. "I'll pack the pup tent."

They parted, Kara to her newspaper office and Salazar to the Museum, where he reported to Skanda Patel that he had visited Empress Gariko to warn her of the Chosha invasion.

"What is Mr. Bergen doing now?" asked Patel.

"Brought a big tractor out to bulldoze; but yesterday it broke down. Looks as if it would be some time before it's fixed." Salazar sternly suppressed his lips' tendency to twitch into a triumphant smile.

Patel drummed his fingernails on the desk. "I wish

I could think of some way to stop him, without breaking the law."

"The Choshas may do that for us," said Salazar.

"But it is rumored that the developer has an agreement with their chief. You had better pack up your equipment and specimens to flee with your people on the minute's notice. It would be bad enough to lose the site; the Museum cannot afford to risk our students as well."

"I've already put my assistants through evacuation drills. Staying late?"

"Yes, indeed. I work best at night, when nobody visits or rings me up."

"Have fun!" said Salazar.

In his own apartment, Salazar activated his poignette: "Cabot, it's my turn to fix dinner."

"Let's eat here," replied Firestone's voice. "I've got the better stove. You can buy the chow and bring it in, if you insist."

Over drinks, Salazar brought his friend up to date. "My present problem," he said, "is to pry Skanda Patel off his arse and out of the building for one little night."

"Which night?" asked Firestone.

"Don't know yet. As soon as possible after Gariko's men and animals arrive, which might be in five or six days; but you can't time these things to the second."

"Especially with our primitive communication systems," said Firestone. "With our small population and limited research and manufacturing facilities, we're centuries behind the home planet. Sometimes I get homesick for good old Terra, even if it's dreadfully overcrowded and overorganized."

"So do I," said Salazar, and continued:

"Spare me a life on Kukulcan,
Where reptiles the coming of man defy,
And dinosaurs play the part of man,
And fishes scuttle and spiders fly,
And critters will eat you whenever they can!"

Firestone laughed, then changed the subject. "How are you and Kara making out with this 'just friends' relationship?"

"She seems to manage all right."

"And you?"

"Just being driven quietly nuts. That leaves unanswered the one more urgent question: How to lure Skanda out of his lair when the time comes?"

"How about a dinner party? If we could get two or three attractive women. . . . I hear that pretty girls are Skanda's weakness."

"Hm," said Salazar. "I haven't entertained anybody for months. I could ask Kara. Or you could ask her, if you'd prefer. Who else?"

"How about that man-eating student you told me about? You know, the gorgeous redhead."

"Penny Molina? Not a bad idea."

"Then during the evening, you could slither away on some pretext and go to the museum. I could see Kara home, leaving poor Skanda to Penny's mercies."

Salazar pondered. "I don't know. She may not even like my workaholic director. She may be furious when I pull a vanishing act."

"Can you think of a better scheme?"

Salazar sighed. "No."

"Does Patel drink? He's considered somewhat austere."

"I believe he's been known to imbibe a thimbleful of bumbleberry wine. You call Kara and tell her to stand by. I'll take on the job of inviting Penny. We'll set the party for a few nights after the convoy arrives."

"Why not as soon as they get here?" asked Firestone.

"Because, after a twelve-day trek, the animals have to rest and feed for a couple of days. If you push them too hard, they'll lie down and die."

"Why don't you use trucks? Won't the roads take them?"

"A convoy of Kookish steam trucks would be more than conspicuous. Miyage would get suspicious and find a pretext to detain them. If this weren't a secret operation, I'd haul the crates down to the station and ship them by the Kooks' teakettle railroad."

Later that evening in his apartment, Salazar buttoned Penny Molina's number. When her "Hello?" floated out of the poignette, he said: "Hello, Penny; it's your old professor."

"Which one?"

"Keith Salazar." The poignette gave a gasp of pleasure.

"Cabot Firestone—you know, the psychologist—and I are planning a little dinner party at his place, with two or three other people, in about an eight-day or so. We can't set the exact day yet; but when we do, would you like to come?"

"Oh, would I! I'd even break a date with Monty Skopas to—"

"Who's he?"

"My, but you're ignorant about some things, Keith! He's that gorgeous actor on the movie cassettes from Terra."

"All right then, I'll call you back when the date's been set."

"Oh, thank you, Keith! Thank you! I'm so happy—"

"Good-night, my dear," said Salazar firmly, since the outpouring of gratitude might go on indefinitely.

His conscience nagged him a little. He was taking advantage of Penny's childish enthusiasm to enlist her on his dark scheme under false pretenses. But, he sternly told himself, the salvation of the dig justified such small deceptions.

Days passed. Salazar spent his time working at the Museum, keeping in touch with his assistants by poignette. Galina reported:

"They came back today, with a gang of Kooks and a dozen kyuumeis. They hitched the animals to the tractor and tried to haul it out; but no matter how they beat the beasts, the machine remained in the hole. The kyuumeis' hooves tore up the surface layer in that part."

Salazar said: "Has Bergen been out there yet?"

"No; at least we haven't seen him."

"When he comes, which could be tomorrow, he might organize a raid to wipe out the lot of you. He'll guess that pitfall wasn't put there for archaeological research. So we'd better bug out. Tell Ito to go to Neruu this evening, avoiding Terrans, and hire Kooks and animals to carry our stuff back to Henderson. Leave the labeled bags of specimens in the bush. We'll recover them later. You and Marcel start dismantling everything else, with Kono's and Uwangi's help. I want all of you out by sunrise."

"You mean work all night?" squeaked Galina.

"Yep. Get going. It's your lives you're saving."

"What shall we do with Kono and Uwangi?"

"Bring 'em back to the Museum; their contract covers packing and moving. And don't forget my rifle, my bike, and the ice maker!"

The following afternoon, the fugitives materialized, followed by a score of Kooks bearing bundles and leading laden kudzais. For the rest of the day and far into the night, Salazar, Patel, and all the other museum personnel they could catch were drafted for the task of unloading, unpacking and storing.

Returning late and exhausted to his apartment, Salazar found a note pressed into the jamb of his door. He bent to pick up the paper, almost collapsed with fatigue, but managed to recover both note and balance and insert his key in the lock. In the lighted room he scanned the paper. It read:

"Let's get together some time. Diane."

Angrily, Salazar crumpled the note the better to hurl it into the waste basket. Contact with his second ex-wife was all he needed to complicate his life to the screaming point!

Then prudence reasserted itself. The note contained an address and a poignette number, both of which might some time prove useful. He smoothed out the paper, scribbled "No answer" across the face, and filed it in his current letter file under M for Diane's maiden surname of Morrow.

A few days later, Salazar called Firestone on his poignette. "Cabot? Keith here. They've arrived, and I'm going out to see them."

"Want to borrow my car?"

"Thanks, but I'd rather use my bike."

Salazar returned to town late in the evening. He parked his bicycle in the rack outside Firestone's apartment and went in, saying with ill-concealed excitement: "Vittorio insisted on my baring a fang with him. The caravan leader thinks the animals need three full days to gather their strength."

"Does that mean you'll bring them in the evening of the third day, counting tomorrow as the first?"

"Yep. If you'll call Kara, I'll take care of Skanda

and Penny—though maybe not quite the way they expect."

On the appointed evening, Salazar rang the doorbell of Firestone's apartment with Penny Molina on his arm. When the door swung open, he glanced around. "I see we're the last. Penny, this is Kara Sheffield, and this is our host, Cabot Firestone. Skanda Patel I believe you know. This, people, is my prize all-A student, Penny Molina."

Salazar's sharp ears caught a sudden intake of breath—Kara's, he suspected. Penny Molina was not a girl to be dismissed with a casual glance. Reddish-gold hair cascaded down her back. Taller, younger, and more voluptuously formed than Kara, she made the attractive journalist look almost drab by comparison.

In acknowledging introductions, Penny seemed to bubble with scarcely suppressed excitement and good humor, now and then breaking into a little giggle. *She expects,* Salazar thought sardonically, *that after the party I'll take her home and screw the spots off her.*

Firestone gave Salazar a raised eyebrow that said: *You turned down advances from this?* Patel simply goggled, while Kara's expression remained sphinxlike.

While Firestone busied himself with drinks, Patel came out of his daze. "Miss—ah—Molina, as I understand it, 'Penny' is a shortened form of a longer name. It is a nickname. Please tell me: What is it the nickname for? Penelope?"

"Worse!" cried Penny, laughing. "It's Penthesileia, also out of Greek mythology. How'd you like to be stuck with a label like that?"

"I was," said Patel. "My misguided parents inflicted 'Skandaguptakrishnalal' upon my innocent infant head. For practical reasons, I have abridged it. Your excellent health, my dear Mistress Penny!"

He hoisted his glass of bumbleberry wine and sipped. Thereafter, the party went swimmingly. Firestone's cooking was in fine form. Penny, thought Salazar, would make a better impression if her laugh were not quite so boisterous.

Salazar and Kara were pressed to tell the tale of their captivity by the Choshas and their escape. This they did, with tactful omissions. Penny said:

"Why must Terrans like your Reverend Ragnarsen always be meddling? Meddle, meddle, meddle, that's all some people think of! One missionary thought it indecent for the Kooks to run around naked; he wanted to use our army to force them to put on clothes."

"True," said Firestone. "You see, my dear, we're primates. I've watched apes and monkeys on Terra when something new is put into their cage—say, a device they're not familiar with. When they get over being afraid of it, their next thought is to take it apart. They push, pull, twist, and bang it against the floor. Like our primate ancestors, we—or at least many of us—are born meddlers.

"The Kooks, to the contrary, are closer to our Terran reptiles—stolid, single-minded, and coldly unsentimental. They're what our Terran dinosaurs might have become if the Cretaceous catastrophe hadn't wiped them out. Their needs are simpler and their curiosity less. When they want something, they go straight for it, without letting anything distract them.

"They also hold tight to what they think they know. That's why it took them a hundred thousand years to move from the hunting-gathering stage to the beginnings of industrialization, when it took us only ten thousand. Yet their brains are as big and well-developed as ours."

Under the benign influence of wine and pretty women, Patel rose to the defense of the extraterrestrials. "You must not ignore that the Kukulcanians also have their virtues. They have little crime, and their wars are piddling affairs compared to those that Terra has seen. They do not fight over obscure abstract questions like the precise nature of the gods."

Salazar, helping Firestone to clear the table, interjected: "You may not be able to say that much longer, Skanda, if Terrans like the Reverend Ragnarsen put their teachings across." After a pause, he added: "Sorry, folks, but I've got to leave you for a while. Got an errand to run—a small job but necessary." He held out a hand to Firestone. "May I, Cabot?"

Firestone placed the car keys in the hand. "I left the pilot light on; you can get up steam in a few minutes."

"But Keith—" began Penny in tones of surprise and disappointment.

"I shall be back soon," said Salazar, smiling. With calculated composure, he bowed his way out.

Once out of the apartment, he hurried down the stairs, started Firestone's car, and drove off toward di Pasquale's farm.

An hour later he chugged into the Museum court-yard, followed by a train of sixteen kyuumeis and their attendants. They found Kono and Uwangi waiting before the main entrance; for Salazar had persuaded his camp servants to sign new contracts, to go on working for him.

Salazar conferred in low tones with Chensoö, the caravan leader. Then he gathered several Kooks, unlocked the main door, and led them all into the building. There was no watchman on the premises because Salazar had, on his own responsibility, given the man the night off and the money to take his wife to a show.

Presently Kono and Uwangi staggered through the entryway, each holding an end of a heavy crate. Another crate followed, borne by another pair of Kooks. As each crate appeared, Chensoö directed its tying up with iron wire, the ends of which were twisted together and secured with a leaden seal bearing the symbol of the Empress. Salazar supervised the lashing of crates in pairs, one on either side of each kyuumei.

The loading took over two hours. It was past midnight when, having seen the caravan off on the road to Neruu, a weary Salazar returned to Firestone's apartment. He expected the party to have ended as he parked Firestone's car and rang the bell. But when Firestone opened his door and Salazar held out the keys, Firestone said: "Come in! The party's not over yet."

"Huh?"

Firestone waved toward the bedroom door. "They're in there."

"Who are?" Salazar's voice rose as he conjured up a horrid vision of Kara with . . .

Firestone interrupted the fantasy. "Penny and Skanda, of course. Has this been a night! It would have done Caligula proud."

"What happened?"

"Sit down. For an hour or so it was just talk and some drinking. We played games and told stories. Then Skanda, who had shifted from bumbleberry wine to whiskey, began to show symptoms. We were still a little high, I guess, when somebody proposed penny-ante poker.

"We played for a while and drank some more. When I ran out of whiskey I opened a bottle of filegrass rum. Then your Penny Molina—"

"Not *my* Penny Molina!" said Salazar sharply.

"Anyway, having lost her stake, Penny offered to bet a shoe. Pretty soon we were all playing a game of strip poker. By now Skanda was pretty exhilarated, not at all like his usual sober self."

"He's not used to liquor," muttered Salazar.

"The time came when I still had my pants on, and Kara her underwear; but Skanda and Penny were both—well, you might say dressed for an orgy. Skanda began doing all sorts of foolish things. He performed a kind of bow-legged dance around the room, saying he was an incarnation of Krishna. He rolled up a piece of paper and held it sideways, pretending it was Krishna's flute.

"Then Penny, also in an advanced state, joined him. The pair did some kind of erotic Tantric dance; he was expert, while she followed as best she could. Then she picked him up and carried him—"

"Did you say *she* picked *him* up?"

"Yes; she's bigger than he and a strong girl. In they went to my bedroom, and she kicked the door shut behind her.

"Kara and I got dressed, and I walked her home and came back here. The door was still closed, and I heard a faint murmur of voices through it. Then all was silent. I'm wondering what to do with them."

Just then the bedroom door flew open. Within the frame stood Penthesileia Molina, every inch a queen of the Amazons. Staring at her frontal exposure, Salazar felt himself flushing. The sight, he thought, would arouse a marble statue.

"Well!" she said. "Your little Hindu god pooped out on me!"

"What happened?" The two men spoke at once.

She strode across the room and began to dress. "The silly man drank too much, that's all. When the time came for action, he couldn't get it up. He said if we just rested and talked, he'd get his powers back. Instead, he passed out. Now, not even shaking can wake him. Oh, Keith, if only you hadn't been away so long!"

"Sorry," said Salazar, "but I had a job to do. Shall I walk you home?"

"Sure! Thanks for the party, Cabot, even if it didn't turn out quite the way it was planned."

On the street, Penny compensated for unsteadiness by clutching Salazar's arm in a muscular grip. She asked: "What's that Kara Sheffield to you, Keith? Some things that were said made me think she's more than just an acquaintance."

"Smart girl! She's my former wife."

"Oh! What a fool she must be, to let a prize catch like you get away!"

"I'm afraid that was my doing. I'm the villain."

"She must have done *something* to drive you away. Did she have an affair? Or nag? Or—"

"No. She did nothing wrong. It's a painful subject; I'd rather not discuss it."

Penny prattled on. "I understand. But I'm interested in relations between former spouses. I may do my master's thesis on them. They range all the way from people who bitterly hate each other to divorced couples who return to living together as if they were still married. In your case, for instance, do you and she get together now and then for a horizontal workout, just for old times' sake? Do you—"

"Just friends. No liaison, no plans." His voice sharp, Salazar changed the subject. "Please promise me one thing, Penny. Don't say a word to anybody about Skanda's part in this abortive orgy!"

"Is that excessive loyalty to your boss, or what? If Skanda lost his job, wouldn't you be the next director?"

"I might; but that's exactly what I don't want! I want to stay with field work and publication. I love real dirt archaeology; it's the most fun you can have with your pants on. As director my time would be taken up with paper shuffling and wangling money for the Museum, and that sort of thing makes me feel as if I were wrestling with pythons. So be a good girl and clam up about this evening, will you?"

"All right." She giggled. "But that poor little Skanda Patel was funny!"

They arrived at her door. She said: "Won't you come in, Keith? I'll make you a nightcap."

"Thanks, but I—"

"Oh, come on! This has been a frustrating evening for all of us, and we deserve a little real fun!"

With a powerful tug, she hauled him over the threshold and closed the door. Then she faced him, sliding her hands slowly up the front of his jacket as she murmured: "Isn't it time we *really* got to know each other better?"

A moment later, locked in an ardent embrace, Salazar felt his blood pound. Then the girl abated her incandescent kisses long enough to add: "Especially since I'll be in your graduate class next month?"

Like an exorcism, these words broke Penny's spell. Although a bit of a puritan, Salazar would have been overjoyed by such overtures from Kara. But a sexual encounter with a student filled him with distaste. He despised instructors who took advantage of their pupils.

Still, Salazar hesitated to make an enemy of Penny Molina, a gifted and forceful young person accustomed to getting her own way. Neither was he willing to make himself vulnerable to charges of sexual harassment, or to foreclose all chances of reconciliation with Kara. Thinking fast, he said:

"Penny dear, I fear I must tell you the ghastly truth."

"What's that?"

"I lately went deep into Kookish country."

"I know; you saw the Empress."

"Well, along the way I acquired a kind of Kook called an onnifa—a sterile female, living a warrior's life. Although I didn't know it at the time she became my retainer, Kookish rules say that the master of an onnifa is expected to service her sexually whenever his legal mate is absent."

"Sort of like the Biblical handmaidens?"

"Yep. Anyway, she put it to me: If I didn't come across, one of us would have to kill the other."

"Good heavens! Why?"

"It's a long story. Anyway, I thought: Why not? But Kook organs differ from ours. In any case the result was—" (Salazar stepped back with a woebegone expression) "—that my manhood was destroyed!"

"Oh, my God! You mean you lost your—"

"Yep. Luckily the Empress's physicians saved my life."

She lowered her gaze with a puzzled expression. "But when we kissed, I thought I felt . . ."

Wordlessly, Salazar drew his small in-town pistol from his pocket, showed it, and replaced it.

"You poor, poor man!" cried Penny, throwing herself into his arms and covering him with tears and kisses. "So that's why you and Kara have to be 'just friends'!"

"There, there, my dear," said Salazar, trying tactfully to fend her off. "We must all bravely face the vicissitudes of fortune. And now good-night!"

Salazar stopped at his apartment to pick up personal effects, including his new binoculars. While packing toiletries and a change of clothes, he stared uncertainly at the poignette on his wrist. He could not decide whether or not to tell Kara that the caravan was about to leave. There were arguments for and against. In the end he buttoned her and said:

"Kara, I'm setting out tonight. The kyuumeis are on their way to the farm. I'm heading for the Museum to pick up Kono and Uwangi, and we shall be on the road by first light. Want to come?"

"Certainly!"

"Your juten is still stabled at Vittorio's farm. I'll tell him to have it saddled and ready for you."

"Good; I'll bike out to the farm at daybreak."

"Fine! And please, not a word about tonight's events. I'll explain when I see you."

THE
CARAVAN

A few stars lingered in the paling sky as Kara Sheffield pedaled down the lane to di Pasquale's farmhouse. Four of Kukulcan's moons hung like paper lanterns above the horizon; but they little resembled Earth's Luna. The largest, Tlaloc, unveiled a small visible disk to the naked eye, while the others appeared little more than luminous dots.

In the courtyard, heavy-laden kyuumeis stamped and pawed while their Kookish teamsters, with muskets slung across their backs, adjusted loads and lashings. Chensoö strolled about, croaking orders; Keith Salazar, holding the lead rope of his juten, stood with Kono, Uwangi, and their mounts.

As Kara braked her vehicle, di Pasquale led a saddled juten from his barn. "Ah, Miss Sheffield!" said the stout, fierce-mustached farmer. "Always a pleasure!"

"Hello, Vittorio," said Kara.

Di Pasquale laid a finger along his nose. "Keith must be mad to take a beautiful, delicate woman out into the wild back country."

Kara laughed lightly. "I've survived worse hazards."

Dawn saw Salazar and Kara jogging along the road to Neruu, followed by the rest of the caravan. Kara said: "What happened at the party? Cabot acted evasive when I called to thank him for taking me home."

Salazar told the tale, ending with his escape from Penny's amorous clutches. With anyone else he might have withdrawn into his shell; but confiding in Kara was a habit that he had never broken.

"Poor thing!" laughed Kara, "or I should say, poor both of you! Penny must have been red-hot, and you—I don't see how you withstood her. You exaggerated the—ah—"

"If I'd given in, would it have made you jealous?"

"No."

"Not one teeny bit?"

"Not one bit. I'd assume it was good for you. You were virile enough when we—when I knew you before."

"A compensation of maturity is that one learns to restrain one's passion in consideration of future consequences."

"But you're still young!" exclaimed Kara. "It's only a couple of years since we—"

Salazar cut her off. "As La Rochefoucauld said, when a man controls his passions, the reason is not that he is strong but that they are weak. I don't know which applies in my case. If a certain other had acted as Penny did, I'd have leaped to it—"

It was Kara's turn to interrupt. "Wouldn't it be safer to go by the western road to the ford? It's roundabout, but we avoid Conrad's people. Besides, the Sappari bridge will never hold all these pack animals at once!"

"I've thought of that," said Salazar. "You and the rest will go by the west road; I shall catch up with you."

"What are you going to do?"

"Just a quick recon to see what they're doing to the site."

Kara said, "If you run into Conrad, promise me you won't shoot him!"

"Why not? After all that's happened, shooting him sounds like the best idea since shredded wheat. He's one who never would be missed."

"I know; he's a scoundrel and a beast. But I couldn't bear it! A woman like me has enough problems without being the cause of a murder."

"I'll try not to do anything foolish; that's all I promise. Here we are!"

Kara would have continued her protests; but at this point the road divided. Chensoö stolidly led the kyuumeis along the right or main fork. Salazar vanished down the lesser trail with his mount at a run.

Two hours later, with the sun high, Salazar rejoined the caravan. He told Kara: "I went to our former camp, tied up Daffodil, and wriggled through the brush until I could see the site. Bergen was yelling orders, with Charley Ma translating, while his Kooks hitched up kyuumeis to a dragline scraper. I resisted the temptation to take a shot."

"Thank goodness for that!" she said.

"Oh, I don't know. I suspect I should have potted Bergen while I had the chance, after all he's done. But I held off, because I hadn't figured out all the angles—how it would affect the Museum and such. Then Bergen drove off in his steam car. That's the trouble with us damned academics; all thought and no action." He did not add that he had restrained himself partly to please her.

"Did any of them see you?" she asked.

"No. I passed a couple of Kooks on the trail, but they just looked at me and went about their business."

"Where are we stopping tonight? Neruu?"

"No. It's full of Bergen's people. At the rate these critters move, we shall have to camp out in the pup tent."

Having, like many leaders of field expeditions, a reliable internal clock, Salazar awoke at dawn. He unzipped his bag and reached out to tease the tent flap open a a crack. By the augmented light he saw that Kara was awake. He gazed at her with tender memories.

"No, Keith!" said Kara sharply.

"Huh? I haven't said a word—"

"You didn't have to. I know you too well."

With an angry grunt, Salazar hauled himself out of his bag and started pulling on his outer clothing. He told himself: Keith Adams Salazar, can't you do anything right? You were the world's prize ass to leave her two years ago, and now you're a bigger fool for bringing her along on this jaunt. You must enjoy self-torture.

The second night they camped, Salazar saw that Kara was comfortably settled in her sleeping bag. Then he laid his own bag on the ground outside the tent.

"Keith!" she called. "What are you doing?"

"Going to sleep," he said grumpily.

"But why out there?"

"Try to guess." Controlling his vexation, more at himself than at her, he added: "Good-night, Kara."

*   *   *

Sending the caravan on ahead, Salazar and Kara stopped in Shongaro long enough to speak with Chief Sambyaku, who warned them: "Beware, honorable Sarasara, of soldiers on the roads. The air is thick with rumors of trouble with the Choshas, and the High Chief has ordered some of his men to the eastern border."

"I tried to tell Miyage—" began Salazar, but Sambyaku cut in:

"Aye, so you did. But the High Chief has had experience with Terrans. The only Terran whom he trusts is this developer, Bergen."

"With whom he will become disillusioned. But why should I fear Miyage's soldiers?"

"Many are not well-disciplined. One never knows what such persons might do if surprised."

Salazar and Kara remounted and rode off. Less than a kilometer outside Shongaro, they caught up with their caravan. The kyuumeis were munching vegetation along the roadside, while the teamsters, muskets in hand, clustered behind Chensoö. The caravan leader was in furious argument with a Kook, a soldier from his body paint and an officer from the fact that he bore a sword instead of a musket. Observing the sixteen soldiers of the detachment, it seemed to Salazar from the movement of their neck bristles that they were spoiling for a fight.

"What is this?" Salazar called out as his juten reached the scene of the dispute.

"These," said Chensoö, "are High Chief Miyage's men. They wish to know about the crates."

"Tell them the crates contain agricultural implements," said Salazar.

"I have so said, but the officer wishes to pry one open to confirm this fact. I have told him that we may not permit the Empress's seals to be broken, but he is not convinced."

Salazar dismounted. Confronting the officer, he said: "I am on a mission for the Empress, and I do not think that your High Chief wishes to antagonize her."

"I have my orders—" began the officer.

"We are on our way to Machura by way of Biitso. If you have questions about our cargo, accompany us to Biitso and lay the matter before High Chief Miyage himself."

The officer's tongue flicked. "We cannot! Our orders are to proceed eastward forthwith, to take up a position near Neruu. This matter must be settled here and now—"

Salazar was standing beside one of the spare kyuumeis. It was a big animal, as tall at the shoulder hump as Salazar, and its dark-gray scales bore the butter-yellow symbols of the Empire of Feënzun. As the officer spoke, a thunderous *boom* made everyone start. With an earth-shaking impact, the kyuumei beside Salazar fell over on its side, its legs pawing the air before its eyes glazed in death. The grazing animals snorted and danced in alarm. Some were barely restrained from bolting.

"Uwangi!" yelled Salazar. "The rifle! Get down, Kara!" He added in Shongo: "Take cover, all of you!"

Uwangi dashed up with Salazar's gun, whereupon the archaeologist sprawled on the ground behind the dead beast, with his rifle barrel resting across the carcass. The soldiers, with apparently no concept of taking cover, formed a ragged line behind Salazar, facing the forest with cocked muskets.

Salazar, sure that he recognized the sound of Bergen's big-game rifle, swept the foliage with searching eyes. On the road behind, a flicker of motion caught his attention. For less than a second he glimpsed a juten and a rider, pounding away to eastward. Before he could bring his rifle to bear, the target was out of sight. So brief had been his glimpse that he could not even be sure whether the rider was a Kook or a Terran.

Salazar set his straw hat, Pokrovskii's gift, on the muzzle of his rifle. When this failed to draw fire, he said: "I believe our attacker has gone; but I suggest, Captain Tuskei, that you send some of your men to search the woods."

"Aye, sir; that I shall do. But about these crates—"

"Just a moment, Captain. Kara, I think Bergen shot at us; but I don't see how he could still have his fourteen-millimeter gun. Kampai would have kept it, along with the other Terran firearms, when he let Bergen go. And you carried off the ammunition for that rifle."

Kara thought for a moment. "Didn't Conrad and Pokrovskii stop at your camp on their way to Henderson? Maybe one of your people noticed."

"Good idea!" said Salazar. He buttoned Galina Bartch on his poignette, told of their situation, and asked: "When Bergen and the others came by our camp after the Choshas released them, do you remember whether Bergen was carrying a heavy rifle?"

After a thoughtful pause, Galina said: "Yes, he was. I remember because, at dinner, he boasted of how he got it. He asked Kampai for it on the grounds that it would be useless to the Choshas. To prove his point, he let one of Kampai's sub-chiefs shoot at a target. The recoil knocked the Kook flat and injured his arm, since they are not so solidly built as we. Then Kampai let Bergen take the gun but not the cartridges."

"Thanks, Galina." Salazar chuckled. "That explains the mystery. Not being used to repeating firearms, Kampai didn't think to make Bergen unload the magazine. I told you I should have killed the bastitch when I had him in my sights. Now, how to prove to Miyage that Bergen is not to be trusted?"

He frowned in thought. "I have it! Chensoö, I want to recover the bullet from the dead kyuumei. You will butcher the animal for meat; so tell your men that I will pay one sovran, in Henderson gold, for that bullet." Salazar held up the coin between thumb and forefinger, setting it ablaze in the sunshine.

The next hour saw the bloody spectacle of the drovers hacking at the carcass with hatchets and bush knives. While they were so engaged, Chief Sambyaku appeared from Shongaro with his escort, saying:

"Sarasara, I heard a shot. One of our townsfolk told me that he had passed your party with these soldiers standing by a dead kyuumei as if expecting attack. I have come to investigate."

Salazar explained the contretemps over the crates. Sambyaku replied: "I shall go to see my High Chief at Biitso. Proceed on your way, Sarasara; I shall return to Shongaro for mounts and overtake you. Continue to your destination, Captain; I will be responsible for the Terrans. May your life be tranquil. . . ."

After the departure of Chief Sambyaku and the soldiers, one of the drovers cried: "Honorable Sarasara, here it is!" He straightened up with a bloody cylindro-conical bullet in his claws.

Salazar took the object, wiped it on a paper handkerchief, and held it up. "Sure looks like fourteen millimeters!" He handed over the reward and pocketed the find.

When the caravan arrived at Miyage's palace in Biitso and Sambyaku sent in a message, High Chief

Miyage himself appeared, exclaiming: "By our ancestral spirits, what is this? You, Sambyaku, all these beasts, and that tricky Terran Sarasara! What do you here?"

Sambyaku began an explanation, but the High Chief raised an admonitory claw. "Let us go inside for details. Not you, evil alien; we do not wish converse with you; nor shall you fill our house with your Terran stench."

"But, Your Highness!" expostulated Sambyaku. "The alien has evidence of dire events, which do affect the welfare of Shongosi. Besides, I have known him for a year and more and find him honest and truthful for a Terran."

Salazar hid a smile at the memory of the whopping lies he had lately been compelled to tell. The High Chief nodded skeptically, as if but half-convinced, saying: "Very well, but the proof must needs be as solid as Mount Nezumi to change our mind about this Terran. We never trust monsters from outer space."

"Your Highness," said Sambyaku, "I do assure you that this monster is not really *very* Terran. It is as if he had the mind of a civilized human being, like you and me, in his alien body."

Miyage grunted. "This we shall see." His forked tongue lashed the air.

In his chamber of office, Miyage squatted on a cushion with his visitors kneeling before him. "Now, tell your tale," he said. "Silence, Sarasara! We do not wish to speak with you; you would forget the honorifics proper to a being of our rank. You may instead speak to Sambyaku, who will relay the message." He used the inflections employed in speaking to a person of the lowest caste.

Salazar told briefly of the shipment of agricultural implements to the Empress and the attempt on his life. When he named Bergen as his assailant, Miyage burst out: "There you go again, trying in your perfidious Terran way to stir up trouble between us and our staunchest ally! Utter no more of these fabrications, unless you wish to lose that hideous Terran head!"

Salazar exchanged glances with Sambyaku. Miyage, he knew, was quite capable of having him dragged out and slain, despite the risk of hostilities with the Terrans of Henderson.

Wordlessly, Salazar dug into a pocket and retrieved the bullet carved from the dead kyuumei. Wordlessly he held it up between thumb and forefinger.

"What is that?" snapped Miyage, flicking his tongue.

Salazar remained silent until Sambyaku spoke: "Your Highness threatened Sarasara with death if he spoke. Do you withdraw that command?"

"Oh, very well," grumped Miyage. "You may speak to us directly, Sarasara; we cannot wait for Sambyaku to pass on every word."

Salazar explained where the bullet had come from. Then he asked: "Will Your Highness have the goodness to repeat Bergen's story of his escape from the Choshas?"

"He said that he dug a burrow under the bars of the cage wherein you were confined. During the night, he and his companions wriggled through and fled. You and the female Sheffira followed but were recaptured."

"Miss Sheffield and I tell quite a different story, Your Highness, But tell me, did Bergen say anything of being armed during his flight?"

"Not specifically. He did speak of beating off an attack by a fyunga with a club made from a fallen tree branch."

"And he would hardly have defended himself in that manner if he had possessed a gun, would he?"

"We suppose not. But what does all this signify, Sarasara?"

With a smile, Salazar tossed up and caught the bullet. "The gun for this bullet is the only firearm of its kind on this world; Bergen imported it from Terra. The guns that Terrans make here, like that which your guards took from me when we entered your palace, shoot smaller bullets. This did not come from one of the muskets your people make, as you can see from its shape; your guns fire only spherical shot. So, obviously, Bergen still possesses his heavy rifle despite his tale of fleeing unarmed."

Flick, flick, flick went the forked tongue. At last Miyage said: "How do you know that Bergen did not order another gun of this kind from Terra as soon as he reached Henderson?"

"Because, Your Highness, it takes eleven or twelve years for a space ship to travel to Terra, and an equal length of time to return."

After another silence, Miyage persisted: "But how know you that Bergen did not own a pair of these guns, and that this bullet came from his second weapon?"

"He repeatedly assured us, Your Highness, that his heavy rifle was unique on this planet."

"If he lost all his ammunition to the Choshas, how could he shoot that kyuumei? Another of you Terrans may have a firearm of this kind."

"Bergen doubtless had a reserve supply of cartridges at his home, and to make more of this kind is not beyond the ability of our machine shops."

Sambyaku broke the following silence: "Your Highness, there must be more to this tale than meets the eye. Since the conflict between Bergen and Sarasara is mainly over the ruins of ancient Nomuru, were it not wise to stop all actions at that place until we have sifted this matter and discovered the exact truth?"

Miyage gave a long, serpentine hiss. "We fear you are right, Sambyaku; albeit we are sure, when we solve this problem, that Bergen will be proved the more honest of the two aliens. May our ancestral spirits curse these Terrans! Would to the Universal Law that they had never come to our world; they give us nought but trouble. Common courtesy is wasted on them.

"We shall send soldiers with orders to guard the ruins of Nomuru and allow no Terran activity there. May you lead tranquil lives. . . ."

When the caravan left Biitso, nothing more had been said about the sealed crates. The chieftains had evidently forgotten the matter, and Salazar had better sense than to remind them.

"Don't Kooks have such a thing as an inn or hotel?" asked Kara as Salazar, with the help of Kono and Uwangi, set up the tent.

"Guess not," he said. "If one goes traveling, either he stays with someone connected with him by their complicated rules of caste and kinship, or he squats down wherever he can find a wall to rest his back against. The idea of bothering about physical discomfort is foreign to them. Even if they had inns, their caste rules about eating and sleeping would present innkeepers with an impossible problem."

On the second night after leaving Biitso, thunder rumbled and rain began to fall. Kara said: "Don't be silly, Keith! Drag that bag in here and spend a dry night."

"Are you sure—"

"I can't have you getting sick on me." As Salazar,

grumbling under his breath, brought in his sleeping bag, she added: "Now, repeat after me—"

"Eh? What's this?"

"Never mind. Just repeat after me, loud and clear: I will not . . ."

"I will not . . ."

"Make a pass at . . ."

"Make a pass at . . ."

"Or make love to . . ."

"Or make love to . . ."

"My platonic friend Kara Sheffield."

"My platonic friend Kara Sheffield. Say, what is this? Some sort of magical incantation?"

"In a way. I know you pretty well, Keith. In most matters you're punctilious, literal-minded, and—with one unfortunate lapse—a man of your word. So if you promise, right out loud, not to try any intimacies, I'm pretty sure you'll keep your word."

Salazar gave a snort of laughter: "But what if *you* make advances to *me?* What am I supposed—"

"Mount Nezumi will dance a pachanga before that happens!"

After a long pause, Salazar spoke:

> *The lady so clever*
> *Avows she will never*
> *Throw open the gate*
> *To her recreant mate;*
> *But can one dissever*
> *All bonds whatsoever*
> *With the veriest drone*
> *Whose love one has known?"*

"Keith! Go to sleep!"

At Machura, the Empress, surrounded by muske-

teers and spearmen, said: "Hail, honorable Sarasara!
Is your health good?"

"Hail, Your Imperial Majesty!" said Salazar, down
on both knees. Beside him Kara knelt likewise. "My
health, thank the Universal Law, has been excellent.
Has Your Majesty's health . . ."

After completion of the long exchange, the Empress said: "Are these the promised Terran guns?"

"They are, Your Imperial Majesty."

"Come inside, with your companion. Arrangements
will be as before."

Hours later, bathed, groomed, and rested, Salazar
and Kara found themselves alone in the audience
room with the Empress. Gariko said in English: "I
am pleased with your success, Sarasara. Is this loan
of Terran weapons known to any other Terrans?"

"Only two others in Henderson, whose discretion
I can vouch for. What has Your Majesty done with
the guns?"

"The crates are stacked in the armory. But I must
tell you that your plan has met objections from some
of my ministers."

"What objections, Your Majesty?"

"My Minister of War—or you could call him General Shta—opposes any sort of dependency on Terrans. He has read a history of Terran civilization and
avers that to give them the slightest grasp upon us
will result in our being conquered and reduced to
servitude. He cites many instances."

Salazar said: "Your Majesty, the events that Minister Shta refers to occurred centuries ago. On my
world, we have learned to be more scrupulous in
observing the rights of other peoples."

"Ah, but here you Terrans are not on your world;
nor has your species evolved appreciably since the
earlier days of which you speak. You are at bottom

the same excitable, impulsive, aggressive creatures
that you were back then. And now you are in the
position regarding us that the people of Yura—Yero—"

"Europe," Salazar prompted.

"The people of Europe were when they invaded
the other continents of your world. Having technical
advantages—well, we shall discuss this further. The
final decision shall be mine.

"Meanwhile I must know more of your plan for
putting the Terran guns to use. My spies tell me that
the Choshas will soon invade Shongosi. How shall
we transmit news of this invasion to our forces in
time to enable them to meet the Choshas before the
latter have overrun Shongosi and perhaps entered
Feënzun as well?"

Salazar thought before replying. "Your Majesty's
people have no electrical communications. Lacking
these, what method swifter than a rider on a fast
juten would serve? On Terra, men once set up lines
of signal towers, by which they sent messages from
one tower to the next by means of a device with arms
that could be set to symbolize the characters of our
system of writing."

"That is not feasible here, Sarasara. It would take
much too long to build the towers and train the
signalers. Secondly, while your system of writing, I
understand, makes do with a mere thirty or forty
symbols, ours employs hundreds. These could not
easily be conveyed by wagging the arms of your
device. What else?"

"Your Majesty, on Terra we have many species of
small, flying creatures called 'birds,' somewhat like
your zutas. A few of these have been trained to bear
messages."

"None of us has, to my knowledge, ever sought to
employ zutas thus. It is a possibility, but for the
future. Is there aught else?"

Salazar pondered. "As Your Majesty knows, we Terrans communicate afar by electrical devices. I know your people believe that such devices distress your ancestral spirits; but if, of myself and Miss Sheffield, one were in Shongosi and the other at your army headquarters, the invasion could be reported instantly."

After a silence, Gariko said: "It is too late to call a special meeting of ministers today; but perhaps I can arrange one for tomorrow afternoon. You shall be informed, and your presence is expected."

"May my companion, Miss Sheffield, attend also?"

"Surely. Do you require anything for your comfort?"

Salazar said: "We should be grateful for a few more cushions, Your Majesty. Your floors are of an admirable hardness."

Gariko could not smile; but the rippling of her cervical spines implied that she might have done so if furnished with human lips instead of a turtle's beak. She murmured: "It amazes me that creatures, so soft-skinned and sensitive to the slightest discomfort, should ever have conquered the vast distances between your world and ours. But cushions you shall have. May you be in good health. . . ."

Salazar strolled the streets of Machura with Kara, taking in the limited sights of the town. Kara said: "I find the monotony oppressive. All the houses look alike, as if they had come out of the same cookie cutter."

Salazar shrugged. "An infinite number of apartment blocks on Earth are just as uniform."

"And the people don't seem in the least interested in us."

"Kooks decide what they intend to do and concentrate on that goal. It takes more than a mere pair of monsters from outer space, like us, to distract them. . . ."

A young Kook planted itself before them, saying in Feënzuo: "May your health be good! You are Terrans, are you not?"

"Yes," said Salazar.

"And you are a male, and the smaller one a female?"

"You are right, young fellow."

"Have you twain traveled hither together?"

"Yes." Aside, he added to Kara: "Here's an exception to my rule, I do believe. He actually has curiosity."

The Kook continued: "My parents have told me that Terrans have no sexual morals. Whenever a male and female of your species are alone together, they go to it at once, like other lower animals. Tell me, then, how often do you copulate?"

A sputter of suppressed laughter told Salazar that Kara had caught the drift of the conversation. He said: "That must forever be a secret among Terrans. If I told you, I should shrivel up and blow away. May you be in good health!"

THE
COUNCIL

At the morrow's meeting, Minister-General Shta arose from his cushion, declaiming in rhythmic, rhyming Feënzuo: "I will accept, provisionally, that the words of our honorable Terran guest are true and his intentions honest. I concede that we are threatened by the Chosha invaders and that we shall be hard pressed to repel them.

"But in accepting Terran instruments of war, we are defeating the lesser evil by exposing ourselves to the greater. I have learned how Terrans act on their own world." He held up a Kukulcanian book in its glass-fronted wooden frame. "This is one of ten scrolls comprising the Terran *History of Civilization*, composed by a Terran named Dikran Gregorian. My colleague, Minister Gakki, has translated it.

"I was struck by the extraordinary variability of this species; individuals differ far more widely, one from another, than do we. One meets a Terran who speaks to him fair and uses him with probity; so he thinks, all Terrans must be worthy beings. He meets another Terran, who lures him to destruction by crafty, perfidious treacheries. How can an honest human being, like one of us, distinguish one kind from the other? Neither size, nor shape of skull, nor texture of hair, nor color of skin provides a clue. By the time one has come to know a Terran well enough to judge its character, it is too late to escape the toils of an evil alien.

"A second trait is the extraordinary ferocity that Terrans display when roused. They are incredibly emotional. We are not a species of pacifists, as witness the coming struggle with the Choshas. But when the battle is over and the dead are buried, we put hostilities behind us. Not so the Terrans! When two groups claim possession of a single patch of land, they foster a mutual hatred that forces them to fight for centuries. The young grow up possessed by these bitter hatreds and with them infect the minds of their children and grandchildren.

"Finally, they are restless and unstable, lacking respect for the customs of their forebears. Hence their culture changes with dizzying rapidity. Gregorian tells us that Terrans were a relatively stable folk until a few centuries ago, when the growth of technology became a self-powered engine of change. We human beings have so far kept this mighty force within bounds, by limiting innovations. If we permit random changes to take root at the whim or by the greed of the innovator, we shall develop social pathologies like theirs.

"To accept this martial material, therefore, is to expose ourselves to the disasters that have befallen Terrans of conservative cultures when confronted by persons in possession of deadlier methods of war and conquest, whereby whole continents have been subdued."

Salazar interrupted: "Your Honor refers to events of centuries past. In recent times, we have learned to do things in a more peaceful and orderly way, better to protect weak groups and individuals against the strong."

"Aye?" said Shta. "When I believe that, I shall also believe that Terran tale of a prophet who walked on water. To continue: Terrans, to aggravate matters, have a compulsion to force their beliefs and customs upon those within their power, with no regard for the suitability of such ideas and usages. Many Terrans, for example, believe that their world is ruled by one or more Great Spirits, who require constant flattery. Terrans initiate bloody wars to settle the question of which spirit is supreme and what form of ritual flattery it demands. For a while the followers of the spirit Kraista fought those of the spirit Muhamma; then the followers of Kapitara fought those of Komiunisma. Demands for conformity to the ideas of the dominating group extend to such paltry matters as the design of the coverings wherewith they drape themselves in lieu of painted insignia. They even dispute which bodily parts may properly be exposed.

"For centuries, Terrans have been burning one another alive, feeding one another to flesh-eating beasts as a form of public entertainment, and otherwise ingeniously disposing of those with whom they disagreed over some abstract doctrinal question. Baneful effects of such Terran thinking have already transpired on our world. Chief Kampai bothered no one until a Terran preacher convinced him that his nomadic way of life was the only proper one, and that all those who refused to adopt it should die. Today we must cope with the results of this conversion."

"That is not quite correct," ventured Salazar. "The Reverend Ragnarsen preached peace and love, but Kampai distorted his teachings."

"So?" said Shta. "Teachings so easily bent to destructive ends—"

The Empress broke in: "Minister Gakki, you stated that you also wished to speak. Pray do so now."

"Your Imperial Majesty and honorable fellow ministers," began Gakki, the female Minister of Culture. "I am in accord in general with Minister Shta. We agreed that he should present the case against the Terran guns, and I should speak against Terran devices for electrical communication.

"Our scientists are not unfamiliar with electricity. They know, for example, that the force that causes a little flash and click when certain substances are rubbed and brought into near-contact is the same as that which causes lightning and thunder. They know, too, that electricity is somehow connected with magnetism, which makes a compass needle align itself.

"Long before these facts were known, however, we human beings realized that lightning destroys the spirits of our ancestors. Every year, we estimate, hundreds of these spirits are thus disintegrated. While most spirits prudently avoid storm clouds, accidents will happen. It is my understanding that Terran communication devices employ electricity to send out invisible rays, and similar devices to receive these rays. Since such phenomena are like unto those brought about by lightning, albeit on a smaller scale, ancestral spirits near such devices would be pained and distressed if not slain outright. If we so harm our ancestral spirits, they may leave this land and settle in a clime that is innocent of these inventions. Then who would counsel us in dreams?"

Salazar whispered to Kara, to whom he had been giving a running translation: "How do I answer that? If I say the spirits don't exist, we shall be thrown out or worse."

"I'm getting an idea," she murmured. "See if the Empress won't call time out."

"Your Imperial Majesty," said Salazar, "may my colleague Miss Sheffield and I have a recess to formulate our argument?"

"Very well," said the Empress, rising. "We shall reassemble in one hour."

Alone in their spacious two-room apartment, Salazar asked, "What's your idea, Kara?"

"A year ago," she replied, "I wrote for the *News* a series of exposés of mediums and occultists in Henderson and Suvarov. I learned some of their tricks; for instance, you can grip the leg of a light table with your toes and rock it to give off raps. You can make vaguely comforting prophecies that will bring in the money. And when things don't work out, you can blame the skeptics in the audience, whose presence offends the spooks."

"I must have missed that story," said Salazar, "although I read most issues of the *News*."

"Only one installment appeared. Then all the mediums and their clients made a fuss, and McHugh cancelled the series. That made me furious, and now I'm trying to persuade Knebel to bring it out as a book."

"So much for our vaunted freedom of the press!" snorted Salazar. "Knebel had better be careful if he doesn't want to lose his shirt. Skeptics have been exposing such tricks for millennia, but people will still pay anything to be bunked and nothing to be debunked. What have you in mind now? A séance in the palace?"

"That's right."

Salazar wrinkled his face. "To a scientist, that's like asking a pious Jew or Muslim to eat pork; but I guess there's no help for it. How do you propose to stage it?"

"If we could collect Gariko and her ministers, we might induce some ancestral spirits to say that poignettes and rifles are fine with them. Name me some influential Kukulcanian spooks."

"I'll try to remember some Kookish history and mythology," said Salazar. "Let's see—Gariko's predecessor was her father Odzi. His predecessor was his mother Datsimuju; her predecessor was her father Hamashti, he of the boundary stones. It goes on and on, back to their mythical ancestor Simmo, who's their Abraham or Romulus. I don't remember much of it. Where shall we have the séance?"

She peered at the little low table. "Right here. I can handle this table with my toes, but the one in the meeting room is too heavy."

"How are the spirits to communicate?"

"Let's think. . . . In this language, 'yes' is *wa*, and 'no' is *yao*. Since the first word has two letters and the second word three, we'll let two raps stand for 'yes' and three for 'no.' "

"Fine so far. But if we want to go into details, we might spend the whole night asking questions. We'd be like a lawyer on cross-examination, probing and fishing until he hits pay dirt."

"A mixed metaphor if every I heard one," said Kara. "Since we know the answers we want, we shouldn't have to fumble around."

"Still, it might take more time than the Kooks may

be willing to spend. How would it be to have the spirits speak directly on our poignettes?"

"Who'll do the talking? It has to be someone outside the room, who's in on our scheme and speaks good Feënzuo."

"Guess I'm nominated," said Salazar. "Suppose the ghost takes offense at me and orders me banished? You've turned your poignette on, and I go to the other room and say the spirit's speech."

"How about your accent?"

"Pretend that the language has changed since the spirit was mortal." He glanced at his poignette. "It's almost time for me to sell those jokers on the séance, and I'm no salesman."

Again, Keith Salazar and Kara Sheffield faced the council of ministers. Salazar said: "My lords and ladies, since there is a difference of opinion as to whether your ancestral spirits would be displeased by my proposals, let us ask the spirits themselves."

"How can we?" said the Empress. "They appear to us only in dreams, and then their messages are often garbled or obscure."

Salazar smiled. "We Terrans have among us some who are sensitive to the spirit world. Spirits speak through them."

Fosku, the Minister of Commerce, said: "I have heard of these spiritually sensitive aliens. But, honorable Sarasara, would you have us defer our decision until you fetch such a person from a Terran city?"

"No, my lord. We have such a person here, my associate Sheffield. She needs a few hours to prepare her mind for spirit communication. If you will return this evening, at about two hours after sunset, we shall receive you in the rooms Her Majesty has generously placed at our disposal."

There was a murmur of agreement. Shta was opposed, with Gakki doubtful; but the others evinced enough curiosity to carry the vote.

"I shall be present," growled Minister Shta, flicking out his tongue. "If there be any trickery, be assured that I shall detect it!"

Back in their two-room suite, Salazar and Kara arranged cushions around the low table. Salazar halted, saying: "I just had an idea. To add a touch of theater, we could rig up a thread to pull over one of those torchères."

"Wouldn't that set the house afire?"

"No; the flame will be out when we darken the room. We shall merely spill a little oil."

"Let's hope this rug isn't a priceless antique." Kara rose and examined a torchère. "This is too heavy to be pulled over by a mere thread. But—I know!"

She rummaged among her toiletries and produced a dispenser of dental floss.

"Just the thing!" said Salazar. "I'll rig it so the string isn't visible until you start to pull, and then it'll be dark. If we run it under the edge of this rug . . ."

Around the low table, on their cushions sat Salazar, Kara, the Empress, and eight ministers hip to hip. The room was totally dark save for a minute trace of light that escaped around the edges of a rug hung over the window. Since moonlight on Kukulcan was negligible, the only source of this illumination was a few lanterns hung outside the palace. Even when his eyes had adjusted to the gloom, Salazar could barely distinguish the shapes of his table mates. He was glad to know that the shape on his left was Kara, for in the blackness he could not have distinguished her from the Kooks. She sat where, by shedding a slipper, she could grasp a table leg with her toes.

After a while, Kara moaned and spoke: "I feel the power rising within me. . . . Entities gather in the room. . . ." Salazar murmured the translations.

At last she said: "If there be an intelligence in this room, other than those with hands upon this table, let it manifest itself by rapping once."

The table tilted slightly and returned to its position with a thump. There was a serpentine hiss from the Kooks as Salazar translated the question. The voice of the Empress spoke:

"Have her ask if the spirit be that of my sire Odzi."

Salazar passed on the question; Kara repeated it. The table rose and fell thrice. "It means 'no,' " said Salazar.

"Ask if it be that of his dam, Datsimuju."

Again the reply was no. Salazar said: "Your Majesty, it will take all night if you go through the entire list of your honorable forebears. Permit me to ask a daring question: Is this the spirit of the great and glorious Simmo himself?"

The table tipped twice, thump, thump. "It means 'yes,' " explained Salazar.

Again the hiss of indrawn breaths. Salazar could imagine the nine forked tongues darting. He said: "We are honored, Your Ghostliness. May I question you?"

Thump, thump, thump.

"No questions?" said General Shta. "What good is communication with a spirit who refuses to answer?"

"A moment, my lords and ladies," said Salazar. "Emperor Simmo, is it that something or someone in this room offends you?"

Thump, thump.

"Is it the presence of myself and my fellow Terran?"

"Thump, thump, thump; pause; thump, thump.

"Yes and no," said Salazar. "Is it only one of us?"

Thump, thump.

"Is it I?"

Thump, thump.

"Is it that you dislike a Terran's questioning you?"

Thump, thump.

"If I depart, will you then answer the questions of others?"

Thump, thump.

Salazar rose. Minister Gakki protested: "Honorable Sarasara, if you leave, how shall we communicate with the spirit? Sheffira speaks but little Feënzuo."

"My lady, he will understand when one of you speaks," said Salazar.

Careful not to trip over the dental floss, he stalked into the other room of the suite and closed the door. Then he clicked on his poignette and spoke into the instrument, pitching his voice in imitation of the harsh, rasping Kookish speech and using an archaic form of the language, of which he had a smattering.

"Hail, mortals! The shade of Emperor Simmo asks: Wherefore have ye disturbed our rest?"

Through the door Salazar could hear a stir among the Kooks. There was a murmur of voices; then one spoke up: "O great lord, we wish your guidance."

"We offer it. Speak!"

Minister Shta's voice wafted from the poignette on Salazar's wrist: "We are, as Your Imperial Majesty knows, faced by an invasion. Terrans have offered us the use of their rapid-fire guns and of electrical devices for swift communication. But we fear such alien aid. . . ." Shta then summarized the arguments that he had set forth that afternoon.

When Shta ran down, Salazar said: "We hear thy words, O mortal, and shall consider them. Let the next minister speak!"

Gakki in turn advanced her argument, that electronic devices harmed ancestral spirits. The ghost retorted: "We speak to thee over these same devices. If the machine cause us pain, should we not know it? We do assure thee that these things be harmless to us who dwell beyond. Let the next minister speak!"

After the last minister had had a say, Salazar rasped: "Ye are right to suspect the Terrans and hold them at a distance. Yet in this case, the use of Terran guns is the lesser evil; without them ye shall surely be overborne and slaughtered."

Shta burst out: "But, great lord, do consider . . ." He began to repeat his previous argument.

Knowing the Kookish tendency to orate by the hour, Salazar thundered: "Silence, O mortal! Thou hast had thy say. Know that we seldom meddle in the affairs of the living; but when they summon us from our well-earned rest to beg advice and then flout our counsel, we wax wroth! Moreover, we can make our displeasure manifest on the material plane, *thus!*"

Salazar listened tensely through long seconds of silence. Then a mighty crash announced the toppling of the torchère. Guttural cries and scuffling ensued as a couple of Kooks leaped up from the table and bolted out the door that led to the main corridor.

Feigning concern for the welfare of the Empress, Salazar rushed into the séance room, now bathed in light from the lamps in the corridor. Kara remained seated, leaning back with her eyes closed and gasping as one just rescued from drowning. Salazar went solicitously to her, feeling her forehead and patting her hands, saying:

"Are you all right, darling?"

"Don't spoil my act," she breathed. Little by little she gave the appearance of returning to normal. At last she turned to the Empress, saying:

"Your Majesty, the spirit of Simmo has departed. May I rest now?"

"I should hope so!" said Gariko in English. "You have frightened us more than the Choshas ever could." In Feënzuo she added: "The meeting is adjourned. We shall expect our ministers tomorrow at the usual time. May you all enjoy good health! . . ."

Two mornings later, on the drill field, Salazar inspected the soldiers chosen for him by the Minister of War. At length he asked General Shta: "Are these your picked companies?"

"Aye, they are," said the general coldly.

"Then I should hate to see your discards," growled Salazar, for the line of 120 Feënzurin was the most unsoldierly lot of Kookish soldiers he had seen. Although they were supposed to be standing at attention, they slouched and squatted and held their muskets every which way. Salazar was sure that to demand another lot from the hostile Shta would effect no improvement.

"Where are my officers?" he asked.

The Kooks's tongue flicked. "I must tell you that none is willing to serve beneath an alien."

More likely, the archaeologist thought, Shta had quietly passed the word that any officer who served under Salazar would thenceforth find himself in the Kookish equivalent of the doghouse. He addressed the line of soldiers:

"Attention! Right, face! Left, face! About, face . . . !"

After some more commands, Salazar went down the line and pulled out six soldiers who had obeyed with more snap than the rest. These he lined up and commanded: "Forward, march! To the rear, march! Halt! . . ."

Eventually he chose three of the six, made one his captain and the other two his lieutenants—or his sergeant and corporals, depending on how one translated the Kookish terms.

"Now," he told his new officers, "arm yourselves with those sticks used for punishment." When this had been done, he led the trio down the line. Whenever they passed a recruit who was not standing correctly, Salazar said: "Hit him!"

Salazar knew how tough Kooks were; a blow that would cripple or kill a Terran would merely sting a Kook's leathery hide. Nonetheless, after a few had been whacked, the rest straightened up remarkably.

Later, lying exhausted on the cushions in their suite, Salazar told Kara: "May I never have another such day! I wish my predecessors at the Museum had bought a few machine guns instead of a gross of rifles. A machine gun has the firepower of a section of riflemen, without the riflemen. As it is, Shta is determined that the experiment shall fail. So he sent me picked men all right; a selection ranging from bad to worst."

"Seems he'd rather lose the war than see someone else get the credit?"

"Not exactly. Such a leader often rationalizes his jealousy by assuming that his way is necessarily the best. Terran history is full of examples of this self-delusion."

"Think you can make soldiers out of that ragtag collection?"

"I intend to try. Been thinking of ways to boost their morale."

"How soon will they be ready to fight?" she asked.

"Depends on how fast they shape up and learn to hit a target. A week at least."

"But the Choshas may invade any day!"

Salazar shrugged. "Nothing I can do about that. Sending this gang against them without training would be throwing them away, the way a British general threw away the Light Brigade."

"But if you use up your ammunition in target practice, you won't have any when the real shooting starts."

"Luckily, the people who stored the rifles did one thing right; they packed a couple of hundred rounds for every rifle. If I use twenty or thirty rounds for practice, there will still be enough for a battle, provided my Rangers aim their shots. Untrained soldiers tend merely to spray landscape with lead."

For nearly a sixtnight, Salazar sweated to whip his raw companies into shape. Mornings were given to drill—simple commands for marching and more complex maneuvers in open order for fighting. He taught his Kooks to take cover, to advance by rushes, and other features of later Terran warfare. Minister Shta remarked:

"Sarasara, such conduct on the battlefield is unheard of! It is disgraceful for warriors, instead of standing bravely facing the foe, to skulk behind trees and crawl on their bellies!"

"In a Terran war," mused Salazar, "centuries ago, a general named Braddock thought as you do. He was routed and slain."

"Well, play your silly games," said Shta. "Since nought will come of your heretical ideas, it matters not what tactics you employ. You barbaric aliens do no end of crazy things." With his reptilian jaw set in scorn, he strode off.

Afternoons were given to target practice. For the first few days, Salazar's Kooks practiced without ammunition, going through the motions of lying prone, working their bolts, and squeezing triggers. Several times, the Empress was driven to the drill field in her steam car to watch her soldiers' progress.

One evening, Salazar told Kara: "They're coming along better than I expected; Kooks, being very literal-minded, are good at following exact directions. I've forbidden them to touch the button that sets one of these guns on full automatic, lest they shoot off a whole clip in a couple of seconds." A knock interrupted. "Yes?"

A palace flunky bowed. "Her Imperial Majesty desires the honorable Sarasara's presence."

"Get on with your notes, Kara," said Salazar. "I'll return as soon as I can."

The Empress received the archaeologist in the audience room. "Sarasara, I have had word from a spy that Kampai is massing on his border. Are you ready to march?"

"If occasion demands, Your Majesty. I could spend a year training your soldiers and see improvement every day; but we shall do the best we can."

"Can you march tomorrow?"

"Perhaps not at dawn, but soon enough. Where do we go?"

"You shall go to the headquarters at Tuui of the Frontier Force and report to General Jidsho. Then, I suppose, you must turn over command of these companies to your highest officer, while you proceed on to the Shongosi-Chosha border. Will he be competent in your absence?"

Salazar shrugged. "We can only hope, Your Majesty. I have taught him what I could, bearing in mind that I am not a trained soldier either. Will Your Majesty kindly tell me of this General Jidsho?"

Gariko's cervical spines rippled in a way corresponding to a Terran's chuckle. "He and Shta were rivals for the post of Minister of War, or perhaps you would say commander-in-chief. I chose Shta because I deemed Jidsho too conservative and set in his ideas."

Salazar said: "Permit me to suggest to Your Majesty that it were wise to furnish me with a letter precisely defining my authority. Otherwise . . ."

"Otherwise he might waste your companies. Yes, he is headstrong. I will write that letter, Sarasara, and send a separate message by courier, stating the same points. But I worry. If the Shongorin are beaten on their eastern border, then despite your electrical communications, the nomads will overrun Shongosi before our forces can advance even so far as Biitso."

"How about mounting my Rangers on jutens for long marches?"

"It would take several sixtnights to make competent riders of them."

Salazar struck his forehead with his palm. "Your Majesty, I am stupid! I see steam trucks chugging about Machura. Why not requisition some of these and pack my Rangers into them? It woud halve the travel time and leave them fresh for fighting."

Hours later, having routed out his senior officer Kange (on whom he had conferred the Terran rank of Major) and helped to prepare for an early march, Salazar, back in his quarters, told Kara:

"Now the outcome is in the hands of the ancestral spirits or something. Boy, if she picked Genral Shta because Jidsho was too conservative, Jidsho must be a real Neanderthal!"

Kara protested: "My anthropology professor insisted that the Neanderthals were a much-maligned race. Are you still planning to drop me off at Tuui with the Rangers?"

"Yep. One of us must be with the frontier force to relay the messages."

"Good heavens, Keith!" she exclaimed. "How can I manage? I couldn't command your companies. My Kookish isn't good enough even to pass the word to our thick-headed Jidsho. Why don't you stay with the Rangers and send me on to Shongosi?"

"And put you out front like Uriah the Hittite? Don't be silly! You'd be no better off among a lot of strange Kooks. I'll leave my phrase book with you, and Uwangi to help with language drill. I shall be safer among the Shongorin than on the crime-ridden streets of Terra!"

THE
PIT

Upon reaching Tuui, Salazar and Kara rode towards the huge headquarters tent, followed by their two Kook helpers and a string of eleven snorting, smoking trucks, crammed with Rangers and their gear. As they neared the main entrance, lines of musketeers shouted: "Hail, Terrans!" and presented arms in the Kukulcanian manner, turning their weapons muzzle down.

Other soldiers ran forward to hold the jutens' lead straps while the Terrans and Salazar's deputy, "Major" Kange, dismounted. An officer saluted and said: "Follow me."

He led them to the main tent, which loomed above them, its bulbous arms resembling a fat starfish. A Kook identified by his painted insignia as General Jidsho received them with un-Kookish effusiveness:

"Ah, Terrans who come from across the nighted gulfs of space to save us from the bloodstained nomads, thrice welcome! May you lead tranquil lives! Major Kange, return to your command, whilst we discuss the impeding campaign. My troops will assist you in promptly quartering your men."

When Kange had departed, Jidsho continued: "In your honor we have prepared our best food and drink to refresh you after your toilsome journey. We have imported from Henderson a human being who, having worked for Terrans, can cook in the alien fashion. Follow me, please."

As they trailed through the curtain that divided the main part of the tent from one of the starfish arms, Salazar muttered in English:

"Curiouser and curiouser! Upper-caste Kooks lose face if they eat with a Terran."

"Maybe they'll just watch us eat," Kara whispered.

As Salazar let the canvas flap fall behind them, he saw that he was in an elongated sub-tent at right angles to the axis of the main accommodation, and nine or ten meters high. Midway between the two poles was a circular pit a meter deep and seven or eight meters in diameter. In the center of the pit rose a post somewhat higher than a man.

"Now what?" murmured Salazar. "I don't see any sign of a buffet—"

At that instant, Kooks on both sides of the Terrans seized their arms in scaly, steel-muscled hands. Kara screamed.

"Hey!" shouted Salazar, resisting. "What the hell—"

Kooks swiftly relieved Salazar of his rifle, pistol, and sheath knife. Others took Kara's small pistol. General Jidsho stepped before them, his neck spines rippling satisfaction, saying:

"You clever aliens intended, by pretending to aid us against the Choshas, to seize the rule of our Empire? But we are not so stupid as you thought!"

"Whatever makes you think that?" retorted Salazar hotly. "If this be the treatment you accord those who come to help you—"

From a pouch, Jidsho drew a roll of native paper. "This letter arrived by courier from General Shta. It gives the particulars of your plot; you plan not to march against the Choshas but to slay me and my subordinates, seize command of the frontier force, lead it back to Machura, overthrow the Empress, and make yourselves rulers! You would destroy our venerable traditions and noble principles! You have already begun your subversion by wheeling soldiers about the land in trucks, instead of marching them about as warriors have always marched. You wish to soften them to the point of uselessness."

Privately, Salazar though the Kooks were right to fear the expansionist tendencies on the part of the Terrans on Kukulcan; but under present circumstances he could not admit this to Jidsho. He said:

"That is a fantastic fabrication. Will Your Gallantry hear the true story?"

"We shall give you your say ere you pay the penalty of treason." Jidsho snapped a clawed finger. "Tie their hands behind them and fetch a brace of stools. These feeble aliens cannot stand for long without extreme distress."

When this had been done, Jidsho stood towering over the Terrans. "Very well, now speak!"

"Do you know the work I have been doing at Nomuru?" said Salazar.

"Aye, digging for treasure, albeit I am not familiar with petty rumors in Shongosi."

"My treasure is one that Your Gallantry would never recognize. I am an archaeologist, whose work is to unearth, study, and interpret the material remains of ancient cultures and to learn the lives of the people of former times."

Warming to his subject, Salazar gave an impromptu lecture on the aims of archaeology. He explained why he did not wish the Choshas to rule the site of Nomuru and told of his negotiations with the Empress. He feared that he might be boring his hearer if he went on too long; but Jidsho's neck spines showed rising interest. Salazar concluded:

"As Your Gallantry can see, so far from overthrowing your venerable customs and traditions, I strive to bring back into the light of day those that have been buried and forgotten. If I can continue my excavations, your traditions will be strengthened, amplified, and reinforced. If you doubt me, go look at the ruins of Horenso, where workers under my direction replaced fallen stones, restored half-obliterated inscriptions, and returned the city, as far as possible, to its former aspect."

When Salazar paused, Jidsho said: "General Shta also warns me that you and the female Terran propose to use some spirit-destroying electrical device in connection with your plan. That we cannot permit."

"Your Gallantry is misinformed. Miss Sheffield and I can communicate faster than can be done by any courier, to warn you when the Choshas invade Shongosi. Our method has nothing to do with electricity."

"What is it, then?"

Salazar thought with furious intensity. He did not believe that he could quickly convert General Jidsho to the use of Terran electronics by citing the approval of Emperor Simmo's ghost. At last he said:

"Your Gallantry, Miss Sheffield and I are cousins. To communicate across long distances, we call upon the spirits of our common ancestors such as our great-great-grandparents. They carry our messages to preserve family solidarity."

Salazar fell silent, while Jidsho stood for a long minute with his chin on his talons. He turned to the Kook holding Salazar's rifle. "Let me see that!"

After turning the gun over in his claws, Jidsho said: "This is one of those Terran firearms that shoot again and again without reloading. Such inventions have ruined the noble art of war, making victory not a matter of strength or bravery but of blind luck, slaying by missiles launched from afar. I wish the gun had never been invented and that we still fought in the old heroic way, with swords and spears. I am told that Terrans have developed this evil art to the point where they can wipe out all life on a planet."

"But, Your Gallantry," said Salazar, "if you sent your men with swords and spears against the Choshas' guns, what would happen? Then consider the use of Terran rifles against the nomads' muzzle-loaders. It is a choice between disagreeable alternatives."

Jidsho gave a hiss that might have been a Kukulcanian sigh. "Your words contain a bitter logic, Sarasara; and your story has a plausible ring. But I am not so simple as to take it at face value. I shall therefore call upon the Universal Law to decide betwixt you and General Shta. I shall let your veracity be determined by the ancient and honorable ordeal of *hurui*, which, sadly, has fallen into disuse in recent centuries."

He croaked a word to his servitors, who seized Kara and began stripping her. Others pinioned Salazar's arms.

"Hey!" yelled Salazar, futilely struggling in his captors' iron grip. "Stop! You cannot do that! You will rob us of our dignity! Your thus disgracing a Terran woman will enrage every Terran on the planet!"

General Jidsho paid no heed, and the servitors

continued roughly with their work. Unused to Terran clothes, they had trouble with buttons and slide fasteners. Some of the garments were torn by their claws.

Soon Kara was as naked as Penny Molina had been the night of the party. Four Kooks carried Kara to the central pit, sprang down to its floor, and tied her to the post.

"What are you going to do?" demanded Salazar. "Burn her?"

The general croaked the one word: "Nay!"

"What, then?"

The forked tongue flickered. "You shall see."

Two Kooks came through a side entrance, carrying a huge basket with a lid. They set the basket down on the edge of the pit, whisked off the lid, and tipped the basket forward. Out poured a dozen or more slender, wriggling, black-and-white striped shapes, which fell to the floor of the pit and scuttled about, hissing angrily.

"Kara!" shouted Salazar. "Freeze! Don't move a muscle! They're venomous boshiyas!"

General Jidsho spoke again; two Kooks untied Salazar's arms. "Now," said Jidsho, "if you succeed in rescuing your fellow alien, your words will have been proven correct by the Universal Law."

"If you'll give me back my guns, or even my knife—" began Salazar, but the general held up a claw.

"Nay, you must save her just as you are. The ordeal would not prove your veracity otherwise."

Salazar stepped to the edge of the pit. He could see Kara's eyes following his movements, but otherwise she held herself as rigid as a statue. The boshiyas, resembling Terran lizards with long, snaky necks, four legs apiece, and long tails, scuttled about, hissing and tongue-flicking. Most were less than a meter in length; but a couple of the largest were longer and capable, should they rear up, of biting Salazar above the tops of his boots.

He walked slowly around the pit, his glance darting about for some stratagem that he could use. From each of two tall tent poles, many ropes led down to the ground inside the canvas and were tied to the tent pegs. The canvas lay upon these ropes, which had not been sewn into the fabric.

If, Salazar thought, he detached a rope from the peg to which it was belayed, he could use it to swing across the pit. He knew that he could not snatch up Kara during his swing, since she was bound to the post.

He felt in his pockets. Lacking clothes, the Kooks were unfamiliar with pockets; they carried their petty personals in pouches slung from belts and straps. Once they had relieved him of his big sheath knife, it had never occurred to them that he might also have a clasp knife in his breeches.

He squatted at the lower end of a tent rope with his back to the Kooks, so that they could not see what he was doing. With the clasp knife he sawed at the rope until it parted. Putting away the knife, he rose, grasping the rope at man height.

Since the rope slanted from the top of the tent pole to the edge of the tent, Salazar knew that he must make a short run to swing across the pit, and that he would follow a curved path. Stepping to within a couple of meters of the edge, he ran towards Kara and swung across.

As he passed over them, the boshiyas craned their necks upwards, hissing. In the middle of his swing, at the low point in his arc, he brought his boots down on a boshiya, smashing it into the hard-packed earth and leaving it broken and writhing.

Salazar had intended to make repeated swings across the pit, stamping one of the pseudo-lizards to death on each swing. But he had miscalculated the length of run he needed to bring him safely out on the other side. The swing slowed and stopped just as he passed over the edge, a third of the way around the pit. He scrambled with his boots for a foothold; but the earth of the edge crumbled, cascading into the pit.

Failing to secure his footing, Salazar found himself swinging back across the pit like a pendulum. Because of the angle of the rope, he saw that his swing would quickly bring him up against the edge, where he could scramble up for another try. . . .

There was a flash, a puff of black-powder smoke, and a loud report. The rope went slack, dropping Salazar to the floor of the pit. He almost fell but by a desperate effort staggered to a balance as coils of rope fell on him. He realized that a Kook had fired a musket to sever the rope.

He sprang back as a boshiya reared and struck. All around, other boshiyas advanced, hissing and rearing their serpentine heads. These animals would ordinarily flee from any creature as large as a man; but now they were enraged.

For some unexplained reason, the tune of Bizet's *Toreador Song* flashed through Salazar's mind. He whipped off his bush jacket and held it before him like a matador's cape, while with the other hand he gathered up the severed part of the tent rope, now lying partly in and partly out of the pit. He had about three meters of rope, which he grasped by the bight, double, to form a double whip. With the rope in one hand and the jacket in the other, he confronted the boshiyas, turning about to ward off those behind him.

One of them struck at the coat. Its fangs caught in the fabric, so that when Salazar whipped the garment away, the beast was thrown across the pit. He slashed with the rope at another, knocking it writhing; then sprang forward to stamp the coiling creature until it merely twitched. Whirling the rope, he cleared away a couple more before him and finally got all those still active on one side.

Still full of fight, they came at him in a tongue-darting, wriggling mass. They were tough organisms; those he had hurled aside returned instantly to the attack. When they were nearly upon him, he threw the jacket over them and leaped upon it.

He did not succeed in covering all the boshiyas; three remained outside the coat. As he stamped on the jacket, he whirled the rope to fend off these, presently joined by another that had escaped from beneath the garment.

He stamped and stamped, until the mass beneath his feet ceased to move. When at last he stepped back and looked around, the four unharmed boshiyas were scrambling up the rough little ramp that he had unintentionally made in the side of the pit.

A chorus of Kookish croaks drew his attention to his audience. Several Kooks fled the tent; others aimed their weapons at the escaping animals. Flintlocks boomed, scattering bloody bits of boshiya about the inclosure.

Ignoring the commotion, Salazar sprang to the center of the pit and cut Kara's rope with his pocket knife. As the last rope fell away, he held out his arms, expecting her to fall fainting into them. Instead, she drew her slender body up, saying:

"Thanks a lot, Keith. Now do you think they'll let me put on my clothes?"

A woman of steel! Salazar thought proudly, as he picked up his jacket, befouled as it was with boshiya blood and guts. He helped her up over the side of the pit, vaulted up himself, and walked with her to the place where General Jidsho stood immobile. Ignoring the general, Kara retrieved her tattered garments and began to put them on. Salazar eyed the general coldly as his hard-pushed heart slowed down to normal. He said:

"Well, Your Gallantry?"

"Honorable Sarasara, you have proved by the Universal Law that your version of events be the true one. Since Shta and I are longtime rivals, I assume he sent the letter to get me into trouble. Such treachery is unheard-of among gentlefolk; Shta has been corrupted by his contact with the Terrans. I offer my apologies to your female and my assurances to you that I accept your soldiers with their newfangled guns; although, if such execrable devices spread amongst us human beings, I shall quit the trade of soldiering. It will no longer be an occupation for genteel persons."

"We thank you," said Salazar with a tinge of sarcasm. "May I ask why someone fired the shot that cut the rope?"

"Had he not, the test had not been fair. We knew not that you, in your sly Terran way, had a second knife concealed on your person."

"If you did not think to inspect my garments, the fault was yours."

Another long hiss floated across the silence.

"True. Although you are a mere animal, honorable Sarasara, and at death you will perish utterly without leaving a spirit to guide your descendants, your logic almost ranks you as a reasoning being like us. Now you and the female may return to your command. An officer will show you the way to your quarters. May good health pursue you both!"

"May the general likewise enjoy good health," growled Salazar as he began the tedious ritual. A Terran could have told from the archaeologist's tone that he wished General Jidsho anything but health, wealth, and happiness; the general, fortunately, was incapable of drawing such subtle inferences.

At last Salazar said: "Ready, Kara?"

"Yes, Keith. Your jacket's a mess, and I'll have to spend the rest of the day mending my own things."

Salazar grinned. "Remember those baths in the creek, when we killed the porondu?"

"What about them?"

"Well, I must say that your shape is as splendid as ever!

> "He's a fool to deny
> That the loveliest lass,
> When of garb she is shy
> Will her beauty surpass!"

"Damned old satyr!" she muttered, following Salazar out of the tent.

As they emerged into the slanting shafts of the afternoon sun, Kara said: "I—I'm sorry, Keith. I really am eternally grateful. You were brave and clever—a real hero!" Her voice trembled, and Salazar though he saw the glisten of an unshed tear.

"No, darling," he said. "You were the heroic one. I did what I did because I love you; and I'd do it even if I never saw you again in my life. Now let's find some better food than was offered at our so-called buffet lunch."

As, following one of Jidsho's officers, they walked
toward the Ranger's tents, Salazar saw a mud-stained
courier pull up his juten and leap down, crying that
he bore a letter from the Empress to General Jidsho.
As the Kook was led into the big tent, Salazar
remarked:

"Lousy timing, eh?"

> *"When Empress is tardy,*
> *And general foolhardy,*
> *We might never again have been fed*
> *But slain in ordeals,*
> *Converted to meals,*
> *And served at a banquet instead!"*

The following sunrise saw Salazar and Kara standing before the main tent. Kono held the lead straps
of three jutens, one for himself, one for Salazar, and
one for gear. Kara and Salazar were concluding a
friendly but heated argument over who should have
the pup tent while they were apart. She insisted that
he take it with him, while he was equally determined to leave it with her.

"After all," he said, "I've been sleeping under the
stars a lot lately—"

"I know. But you'll be traveling alone, and it's
sure to rain. Then you'll get sick, and what will
happen to me?"

"Well—" Salazar weakened.

"Besides, I'll be perfectly fine in with Major Kange;
his tent's big enough for the pair of us."

Salazar grunted. "I suppose it will be all right, if
you can stand the Kookish smell. But don't let him
get too fond of you."

"Silly! I must be as sexually repulsive to him as he
is to me. Think you'll run into Conrad Bergen?"

"Shouldn't be surprised. The route lies past that Nomuru site."

"Promise me you won't try to kill him! Not that I care about *him*, but it would cause us endless trouble."

"I won't shoot unless he tries something first, and he's a terrible shot. Try to practice your Feënzuo on Kange; maybe he'd like to learn a little English."

He half opened his arms, but all he got was a brisk handshake and a gentle smile.

Keith Salazar, with Kono and the baggage animal, jounced expeditiously back to Shongosi on their way to the Chosho frontier. Salazar lingered in Biitso only long enough to learn that High Chief Miyage had gone to the frontier, taking all but a handful of his army. In Shongaro he made a similar discovery when he inquired about Chief Sambyaku.

The forges of Neruu glowed redly in the dusk as Salazar rode through the town, while the smoke of a hundred chimneys dimmed the stars and the little starlike moons. The whirring, clanking machine shops were working overtime on muskets and other military gear.

Knowing the route, Salazar went on to his old camping ground. Kono had lighted a fire, and he and Salazar were putting up the pup tent, when a crackle of twigs apprised them of intruders. As Salazar picked up his rifle, the light of a lantern fell on him and a Kookish voice croaked: "Stand! Who be ye?"

Three Kooks painted with the insignia of the army of Shongosi came toward the firelight, muskets raised. Salazar identified himself.

The Kook wearing the symbols of an officer said: "I am Captain Te of the Biitso Civil Guard. Honorable Sarasara, know that the High Chief has forbidden either you or the other Terran, the large one with a name like 'Boogen,' to touch the site of Nomuru until he decides which of you is legally entitled to do so. We are here to enforce His Highness's command."

"I understand," said Salazar. "In fact, I am here to assure myself that no unauthorized work has been done on the site in my absence. With such alert, dutiful guards as you on hand, I realize that my fears were groundless."

While the beaked face showed no emotion, the neck spines rippled in a pleased way. Even the unemotional Kooks, Salazar thought, were not proof against flattery. "Have you any idea when His Highness's decision will come?"

"Not during the emergency, certainly," said the officer.

"I understand. Where can one now find the High Chief?"

"The army is mustering at the village of Hetori, near the frontier."

Salazar considered. "Is that a little place on the lower Tsugaa, near Mount Zu?"

"Aye, or so I have been told."

Salazar was thankful for Kookish veracity. Kooks were terrible liars. Although they did sometimes lie, one skilled in their ways could detect the lie by the movement of their neck spines. Perhaps, he thought, that accounts for their being so law-abiding. He said:

"Thank you. May you be in robust health!"

"And may the honorable Sarasara's health be robust!"

"May you lead a tranquil life! . . ."

Next morning, Salazar stood on the edge of the Nomuru site, peering across it. A dozen of Captain Te's guardsmen patrolled the site. Three stood near

Salazar. The rippling of their cervical spines betrayed nervous apprehension beneath their stolid exteriors.

Probably, thought Salazar, they have heard of the stunts I've gotten away with lately, mainly by dumb luck. He strolled about the site, pocked by the rectangular test pits. Bergen's tractor still lay half in and half out of one hole.

The chugging of a steam car caused Salazar to turn. The car stopped with a hiss and a puff of white vapor on the edge of the site. Besides the Kook driver, the car carried Conrad Bergen and Oleg Pokrovskii. These climbed down and walked towards Salazar. As they came, several Kooks clustered around them. These the bulky black-browed Bergen ignored and strode straight for Salazar, who unsnapped the flap at the top of his pistol holster. Near Salazar, Captain Te barked:

"No violence!"

Bergen roared: "Go on, Keith, take your hand off your goddam gun! I'm not going to shoot you, even if you deserve it! I just came out to see how the site's doing, so I can get to work as soon as Miyage makes his decision."

"You mean, *if* he decides for you," rasped Salazar, suppressing an urge to draw and shoot Bergen dead.

"I'm not worried. What are you doing here? Thought you were in Feënzun."

"I finished my business there and came by, for the same reason you did. How did you get that car here, with the Sappari bridge in the shape it's in?"

"Oh, hell! I built my own bridge."

"You *what?*"

"Built my own bridge. Had it prefabricated in my shops and strung it over the Sappari a sixtnight ago. Had to wait for the concrete in the dead men to harden before putting any weight on it."

"You do get things done," muttered Salazar. Much as he detested Bergen, he had to admit a wry admiration for the developer's energy.

"Sure. If I waited for Chief Sammy to fix the old bridge, we'd be dead of old age before he got around to it. When we get the resort built, maybe I'll hire you to lecture the guests on Kook history and culture, for the eggheads who like that sort of thing." Bergen gave a contemptuous snort of laughter. "Come on, Oleg!"

Off went the pair with their escort of musketeers. Mentally cursing himself as an ineffectual intellectual, Salazar returned to his camp, got out maps, and studied the route to Hetori. Early next morning he and Kono were on their way before the diurnal species of the leather-winged zutas had begun to squawk and chatter.

They took the road south to Neruu, where they turned east towards Hetori and the Chosha country. Although this road was a mere track, unsuited to wheeled traffic, it was easy to follow. Most of the Shongo forces heading for the frontier had gone this way, so that the surface of the road itself and of the ground on either side was trampled.

Three days later, Salazar and Kono rode past the isolated conical peak of Mount Zu. The road skirted the base of the peak, curving around toward the village of Hetori, which lay between the mountain and the river Tsugaa. At this point, the river formed the boundary between Shongosi and the lands of the nomadic Choshas; and here could be found the only good ford for many kilometers.

The vegetation became scrubby and widely scattered, save for gallery forests along the streams. East of the Tsugaa, as Salazar had noted during his captivity and escape, the trees petered out altogether, and the land stretched into a wide, grassy plain.

On the open spaces along the river, Shongo infantry marched and juten cavalry maneuvered. When Salazar rode into the camp, he was at once surrounded by well-armed guards.

"Who be ye and what would ye?" they barked.

Salazar explained. He asked to see Chief Sambyaku, whereupon the soldiers led him to the headquarters tent, whence Sambyaku presently issued.

"Sarasara!" welcomed the chief. "Is all well with you?"

"Yes, indeed. Is all well with the chief?"

"Indeed it is. Is all well with the honorable Sarasara's clan?"

Salazar and the chief had not finished their formal greetings when High Chief Miyage bustled out of the same tent. "Sarasara!" he croaked. "What in the name of the ancestral spirits do you here?" His tongue flicked.

Salazar said tartly: "Does Your Highness wish an answer forthwith without the usual greetings?"

"Aye; we have no time here for empty ritual. Speak!"

"I am here, Your Highness, to see how things go; since the outcome of the impending conflict affects the practice of my profession. If you should lose, and my site fall to the Choshas—"

"You try by talk of defeat to destroy our spirit ere the battle be joined!" cried the High Chief furiously. "We know not why ye plot against us, unless it be some scurvy Terran scheme to steal our lands. In any case, we will not have you lurking about here, weaving webs to entrap us. Begone, instantly, or we will have you shot!" On command, the bodyguards cocked and raised their muskets.

Salazar looked at Chief Sambyaku. The chief made a vague gesture, while the movement of his neck bristles implied: Sorry, honorable Sarasara, but you know how it is. I can do nothing.

"At least," said Salazar, "let us replenish the food for our journey homeward."

"That were but reasonable," added Sambyaku.

Miyage grunted. "You are a Terran-lover, Sambyaku; but custom demands that the alien be succored. We will spare you a week's rations. If you wish more, you can shoot a wild beast with that newfangled gun of yours." The High Chief turned to his entourage and barked: "Captain Yeron! See to the alien."

An hour later, Salazar and Kono rode back the way they had come. When Hetori and the camp were hidden by the curve of Mount Zu, Salazar left the trampled road and turned toward the mountain. At its base he dismounted, telling Kono:

"Get down, Kono. We shall have to lead the beasts."

"Does the honorable Terran mean to scale the mountain?"

"Yes. Come along!"

The twilight was deepening and nocturnal zutas flitted about, replacing the diurnal ones, when Salazar reached the top of the hill. After resting with his back to a tree to recover his breath, he wandered over the crest.

Eventually he found an outcrop of granite on the eastern slope. By pitching camp above this rocky, treeless surface, he obtained a splended view of the camp of the Shongo army, the village, the river beyond, and the plain across the river. If the Shongorin had known beans about warfare, he thought, they would have posted lookouts on the hill as soon as they reached Hetori.

While Kono set up the tent, Salazar buttoned his poignette. Thin with distance came Kara's voice:

"Keith! Is it you?"

"Yep. Everything okay with you?"

"No trouble so far. How's your job going?"

Salazar told her. "I wanted to ask the chiefs if their spies had any word of a Chosha advance; but they said they'd shoot me if I hung around."

"Keith dear, once you tell me the invasion has started, head for Tuui as fast as you can! Don't get so interested in the battle that you stay up on your mountain until the Choshas arrive to collect your head!"

"Good advice, darling. Good-night!" He silently mouthed: "I love you!"

"Good-night, Keith."

Days passed. Salazar swept the distant plain with his binoculars, seeing wandering dust devils and a few clusters of black specks, like grains of pepper spilled on a beige tablecloth. These turned out to be herds of wild herbivores. Archaeology had instilled in Keith Salazar the virtue of patience.

Between spells of watching, he prowled the mountaintop, making mental notes of the geology and looking for relics of the Kookish Stone Age. He found one projectile point, like that which he had picked up in his flight with Kara. He chuckled at the thought that now, if the Empress proved niggardly, he could at least claim expenses from Patel by calling this expedition an archaeological reconnaissance.

He pocketed the artifact and found Kono cooking a frugal meal. The Kook squatted in a hollow on the western side of the crest, where the rear slope began to fall away. Salazar had insisted that Kono make his fires there, keeping them small and using only dry wood, lest the smoke betray them.

On the seventh day of Salazar's vigil, his binoculars picked up a dust cloud of unusual size and persistence. An hour later, a swarm of black specks appeared beneath the cloud, crawling towards the Tsugaa. Another hour, and the specks grew into Kooks on jutens.

Salazar told Kono: "Strike the tents and start packing." He buttoned Kara and told her the news. She said: "I'll pass the word. Now you ride homeward hell-for-leather!"

Below, news of the approach had reached the camp. Trumpets blew, drums beat, and the Shongorin milled like a colony of ants whose nest has been broken open. With his glasses, Salazar picked out the form of High Chief Miyage, beside a standard bearer. The High Chief was forming up a body of juten cavalry.

Another hour, and the leading elements of the Chosharin were within sight of the Shongo forces on the western bank. Salazar could hear faint war cries above the buzz and chirp of Kukulcanian insectoids. Then, as he scanned the field, he muttered:

"Jeepers! They can't be *that* stupid!"

Although Salazar's military knowledge was obtained entirely from books, not experience, it seemed to him obvious that the course for Miyage would have been to defend the west bank of the river with musketry. He should hold his cavalry, far inferior in numbers to the mounted nomads, in reserve, ready to dash in wherever the Choshas obtained a foothold on the bank. Instead, saber in hand, Miyage was leading his cavalry down to the river and into the ford. Salazar could see tiny diamonds of sunlight sparkling on the fountains kicked up by the jutens.

Evidently Miyage meant to cross and attack the Chosha army head-on. The Shongo jutens splashed across the ford. Through his glasses, Salazar caught the flash of sun on the saber that Miyage brandished. Then the Shongorin plowed into the nomads and were swallowed up in a vortex of circling mounts and whirling blades.

At last Salzar tore his gaze away from the unfolding battle and said to Kono: "Let us go!" Taking the lead strap of his juten, he set off down the steep western slope, man and animal jumping, skidding, and sliding.

THE
RANGERS

As the first day of Salazar's flight from Hetori drew to a close, he called Kara. She asked: "How did the battle go?"

"I left before it was decided, but I'll lay you a hundred to one that the Choshas won." He described the High Chief's charge. "It's Manzikert or Nicopolis all over again. What's Jidsho doing?"

"Getting ready to march."

"He hasn't left *yet?*" Salazar's voice rose.

"No. He's still packing up."

"Oh, hell! At that rate, the Choshas will overrun most of Shongosi. Tell him to hurry, and have Kange load his men into the trucks pronto and take off for Neruu. I shall meet him there. What will Jidsho do if the Shongorin win?"

"He'll say politely, he and his army just came to help. Then they'll march back to Feënzun."

"Has Jidsho any information on the Choshas' route?"

238

"I *think* he said that, according to Gariko's spies, they'll either come by way of Neruu or go up the Mozii past your ruins."

Salazar mused: "Sacking Neruu would be a more direct way to conquer Shongosi; but marching across my dig to the Sappari would cut Shongosi off from any possible intervention by the Terrans of Henderson. Although it's against Terran policy to interfere in native conflicts, in this case, without Terran help, the entire populations of Shongosi and Feënzun may be destroyed. How are you making out?"

"I'm still bunking with Kange. He's a dear when you get to know him."

"Getting a crush on him?"

"Be sensible, Keith! If you were pals with a female shaped like a man-sized octopus, would you call it a crush if you liked her?"

"Depends on how sexy an octopus she was. At least, she'd have eight arms to hug me with—"

"Good-night, silly!"

Next morning, as Salazar and Kono jogged towards Neruu, the Kook made a brave attempt at English: "S-sorjairs c-come!"

Salazar got out his binoculars and twisted in the saddle. Through the broken parkland among the copses wound a trio of juten riders, pushing their exhausted mounts. As the trio shortened the intervening distance, one Kook drew a pistol and waved it, shouting: "Halt!"

By their paint, the three belonged to Miyage's cavalry. They croaked and cawed among themselves: "This is the Terran who arrived in our camp ere the battle. It must be a Terran plot—"

"Nay, he is a spy for Feënzun. It is known that he sojourned with the Empress—"

"You are both mistook; he is the mad Terran who digs up ancient bricks and stones."

"Enough talk!" shouted the first. "I will settle the question at one blow!" He aimed the huge pistol and pulled the trigger.

Salazar had held his rifle pointing near but not at the Kooks. When the first one essayed a shot, by reflex the archaeologist whipped up his gun and fired before he realized that the attacker's pistol had merely clicked. The Kook whose gun had misfired gave a screech, toppled off his juten, thrashed about in the herbage, and at last lay still.

"This Terran," shouted Salazar, "is not too mad to shoot straight, and my gun shoots all day without reloading. I regret this witless death, since your comrade's pistol failed to fire. Now tell me what has happened!"

The Kooks exchanged glances before one replied: "The barbarians have prevailed. They surrounded us riders and cut us to pieces. Then the Choshas charged across the ford in the teeth of our fire. Many fell, but others reached the bank ere our musketeers could reload. There was fierce fighting all along the line. The Choshas rode in, shooting and spearing and swording, while our folk strove to pull them from their saddles to dispatch them on the ground. But in time the nomads' numbers told, and our people broke and ran."

"Will more fugitives follow you?"

"Aye. It was late in the day when our formations broke, and in the dark not even the Choshas could slay us all. We carry word—"

At that instant, the speaker's juten toppled over, spilling its rider, who scrambled to his feet. Salazar said: "You have evidently killed your beast."

"We know that, Terran!" snapped the remaining

mounted Kook. The fallen one limped to where stood
the beast whose rider had been shot. The dismounted
soldier unsentimentally went through his dead comrade's pouches, appropriating articles. Then he
mounted and rode off with the other, calling back:

"May you lead a tranquil life, Terran!"

Salazar returned the conventional response and
spoke to his servant: "Kono, we must push on. The
Choshas may be close behind."

Nightfall on the third day found the hard-pushed
travelers in sight of the ruddy, cloud-reflected glow
of the furnaces of Neruu. They camped amid the
dense shrubbery beside the road. Arriving in Neruu
the next morning, in the central square Salazar found
a Shongo officer, an onnifa, trying to detain fugitive
soldiers and organize them into a fighting force. She
was croaking orders when the sound of steam engines struck her silent.

Along the road from Shongoro rolled a column of
belching, clattering steam trucks crowded with Kooks.
In front, side by side on jutens, rode Kara and Major
Kange.

"Kara!" yelled Salazar. He threw the lead strap of
his juten to Kono and ran to her as she dismounted.
They fell into an embrace; but when he tried to kiss
her, she broke away.

"Thank the Universal Law you're safe!" she said.
"We're the first unit to reach this area; the others
will be straggling in. One of our trucks broke down,
so some of our soldiers are walking. If they can fix
the truck, it'll come by and pick them up."

"I hope General Jidsho can organize a decent defense before the Chosha horde gets here," said Salazar.
He exchanged formal greetings with Kange; then
said to Kara: "Want to move back to the pup tent?"

"I'd be glad. Poor Kange *does* stink. But what about you?"

"I can sleep outside as I did, or I can come in. But I won't promise not to crawl in my sleep."

"Then I'll stay with Kange."

Salazar sighed. "Damn! Why do we get ourselves into these fixes?"

"What do you mean, 'we'?" said Kara. But she spoke softly, with a smile that took the sting out of the remark.

"You're right, of course; but that only makes the predicament worse.

> *"The hero returns*
> *From perils robust;*
> *The lady him spurns*
> *For fear of his lust!"*

Stifling a giggle, Kara said: "Keith, you're incorrigible, tossing off funny little versicles about serious matters! I'll bet you compose one on your death bed."

"I might; why make a solemn fuss over something as commonplace as dying? But remember, you used to like my poking fun at serious things."

It was her turn to sigh. "I remember. It's too bad things changed. Now hadn't you better take over command of the Rangers?"

Salazar directed the Rangers to pitch camp on the outskirts of Neruu. He was inspecting this battalion and checking their equipment and supplies when General Jidsho appeared on the road from Shongaro at the head of a column of juten cavalry. Jidsho dismounted and approached Salazar abject with apologies:

"Honorable Sarasara, I withdraw the hurtful statements I have made against you. General Shta's mendacious letter to me did in time reach the Empress, whereupon she dismissed her faithless servant and appointed me commander-in-chief in his place. So, esteemed savant, I owe my elevation in part to you. To honor you and your Rangers, I shall post them at the place where the Choshas will mount their main assault, wherever it transpires that this will be."

To be posted at the most dangerous place on the battlefield was an honor that Salazar would cheerfully have forgone; but having talked himself into a position of military responsibility, he found no alternative to seeing it through. After the full ritual of good wishes, Jidsho withdrew to set up his own headquarters.

When Salazar reported to Jidsho the next day, the general had just finished interviewing a Shongo soldier, a fugitive from the battle at Hetori. According to this informant, he had seen a long Chosha column moving across the low ridge that separated the watershed of the Dzariki from that of the Mozii.

"Unless this be a feint," said Jidsho, "the invaders plan to take the Nomuru route and seize control of the south bank of the Sappari. Deploy your Rangers forthwith at the ruins of Nomuru; but hold yourself prepared to hasten back to Neruu if it transpire that the main attack will be toward the modern town. Now excuse me; I go to address the assembled Shongorin, informing them that they are now subjects of Her Imperial Majesty, Empress Gariko of Feënzun."

Salazar's Rangers settled into camp along the northern side of the Nomuru site, their numbers spilling out along both sides of the Nomuru-Henderson road. Under Salazar's watchful eye, the squads in turn patrolled the area and performed simple drills. They waited one day, two days, three days. At last Kara asked: "What's holding up the Choshas? From the look of my map, they should have been here on the heels of your Rangers."

Salazar shrugged. "Probably stopped to loot the towns along the way and kill the inhabitants. Jidsho's been questioning fugitives."

"A battle would be easier to bear than all this waiting!"

"You may think different when you see an actual battle. Anyway, the delay has given us time to position all the Frontier Force."

On the fourth day, Salazar was putting a squad of Rangers through a dummy rifle drill when the chug of a steam car brought him around. Approaching the Nomuru site, now serving as a drill field, came the black-browed Conrad Bergen, seated behind Pokrovskii and Bergen's Kook chauffeur. Salazar called to Kara, who was perched on a nearby Kookish milepost writing in her notebook.

"Kara, look!" he said softly, jerking a thumb toward the approaching vehicle. He gave an order in Feënzuo to his squad: "Load your magazines, put one round in the chamber, and follow. Protect me if I am attacked."

As Kara hastened toward him, he said: "Don't you think you'd better go hide somewhere?"

Head up, she replied: "I'll stick with you."

The car drew to a halt in a cloud of vapor, and the two passengers clambered out. Bergen reached into the vehicle and heaved out a large gun, which Salazar recognized as the developer's big-game rifle.

"Well?" said Salazar quietly, as his eight Rangers clustered behind him.

"Whaddya mean, well!" snorted Bergen. "I see

you two have been off in the boonies again. You can't tell me there hasn't been any monkey business between you! And I've told you, she's my woman!"

"I'm not your woman, and you know it!" snapped Kara with a steely glare.

Salazar, more evenly, added: "And it's none of your affair, whether there's been any monkey business, as you call it, or not. We're going to have a battle here at any time; so take your buggy and head back for Henderson, before you're caught in the cross fire!"

Bergen's voice rose: "Goddamn it, you can't order me around! If—"

"Oh, yes I can! I've got the firepower."

"Gentlemen!" said Pokrovskii soothingly. "Please! *Pozhaluista!* We must not make a spectacle in front of natives. Why not walk out on site for talking, where half de Kook army can't hear?"

"Okay, but I'll take my soldiers," said Salazar. He chose four Rangers to stay with him.

"If you're going to talk about me," said Kara determinedly, "I want to be there, too."

Bergen and his construction supervisor, Salazar, Kara, and the four Rangers strode out across the neglected site. Pointing to the useless tractor, Bergen growled: "Look at that goddam thing! I'll sue you for destroying my property!"

Salazar looked surprised. "Neither I nor any of my people ran the tractor into that hole."

"But you goddam well hid the hole with a sheet."

"The tarpaulin was placed there to protect the stratigraphy of the test pit. A heavy storm would have washed down the sides and raised hell with my dating."

"But you didn't have to sprinkle dirt and plants

over the top! You goddam intellectuals are all alike; no grasp of economic reality. You'd spoil a perfectly legitimate business enterprise and kill the jobs it would provide, just to preserve some old stone wall nobody gives a shit about. Just so you can argue among yourselves about your useless theories! And to rub it in, here you are out in the backwoods fucking my dame—"

"Conrad!" cried Kara furiously. "I'm not your dame! So shut up about it!"

"All right," snarled Bergen, "but I still got opinions. Now tell me, what's this about the Empress sending an army into Shongosi and what'll that do to my agreement with Miyage?"

"I think Miyage is dead," said Salazar. "Shongosi is now a province of the Empire. About your resort project, you'll have to ask the Empress or her ministers."

"And you futzed that up when you were in Machura—"

"Please!" said Pokrovskii. "We getting nowhere. If enemy soldiers coming, we better get out of de way."

Bergen flushed a dangerous crimson. "Now look here! I'm not afraid of any two-legged lizards riding featherless ostriches—"

At that moment, the report of a musket nearby made Bergen and his supervisor start. Kettledrums struck up a complex rhythm. Looking round, Salazar exclaimed: "My God, look at that!"

The eastern end of the site was suddenly alive with Chosha warriors, charging on juten-back. A rattle of shots came from the advancing force, with great puffs of smoke. A bullet whistled close by the Terrans' heads. Salazar yelled: "Back to the road, behind the Rangers—no, too late!" The group had, in the course of their argument, wandered far out on the site. Now, even if they ran, the onrushing nomads would catch them before they reached the line of Rangers, lying on their bellies and checking their magazines.

"In there!" shouted Salazar, pointing to a meter-deep test pit. "Duck down, all of you!" He repeated the command to the four Rangers, indicating another pit. "Lie low and don't show your faces!"

The four Terrans piled into the first pit. Salazar peered over the edge, silently cursing himself for having been distracted by a silly argument when he should have been scanning the far end of the site with his glases.

On came the Choshas, waving sabers, lances, pistols, and carbines. As the first ones passed the pit in which the Terrans huddled, Salazar heard Major Kange's croak: "Open fire!"

Mixed with the crackle of rifle fire came the whip-snap of bullets passing overhead. On the masses of Choshas, the effects were devastating. Some jutens pitched forward with earthshaking thuds, spilling their riders. Other Choshas toppled off their mounts, which ran in circles cawing excitedly, sometimes attacking one another. Some dismounted Choshas tried to charge the defense line on foot and were shot down. Others fired their flintlocks, struggled to reload, and were felled as they worked. On the Rangers' right, a Feënzuo muzzle-loading cannon boomed, hurling a charge of grape shot.

Soon the charge dwindled to a few survivors who fled back, mounted or afoot, the way they had come. The site of the ancient city was littered with the bodies of jutens and Choshas, some writhing, twitching, and squawking amid those that lay still.

Presently Pokrovskii ventured: "Think we can make dash for de car now; attack over."

"No; here comes another charge." Salazar's quiet voice rose to a shout. "Wait, you damned fool!"

Heedless, Pokrovskii hoisted himself out of the test pit and waddled ponderously towards the steam car. As he did so, the earth vibrated with the rumble of hundreds of jutens, charging the line of Rangers again. Salazar strained his lungs to scream: "Come back, Oleg!" Then he ducked down as the leaders of the second charge swept past.

One nomad caught Pokrovskii thirty meters from the pit and speared him with a lance. Salazar did not dare to shoot the Chosha lancer for fear of drawing fire from the barbarians swarming around them, thus dooming all those huddled in the pit.

Bergen, who had watched his friend go down, shouted in a strangled voice: "Those—fucking—animals, killing a human being—I'll show 'em!"

Red-faced and panting with fury, Bergen gathered his forces, laid his heavy rifle on the ground outside the pit, and sprang out. A few seconds later, a Chosha rider pointed a pistol at him. Bergen whipped up his gun and fired, catapulting the Kook over the tail of his mount.

Salazar opened his mouth to shout: "Come back, you idiot!" but checked the impulse. If the man whom he most hated, who had beaten Kara and had beaten, betrayed, and tried to murder him, wished to invite death at the hands of the Choshas, why should the archaeologist interfere?

As several Choshas converged upon him, Bergen, screaming an inarticulate war cry, swung his rifle right and left, firing and yelling as each Chosha or juten fell. When he had emptied his magazine, he began pulling cartridges from his bandoleer and shoving them into his gun. Then a Chosha rode up close, fired a carbine at him, and knocked him down. Other mounted nomads clustered around the fallen man, swinging sabers. A moment later, a Chosha rode off with Bergen's bloody head impaled on the point of his lance. Then the Rangers' borrowed rifles opened up again, and sheets of bullets felled Choshas and their mounts.

When the charge petered out, Salazar whispered to Kara: "Before they strike again, I must get back to my troops. Follow me, then crouch down behind that car!"

He boosted Kara out of the pit. Then, vaulting out, he ran back with her to his Rangers. Three of his Kookish bodyguards followed; the fourth lay in the pit, dying of a gunshot.

Arriving behind the line of riflemen, Salazar asked Kange: "How many casualties?"

"Sixteen or twenty; some dead, more merely wounded. Here they come again!"

On came another wave of nomads; but they came more slowly now as they picked their way among the bodies that littered the site. When Kange gave the order to fire, Salazar went down the line of Rangers, nudging each and shouting over the din: "You shoot too high! Keep your eye level with the rear sight. . . . You shoot too fast. Take careful aim, picking your targets. . . . You flinch when you fire. Pull the butt back harder against your shoulder. . . . Your gun is jammed from overheating. Let it cool down before you shoot again. . . ."

In general, the Rangers did better than Salazar expected, squeezing off shots one by one as he had taught them and stopping to replace clips of cartridges. The Kooks' stolid inexcitability made them excellent soldiers when properly led.

Glancing toward the steam car, Salazar saw Kara crouched behind it, holding her pistol in both hands and methodically firing across the vehicle. Salazar used his own rifle only once. Kara had emptied her magazine and was inserting a new clip when a saber-waving Chosha charged towards her afoot. Salazar shouted to the nearest Rangers to shoot the attacker; but the nomad survived the fusillade. When the Kook was within a few meters of the woman, Salazar brought him down with a single rifle shot.

Once more the nomad charge fragmented and fell back like a receding wave. Here and there a dismounted Chosha took cover behind his juten's body to harass the defenders with fire from flintlocks, but with little success. The greater accuracy of the Terran firearms took such a toll of these snipers that the survivors, bent low among the dead and dying, zigzagged back across the site to safety.

Through his binoculars, Salazar spotted small groups of Choshas still moving among the bushes and stunted trees at the far end of Nomuru; but they evinced no desire to attack again in the face of their devastating losses. Presently even these remnants vanished as squadrons of Feënzuo cavalry trotted across the site in pursuit. Salazar saw Pokrovskii crawling toward him trailing a pair of useless legs in bloodsoaked trousers.

As Salazar stood up to go to the Suvarovian's rescue, a flintlock, fired from behind a nearby juten's carcass, sent out a puff of sulfurous smoke. A heavy blow struck Salazar in the ribs, spun him around, and sent him sprawling. He was vaguely aware of a crackle of rifle fire around him and of willing claws carrying him. His side began to hurt abominably, and his daylight faded into dark.

*   *   *

In the hospital at Henderson, Doctor Hajari told Salazar that he might exercise by walking, and that twenty lengths of the main hospital corridor equaled one kilometer. Returning to his room after his first kilometer, he found that, while he walked, Pokrovskii had been moved into the other bed in his room. Pokrovskii said:

"*Zdra'stvuitye*, Keit'! How you feel now?"

"Pretty good, if I don't take a deep breath and split my ribs again. How about you?"

"I be all right in sixtnight; just a little poke with spear in *yagoditsa*—what Americans call de donkey." He parted a bandaged buttock. "Few centimeters higher, and good-bye me! They tell me Conrad dead."

"Yep; I saw his head on the point of a lance. Now, suppose you tell me what really happened to Derek Travers."

"Why, Conrad himself tell your people at dig—"

"I know, but I don't believe that story. Come on, out with it!"

Under Salazar's stern regard, Pokrovskii wilted. "Conrad dead, so is no reason not. We camped, night after Miss Sheff'eld run away. Next morning, Kook guide say: 'Here come big hungry fyunga! Everybody mount and get a hell out!' Fyunga was half a kilometer away but coming fast. Conrad say: 'Hell, I won't run from featherless chicken! Besides, we need meat, since de bitch stole our food.' He grab rifle and get ready to shoot. Guide tell Conrad he foolish; Derek translated. Conrad get mad; call me coward because I mount juten. Everybody yell. Jutens get scared and begin to dance around. Guide start off with me after him. Fyunga get closer; gun go off, one-two-three. Fyunga stagger but keep coming."

"He was no great marksman," said Salazar. "Go on."

"At last minute, Derek start running after guide and me. Fyunga run after Derek. Conrad yell, call Derek yellow. Gun bang again, twice. Derek scream. Fyunga bellow and go off, staggering like he drunk. We came back, guide and me. Derek is lying dead with bullet in him; Conrad sitting on ground crying, saying it his fault his friend was killed. Make me promise not to tell true story. Since he was boss, I did like he said."

"Did Bergen shoot Travers accidentally or on purpose?"

Pokrovskii spread his hands. "How I know? Was looking other way at time. Could be accident, Derek and fyunga being in line; but Conrad once killed another man in one of his mad fits. Had to use money and influence to keep from being tried for murder."

"The son of a bitch deserved everything he got."

"Conrad not really bad; just difficult, with terrible temper."

"Don't try to whitewash a lump of coal!"

"Not all black, Keit'. Did some good things. Gave money for art museum; helped some poor people. . . . Oh, hello, Kara!" Salazar echoed the greeting.

After a quarter-hour of amiable chitchat, Kara dug a sheaf of manuscript out of her handbag. "Here's my story on the Battle of Nomuru. It doesn't mention automatic rifles; just the well-drilled Feënzuo musketeers."

After reading in silence, Salazar handed back the manuscript.

"Looks okay." Seeing Kara's look of disappointment, he added: "Excellent reporting, in fact." Then he turned to his roommate. "Oleg, I'd like a promise from you, not to tell anyone about the Terran guns."

Pokrovskii remained silent for a minute, then nodded. "Hokay, if you promise never to repeat story about Conrad and Derek."

"You mean to let Conrad's official version stand?"

"Yes."

"But why? He's dead and can't mind; and Derek's family deserves to know the truth."

"Just say I sentimental fool. You keep my secret, I keep yours. Otherwise not."

"Oh, all right." Salazar turned. "Kara, will you walk me down the hall? The doc wants me to exercise."

Out in the corridor, he said: "Oleg's a bit of an ass, but one can't help liking him."

Kara asked: "What was the story about Conrad and Derek?"

"You'll have to ask Oleg. I think he's wrong to suppress it; but a promise is a promise."

"Too bad you didn't think of that on that other—"

Salazar interrupted her caustic remark. "Please, Kara! I want to ask you something."

"Yes?"

"I know I've been a louse; but even a louse can learn. Kara, I love you. Will you marry me again?"

She took her time. At last she said: "Keith, I've seen this coming, and I've given the matter a lot of thought. You're a fine man, and I tremendously admire the things you've accomplished. I'm proud to be your friend. And you're the man who thought he could never be a general!

"But a successful marriage needs not only the combination of attraction and attachment we call love; it also needs trust. The main reason for marrying nowadays is for mutual support and protection—for someone on whom one can always rely."

Kara sighed. "You're a very attractive man, my dear. At times during our travels, it was all I could do to keep my guard up. It hurt to fend off your advances when I wanted you as much as you did me; but I felt that to give in would only lead us down the road to another disaster.

"I'm deeply attached to you, as one is to anybody one's lived with for years. I guess one never completely gets over a former spouse. But the other necessary element, trust, is missing."

"Haven't I been straightforward with you?"

Close to tears, Kara said: "Yes; you have, all through this dreadful war. But that doesn't turn the clock back. After you killed my trust, the feeling just isn't there any more." She gave his arm a squeeze. "I really am sorry, Keith; but that's how things stand."

"Even after all we've been through together?"

"Even after that."

After a bleak silence, Kara added: "Don't look so downcast, Keith. There are other women, even on this world."

Salazar's tone was fretful. "How do you expect me to look when the great love of my life slams the door in my face?"

Kara smiled a bitter little smile. "I know how it feels. I've been through it."

"Oh. You're right. I deserved that crack."

"I shouldn't have come out to your dig for that story and then gone on the hunt with you. All that bumming around together was bound to awaken old passions. Despite what you did, I'm sorry to put you through this. Hereafter we'd better keep our distance."

After another silence, Salazar looked up with a sly grin. "But we did have some pretty lively adventures, didn't we? We can dine out on those for years!"

She said: "The nurse will be bringing in your

dinner soon, so I'll say good-night." Head up, she turned and walked away.

After his discharge, Salazar had dinner with his friend Cabot Firestone. Over drinks, Firestone said, "Keith, you've done the Museum and archaeology proud. We ought to play Händel's 'See, the Conquering Hero Comes!' when you appear."

Salazar laughed. "It would make me feel pretty damned silly." More seriously, he continued: "You know, I used to think myself a fairly truthful, upright fellow; but in recent months I've told a lot of outrageous lies. I've lured Skanda into compromising acts so I could blackmail him into running the Museum the way I want. Kara and I have bamboozled the Empire with a phony séance. I've meddled in Kookish affairs, which I condemn when others like Ragnarsen do it. I've killed several Kooks, something I always resolved never to do. I've engineered the imperialistic conquest of a country by the Feënzurin. I've commanded in a battle that was really a massacre, like Omdurman or Ulundi, because of the discrepancy in weapons; so I don't deserve credit for the victory. And all so I can go on digging up an ancient Kookish city, which damned few of my fellow primates care anything about. I wonder if I've been on the right track?"

"Nonsense!" cried Firestone. "We've always agreed on the long-term importance of basic knowledge. Without it, we'd be back on Terra, living in caves and eating nuts and worms. You deserve every bit of the acclaim you'll get."

"But I seem to be such a damned hypocrite. . . ."

"Remember what I said: hypocrisy, like religion and liquor, is one of the lubricants that make it possible for men to live together in vastly greater numbers than the species was designed for."

Salazar sighed and made a small gesture of dismissal. "Good of you to say so, Cabot. Now I shall have to work like a fiend on Nomuru to justify my existence." He paused. "But I'd give the whole thing up if . . ."

"If what?"

"If I could have Kara back. I had the best, and like an idiot I threw it away. She even used to correct examination papers and tabulate grades for me."

Firestone: "And greater love hath no professor's wife! Have you tried . . ."

Salazar shook his head. "I've tried, but she won't have me at fire-sale prices. I thought there was a chance; but I was kidding myself. It's over."

Firestone frowned in puzzlement. "I'm not sure she made the wise decision. As an old couple watcher, I should think, since you two have knocked around together so much lately, that you'd have reestablished some permanent relationship."

"You think we spent our time screwing? No; not a single poke."

"If it were anyone but you, Keith, I might doubt that. It's almost incredible that a healthy, personable pair like you, who'd been intimate before and then were thrown together that way . . ." Firestone shrugged. "Everyone at the university assumes that it's no longer a case of 'just friends.' "

"Then everyone's wrong."

"Aren't you giving up too easily? You were never one to abandon a goal you'd set yourself."

"She convinced me, that's all. Some mistakes you have to live with."

"Why is she so dead set? You're a damned good catch."

"My girl has a spine of steel, and when she makes up her mind . . . Cabot, tell me, what ought I to have done?"

"It's useless advice at this stage, but I should have told you: When you've got a good marriage but feel an itch for another woman, get the hell out with no ifs, ands, or buts. Break all contacts with the new *amorosa*, politely but firmly. Back off. The itch will go away." Firestone looked speculatively at his friend. "If Kara's gone for good, how about that tall redhead, Penny something? Wasn't she in your class?"

"Yep. Got an A, and honestly."

"Well, if you wanted a bed warmer—"

Salazar held up a hand. "Diane cured me of playing house with children. As for Penny, I told her I was impotent."

"Good God! Why?"

"To escape being raped. But you've given me food for thought. Now, must be off. I've got six men's work to do in the coming month: to get the dig started again, first clearing the carcasses off the site; to lay out Gariko's national park; to sneak those rifles back into the Museum while Patel's on vacation. Gariko wants to start her own archaeology department, so I'm to interview some young Kooks as prospective students. Besides, the last ship from Terra brought a new instrument for subsurface mapping—an echo vibratometer. I can't wait to try it out on what may be King Bembogu's library."

"Don't kill yourself!"

"Hard work agrees with me, and it'll take my mind off other things. Come out to the dig soon. Uwangi's cooking is getting cosmopolitan. At least, it won't leave you writhing on the floor!"

"Thanks. By the way, what happened to Prophet Kampai, who started the war?"

"Mutiny. Some of his own Kooks killed him. Good-bye!"

At the Museum, Salazar prepared for the resumption of the summer's field work in the few days left before the start of the fall term at the university. He was in his office, packing papers and instruments, when his poignette buzzed. Kara's voice came from the instrument: "Keith?"

"Yep." His heart gave a jump, but he sternly reined in his emotions.

"Are you alone?"

"Yep. Alone in the office."

"I've been thinking and thinking, and—well—I don't know quite how to say it, but—maybe I was wrong to turn you down so—so—irrevocably."

"You mean—"

"Yes. In spite of everything, I'm awfully fond of you. And, while you make mistakes like the rest of us, I've never known you to make the same mistake twice. So . . ."

Her voice trailed off uncertainly. Salazar threw back his head and uttered a yell like that of a porondu in the mating season.

"Keith!" She sounded concerned. "Are you hurt?"

"No darling. Exuberant. Let's get married this afternoon! Then where? How about a couple of days at the Spaceport Hotel? They've got an excellent Terran chef—"

"Keith, please! Not so fast! We have a lot of plans to make. I sent you back my engagement ring. Have you still got it?"

"Yep."

"I thought you might have given it to Diane."

Salazar almost blurted out that he had offered the ring to Diane, but she had insisted on something showier. Remembering Firestone's words about the benefits of hypocrisy, he said: "No, dearest; I've kept it safe. Shall I bring it around at dinnertime?"

"That would be wonderful. Take care, darling; I—Oh, here comes my editor-in-chief. Good-bye!"

The poignette clicked off. Salazar's secretary knocked and hurried in. "Doctor Salazar, what was that dreadful sound I heard, like a terrible yell?"

Salazar straightened up his desktop as he thought of an answer. At last he said: "Just a tape I made of some animal noises."

"I'd have come in sooner, but just then a woman called you on the Museum's frequency." She glanced at the memo in her hand. "It's a Mrs. Diane Morrow Salazar. I put her on hold. Will you take the call now?"

"No. Tell her I'm living with a Kook at the dig—an insanely jealous Kook."

"Heavens! Male or female Kook?"

"Female, of course. I'm not so eccentric as all *that!*"

NAMES

While the reader may pronounce the names in the story as he likes, and while the sounds of the speech of the natives of Kukulcan (koo-KOOL-kan, named by its human discoverers after an Aztec god) are not much like those of any human language, here are suggested pronuniciations for some of the more difficult names.

Biitso (BEET-so)
boshiya (bo-shee-yah)
Chensoö (chen-SAW)
Feënzun (FEH-en-zoon)
Feënzuo (FEH-en-zwaw)
Frappot (fra-PO)
Gakki (gahk-kee)
Gariko (gah-ree-ko)
Gueilin (gway-lin)
Hjalmar (YAHL-mar)
Kampai (kahm-PIGH)
Kange (kahng-eh)
Kinyobi (kin-yo-bee)
Kovacs (KAW-vahtch)
kudzai (kood-ZIGH)
kyuumei (kew-may)

Miyage (mee-yah-geh)
Mozii (mo-ZEE)
Neruu (neh-ROO)
onnifa (awn-nee-fah)
Pokrovskii
    (paw-KROFF-skee)
poösho (PAW-sho)
Sambyaku
    (sahm-byah-koo)
Sappari (sahp-pah-ree)
Sensao (sen-SOW)
tisai (tee-SIGH)
Tsugaa (tsoo-GAH)
Tuui (TOO-ee)
Uwangi (oo-wahng-ee)
Yukke (yook-keh)

Other Baen Books by these authors:

The Paladin, C.J. Cherryh
65417-9 * $3.95   _____

Twilight's Kingdoms, Nancy Asire
65362-8 * $3.50   _____

*Carmen Miranda's Ghost is Haunting Space Station
Three* edited by Don Sakers, inspired by a song by
Leslie Fish
69864-8 * $3.95   _____

Knight of Ghosts and Shadows, Mercedes Lackey &
Ellen Guon
69885-0 * $3.95   _____

Trouble in a Tutti-Frutti Hat

It was half past my hangover and a quarter to the hair of the dog when *she* ankled into my life. I could smell trouble clinging to her like cheap perfume, but a man in my racket learns when to follow his nose and when to plug it. She was brunette, bouncy, beautiful. Also fruity. Also dead.

I watched her size up my cabin with brown eyes big as dinner plates, motioned her into the only other chair in the room. Her hips redefined the structure of DNA en route to a soft landing on the tatty cushion. Then they went right through the cushion. Like I said, dead. A crossover sister, which means my crack about smelling trouble was just figurative. You never get the scent-input off of what you civvies'd call a ghost. Never thought I'd meet one in the figurative flesh. Not on Space Station Three. Even the dead have taste.

What was Carmen Miranda doing on board Space Station Three?

CARMEN MIRANDA'S GHOST IS HAUNTING SPACE STATION THREE, edited by Don Sakers Featuring stories by Anne McCaffrey, C.J. Cherryh, Esther Friesner, Melissa Scott & Lisa Barnett and many more. Inspired by the song by Leslie Fish. 69864-8 * $3.95